MW01602254

# The Adventures of Lew and Charlie Vol. VI

*By Maurice Decker*

## Forgotten Gold
*First published February 1949*

## Operation Danger
*First published February 1950*

## Caribou Claim
*First published January 1959*

ISBN  978-0-936622-43-9

**Table of Contents:**

# INTRODUCTION:

Lew and Charlie—the ultimate outdoorsmen—hunted, trapped and fished their way from Arctic Alaska to the jungles of Central America and back again. Along the way they also solved mysteries, caught crooks, and rescued the occasional damsel in distress.

The stories ran for 35 years as a serial in *FUR-FISH-GAME* magazine, beginning in 1926. Each novella-length adventure was broken into monthly chapters with cliff-hanger endings. The final chapter of the final story appeared in December 1961.

To mark the magazine's 60th anniversary in 1985, one of the stories was republished in its 12-month entirety. As the story was coming to a close, a new generation of readers who had become hooked on Lew and Charlie flooded the office with letters asking for more. Another of the original serials was republished in its entirety the following year. Then another and another. The magazine's readers are still hanging on every word.

None of the stories had been available in book format before 2012, when the first three were collected in *The Adventures of Lew and Charlie*. Volume II took up where the first volume left off, and then came III, IV, V, and now Volume VI.

The magazine stories had to be edited for a book, but all of the adventure remains.

# Forgotten Gold

## Chapter 1 – The Antique Trunk

The covey of quail flew straight into the little gum swamp less than 50 yards away, just as Lew figured they would. There was only time for one hurried shot, and he felt good when one of the birds crumpled in the air. The lean, spotted dog turned his head, glanced back, and satisfied his gunner was through, moved in to retrieve. Lew rubbed his upper arm. He hadn't quite centered the buttstock to his shoulder and it had instead jabbed the biceps muscle painfully.

He hoped the dogs would find the bird. It was hard hunting the thick sedge fields, live oak and palmetto swamps. But they hadn't lost a quail, which spoke well for the dogs. Both were old and no longer fast on their feet, but age hadn't dimmed their keen noses.

Charlie and their guide Andy came up about the time Lew finished drawing the retrieved bird.

"I'm within three of the limit," Charlie announced. "Suppose we call it a day?"

Lew, who only lacked one, wiped his knife on the grass and replied, "I'm willing."

Andy pulled a silver watch from his pocket and held it close to his weather-beaten face. When his nearsighted eyes made out the time, he protested, "It's only 2:30, the afternoon's just begun."

"This sun gets to me," Lew replied. His face was beaded with perspiration, and he had opened his featherweight hunting coat. "A cool drink would go pretty good," he continued. "Let's go."

Then, sensing Andy's disappointment, he added, "You can go ahead and still get a full day with the dogs."

Partly mollified, Andy whistled for the hounds. "I know a piece of timber over yonder where we could get some squirrels," he muttered to no one in particular. Then he leashed the dogs and started back towards the road, buttoning his old leather jacket across his chest.

Charlie and Lew pulled off their coats and carried them slung over one shoulder. The coarse grass whipped their lower legs. Two crows flapped up from the ground, and suddenly realizing their danger, hammered the air with strong wings. Charlie dropped his coat, swung up the 16-gauge double and fired the Modified barrel. One crow tumbled headlong back into the sedge.

Andy shook his head in disapproval. "I wouldn't waste the shell."

Charlie grinned. "I would. Crows are harder to shoot than quail, and besides, taking them out helps the quail."

"You can't eat a crow," Andy grunted.

They followed the old logging road through second-growth long-leaf pine to the mud-streaked truck. Andy put the dogs in a wire crate in the rear and went around in front to crank the engine. They climbed into the front seat, Andy let in the clutch, and after a series of violent shudders, the truck lurched ahead. Every part of the truck showed the hard beating it had taken from the sand and red clay backwoods trails.

The truck bumped along for two miles and then Andy swung it out on a graded dirt roadbed, shifted from second into high gear. Half an hour later they entered the edge of the village.

Lew pointed to autos, saddle horses and wagons clustered before a one-story rambling house and asked, "What's going on, a wedding?"

"Nope. Auction," Andy replied. "That's Hank Breckenfield's place. He died last month, and they're selling off his goods."

Lew's eyes gleamed with interest. "Maybe they'll put up some old guns. Let me off here, Andy."

Andy applied the brakes carefully and observed, "I guess it's about over by now. Sales generally start before noon."

Charlie pulled out his billfold, removed a $10 bill and handed it to the guide. "Leave our guns with the clerk at the hotel and give the quail to Mrs. Morgan in the kitchen."

Andy pocketed the money and asked, "Same time tomorrow?"

Lew nodded. "Sure. Pick us up at the hotel. And tell Mrs. Morgan we'd like to eat early. I'm starving already."

The truck rattled off, and they walked slowly up to join the crowd gathered about a sagging veranda that reached clear across the front of the house. The auctioneer stood on the porch behind a low table. He was a short, fat man with a red face and loose mouth, wiping his forehead with a blue bandana handkerchief. His assistant set the next piece on the table with a flourish, hoping for the crowd's attention.

It was a small rawhide trunk, stained with age, dirt and mildew. The auctioneer shoved his handkerchief in a pocket and patted the trunk gently. Laying both hands on its top, he leaned forward and confidentially addressed the crowd.

"Ladies and gentlemen," he began. Lew glanced about, failed to see more than one woman and then looked back. "A good auctioneer always saves the best for last. And that is just what I have done. You confuse this priceless antique with the items that have gone before. Friends, this was the personal trunk of Lt. Amos Breckenfield, one of Davis County's most famous sons. He fought and licked the Yankees more times than I can count, and they say some are running still."

Laughter from the crowd checked him for a moment.

"There is nothing new I can say about Lt. Breckenfield's career," he added. "You know how he died for his homeland."

He tapped the lid of the trunk with a thick forefinger. "Here is his name stenciled across the leather, faded but you can still read it."

The auctioneer slowly removed his hat and laid it on the floor. "Friends," he continued solemnly, "the usual methods of an auction cannot prevail now. We must have more dignity as befits the merchandise offered. Please do not insult the memory of its distinguished owner with a paltry sum. What am I bid for the personal trunk of Lt. Amos Breckenfield, now an asset of the estate of his late grandson Henry?"

The crowd shuffled uneasily but remained silent. Lew started to edge forward for a closer look, and a voice cried out, "Five dollars!"

The auctioneer winced.

"My friend," he reproached, "I asked not to be insulted."

Then his face brightened. "I beg your pardon, you are not to blame because I have not told you the amazing circumstances connected with the trunk. See the lock? It is rusted shut, and there is no key. Ladies and gentlemen," he spoke slowly, emphasizing each word with a beat of his hand, "this trunk has not been opened in 75 years. It was just found in the attic, covered with dust and cobwebs. No living man has seen inside it. Henry Breckenfield himself didn't know it was stored away, forgotten under the eaves of his home."

The man got out his handkerchief and mopped his face again. "Unopened for three-quarters of a century. What treasure can it contain?" he tilted one end with exaggerated effort. "Fifty pounds of unknown wealth. Gold? Silver? Precious stones? Real bids now, please. And keep your voices low. Don't shout at this solemn time."

Most of the people were grinning, but a few stared soberly at the trunk. Some felt furtively in overall pockets again counting the change and bills inside. One bid $10. The auctioneer merely nodded and waited. He made no attempt to follow with his usual glib sales patter.

A female voice said, "Twenty dollars." Lew looked around. It was the lone woman. She stood a few feet away, head bare but with the collar of her soft wool gray coat turned up about a slender neck, and he saw that he had misjudged her young age.

A man said $25. Lew located him behind the girl. He wore a brown corduroy jacket and a brown cloth hat. The girl raised his bid by $5. The crowd watched with keen interest and the price jumped up to $110. The girl was beginning to look worried. It was her turn again, and she said in a low voice, "One hundred and twelve dollars."

"A hundred and fifteen," brown coat said triumphantly. The girl brushed a hand across her eyes and looked down at the ground.

The distress in her face made Lew uneasy.

The auctioneer lifted his hand high. "A hundred fifteen is my last bid. Are we all done?"

"Hundred and twenty," Lew said.

The crowd shuffled excitedly. Startled, the man in the brown jacket scowled. The girl glanced up at him surprised. Charlie grasped his companion's arm. "You like antique trunks?" he asked, grinning.

"Sure," Lew whispered. "Sometimes they have old letters in them with valuable postage stamps. I thought I'd take a chance."

"One hundred and twenty-five," brown coat said sharply.

Lew raised him five, and the amount climbed to $150.

That was Lew's offer, and the man in the brown coat bit his lip, hesitated, and then went swiftly up to the auctioneer. He whispered in the man's ear, but the auctioneer shook his head firmly. "Terms are strictly cash," he said aloud. "Cash on the barrel head.

Brown coat—a tall, thin fellow, about 30 years old with sharp features—shot a look of frank anger at Lew. Then he said slowly, "One hundred fifty-five."

Lew met his angry eyes with a grin, then turned to the auctioneer and said easily, "One hundred fifty-five dollars and fifty cents."

"That was dirty," Charlie whispered, and the auctioneer winced.

"Are we done gentlemen?" he demanded. "Are we all done?"

He indicated the trunk for Lew and added,"You understand terms are strictly cash, young man."

"I'm not deaf," Lew replied cheerfully.

He opened his billfold, took out three fifties and a ten and tossed them on the table. The auctioneer's helper counted out the change. Lew pocketed it, picked up the trunk and started through the crowd. The thing was rather heavy and proved an awkward object to carry. He figured it did weigh the 50 pounds stated by the auctioneer.

When he reached a clear space, Lew set the trunk down to give his back a rest. Charlie paused, looked at him and then said, "It's your money, but it looks like you paid plenty for that relic."

A short-legged dog with pointed nose and bushy tail approached to sniff at the trunk. Lew fended the animal off with his foot.

"I'm not worried about the money, Charlie. The fellow in the brown jacket will take it off my hands at a profit if I want to sell. He wanted it pretty bad because he tried to get credit from the auctioneer. All I have to do is give him a little time. That is, if I decide to sell."

"Well, you better start thinking about it," Charlie said, "because he's coming over now."

The man wore a smile that didn't fit very well, but he was doing his best to appear amicable. "I congratulate you on outbidding me," he drawled, "and on acquiring an outstanding relic of the old South. Let me introduce myself. I am Joel Herring."

Lew took the proffered hand, murmured what a pleasure it was and responded with Charlie's and his own name.

"My mother married a Breckenfield," Herring continued. "That is why I am interested in the trunk. I believe it contains papers that concern the early branches of our family tree. They would be of slight interest to a stranger, but they have a strong appeal to me. I am writing a history of the Breckenfields, sir, and it could be very useful."

"I can understand that," Lew agreed, his tone noncommittal.

"I wonder if you would be willing to make a quick profit?" Herring asked. "I can offer you $200 for the trunk as it stands. I will have the money here tomorrow morning. We could put the trunk in escrow at the bank," he waved his hand towards the center of the little town, "for them to turn over to me when I deposit the money to your credit. That would be fair for both parties, I believe."

He raised his eyes from the trunk and met Lew's.

Lew frowned. "I'm not sure I want to sell," he said slowly. "I'm interested in old postage stamps, and there might be some really good ones in the trunk."

The smile on Herring's mouth had started to congeal, but it came back now in a hurry. "I could go a little higher, to cover any old stamps," he suggested. "Say $225? I'm afraid that is all I can give. Or I can guarantee to turn over to you all envelopes bearing stamps. Naturally, I would want to keep the letters. They would be of no value to you."

"I'll think it over," Lew told him. "You might give me your address in case I want to get in touch with you."

Herring's smile went for good then. He took a card from one pocket, found a pencil in another and scribbled furiously. His eyes smoldered as he handed it to Lew. "That will get me," he forced out between set teeth and marched stiffly away.

"There goes a very mad man," Lew said softly.

"A dangerous one, too," Charlie added.

"Say," Lew said brightly. "Looks like another customer."

Charlie turned and saw the girl who had bid on the trunk walking towards them. The sale was over and most of the people had gone. They were almost alone in the big grass yard when she stopped before Lew and said bitterly, "I suppose you fixed it up to sell my great-grandfather's trunk to Joel Herring. Why couldn't you stay up north where you belong and not make trouble for me?"

Lew regarded her mildly.

"Did your mother marry a Breckenfield, too?" he asked.

Dark eyes that seemed too big for her face flashed. "Yes! My father. I am a Breckenfield; Joel is a stepson. What did he offer?"

"Two hundred and twenty-five," Lew replied, eyeing her closely.

"Why didn't you sell? Isn't $70—I beg your pardon—$69.50 enough profit for a minute's trouble? But I suppose rich folks aren't interested in small sums."

Red color started to creep up Lew's neck, but he spoke easily. "Why is it a crime to buy property at a public auction? You, Herring and everybody else had the same opportunity."

"But I didn't have your money," she said bitterly.

"Listen, miss," Lew drawled and Charlie glanced at him, for that tone showed Lew was getting mad. "You're off your trolley if you think I'm rich. We have a little money, sure, but we earned every penny. The hard way, too. We risked our lives to get it. Carrying a few hundred dollars around isn't a crime."

She bit her lip, started to speak, choked, bit her lip again to steady her voice and then said, "What are you going to do with the trunk?"

"Your cousin wants me to leave it at the bank until he can raise the money." Then seeing the anguish in her eyes he said gently, "What do you think it contains?"

Color flooded her white cheeks.

"I'll tell you," she cried defiantly. "You might as well know because I have no chance left. Before the War of the States, the Breckenfield family was rich. Since then, we have been very poor. Somehow my great-grandfather lost his fortune. I think it is inside this old trunk!"

## Chapter 2 – Some Misplaced Money

Lew was considerably surprised to hear that the old rawhide trunk he had just bought at auction might contain the Breckenfield family fortune, presumably lost during the War of the States. He knew it had some value because both the Breckenfield girl and her cousin, a young man named Joel Herring, had been keenly disappointed, even angry, when Lew outbid them. But Lew had supposed the trunk's contents probably consisted of family heirlooms and old letters carrying obsolete postage stamps that might be sold to collectors.

To hide his surprise, Lew bent over, lifted the trunk and set it down. "Not very heavy for a fortune," he suggested.

"What did you expect, gold bricks?" the girl demanded. "My great-grandmother had a diamond necklace, brooch and ring."

She whirled around and walked away. But Lew had seen tears start into her eyes and he called, "Wait. Where are you going?"

"Home!" She flung the word over her shoulder without pausing.

"Come back," Lew said sharply.

She stopped and looked around. "Why should I?"

"You asked me a minute ago why I didn't sell the trunk to Herring. I'll tell you why. I don't like his looks, and when I saw how disappointed you were when you had to drop out, I decided to outbid him no matter how high the price went. I ..." Lew fumbled a moment for words, "I ... bought the trunk for you."

"I don't believe you." Her face displayed stark amazement.

Lew shrugged, picked up the trunk, carried it over and set it at her feet. Then he swung around. "Come on, Charlie. Let's see if we can hurry the hotel cook along with dinner."

"No. You mustn't..." She tried to find words but failed.

Charlie stepped swiftly past Lew and grasped the girl's arm, just in time to prevent her falling. "Sit on the trunk until you feel better," he suggested kindly.

She steadied her swaying body, pushed the hair back from her forehead with her free hand and said, "I'm all right, now. "

"Lew can be a little abrupt," Charlie said. "Even when he wants to help."

"No, I am the one who wasn't nice." she said ruefully.

7

Charlie studied the dark circles under her eyes. He released her arm carefully and asked, "When was the last time you ate?"

Her eyes flashed and then softened. She managed a shaky laugh. "You might as well know it all. Last I ate was yesterday noon. I had a cup of coffee this morning, but that was all. I have been saving my money to buy the trunk."

"We are staying at the Plantation Coffee House," Charlie replied. "Their cook is roasting a dozen quail for our dinner tonight. We would be very glad to have you help us eat them."

"Sold!" she said promptly. "I haven't eaten quail for years."

She walked up to Lew and held out a hand. "I'm sorry."

Lew grinned. "For what? I get flat-out vicious when I miss a couple of meals, Miss Breckenfield."

She hesitated only a moment. "My friends call me Ginny."

The Plantation Coffee House was the only hotel in Plumville, a big sprawling structure with two-story veranda and patches of bare, sun-blistered wood that outnumbered boards still bearing a trace of white paint. It was the sort of hotel you'd expect to find in a small town at the edge of semi-wild hunting country. The beds were a bit hard, the floors uneven. You might find dust on the tabletops and windowsills in your room. But the meals were terrific, home-cooked and served in enormous quantity. Lew's mouth already watered as he walked up the plank sidewalk and thought of the delicately browned birds and light biscuits with giblet gravy that would soon be set before him.

Charlie thought the veranda too drafty for their guest, so they went inside and sat in one corner of a big lobby covered with faded rose-figured carpet. Lew placed the trunk by Ginny's feet and walked on past the desk, through the dining room and into the kitchen at the rear. He had two $1 bills in his hand, and he dropped them on a table before the cook. "Could you hurry our food just a little? We have a guest who missed lunch today."

"I sure can, Mister Lew," she told him. After he left she spoke to her helper, "Anybody who can eat like that boy don't have to pay me for no favors. But," she added quickly, picking up the money, "don't you go tellin' him that."

"So, you don't live here in Plumville," Charlie was saying when Lew returned.

"No," Ginny replied. "My home is at the county seat, Stauton. I am a stenographer in the courthouse. You must wonder why I could only raise $122 for the trunk. My mother died a year ago, and I have just finished paying off our debts. She was an invalid the last three years. I make a good salary, but doctor bills and then the funeral took every dollar I had."

She dropped her coat from her shoulders and continued, "You must be anxious to hear more about the trunk."

"It can wait until after supper," Lew declared.

"No, I want to tell you now. I'm afraid I must repeat some family history to make it clear. Please don't let that bore you. Amos Breckenfield, who originally owned the trunk, was my great-grandfather. He had one son, born while he was away at war. That was William Breckenfield. William had three sons: Henry, whose estate owned the trunk; Jefferson, who married Joel Herring's mother after Joel was born; and my own father, Matthew. Jefferson and my father both have been dead a long time. Henry, who had no other family, passed away last month. It seems he held onto the old trunk for a very long time, although I never knew it even existed until recently. I suppose it came to him because he was the oldest son."

"Today is the first you've seen the trunk?" Lew asked in surprise.

"Yes. I examined it before the sale, came early on purpose."

She shook her head when Charlie held out a glass of water.

"I told you before that the Breckenfields were considered very rich before the war. But since the war, the family has been poor, very poor. My mother and I thought we knew why. We believed that like so many others in the South, my great-grandfather had given his money to his country. And then something happened that changed my mind."

A truck backfired in the street and then limped noisily away on most of its cylinders. Ginny waited until the clamor died in the distance then continued, "The Davis County Historical Society at Stauton occasionally publishes small booklets about early times and especially the war years. Three months ago, they prepared one telling how the county helped the Southern cause. It included a list of residents who made important contributions of money and property, not taxes you understand, but outright gifts. I was astonished when I found Amos Breckenfield wasn't mentioned."

"It may have been an oversight," Charlie suggested.

"Yes, that's possible but not probable. Careful records were kept with the intention of paying the donors back at a future time. The Society has access to all Confederate government records both at Stauton and Richmond. Their papers have always been accurate. But I did check the possibility of error, spoke with several people on the committee responsible for the booklet. They assured me no evidence existed that my great-grandfather had donated money to the South."

Two men came in from the street. One paused, sniffed and said, "Fried chicken for supper like I said, Pete. You owe me two bits."

His bulging eyes swept over the room, fastened on the little group in the corner and then centered upon his companion, who was reaching into his pants pocket. They passed the desk and started up the stair.

"I realized we had been wrong in supposing great-grandfather Amos had given his money away," Ginny continued. "Something else had happened to it. So I set out to find out what."

The white-haired clerk shuffled in from the kitchen and arranged himself behind the desk. Ginny leaned forward and lowered her voice.

"I didn't make any progress for weeks. Mother had a few old letters left from the family, and I searched for something interesting written by my great-grandparents because it might contain some hint about the money. But my great-grandfather was killed in the war, and his wife died a few weeks later when her son William was born. William was raised by a grand-aunt named Amelia. Just when I was getting very discouraged I found a letter from her. In it, she said that money and jewels had been gathered, ready to deliver to the government."

The man who had won the two-bit bet came down the stairs, entered the lobby and sat in a chair near the door. Ginny lowered her voice again. She didn't have to change its quality because it was already soft and low-pitched.

"That letter didn't help a lot, but it did prove there had been a fortune. When Uncle Henry died and the sale bill of his estate listed an old rawhide trunk, I decided I had to buy it. The more I thought about the matter, the more convinced I became that the trunk might contain real clues about the money and jewels, if it didn't actually contain them."

"They could have been stolen," Charlie said. "A lot of looting takes place in war times."

"I don't believe that happened," Ginny said earnestly. "Ever since I learned it had not been given to the government, I have had a strong conviction that the money still exists, and all I have to do is discover where. I almost became obsessed with the idea. It seems so wonderful that I might still have an inheritance from my family."

"What about Herring?" Lew asked. "Where does he fit in?"

"Joel is very clever. He must have read the Historical Society's booklet and got the same impression I did. He attended the sale looking to pick up the trunk. Having more money, he outbid me."

"Think Herring would share anything he found?" Lew asked.

She hesitated and then said slowly, "I don't know. But I hope he would. That was why I was so disappointed when you got the trunk instead of him."

Lew shook his head firmly. "If I have cousin Joel sized up right, the only thing he would give you is his blessing, and he'd cut that down to a few words. But he's your kinfolk, and I don't blame you for preferring him over a total stranger like me." Then, seeing the remorse in her eyes, he added quickly, "You really think the money and jewels could be in here?" He pushed the trunk with the toe of his hunting boot.

"I'm almost sure they are," she declared.

"Well, it won't take long to find out. Shall I open it?"

"Is it really mine?"

"I don't go back on my word," Lew replied.

"I didn't mean that. Oh, I don't know what I did mean. It is so hard to believe anyone would be so generous to a stranger. But I am going to give you a share of whatever we find. You are entitled to that."

"You can give me what I paid for the trunk," Lew told her firmly. "But that's all." He glanced around. The other party to the fried chicken bet had joined his companion. Both were staring at them.

"I don't think we better open the trunk here," Lew said. "Too much audience. How about coming up to our room? We can leave the door open if you wish."

"Don't be silly," she retorted.

Lew stood. "I'll have to go out and get some tools."

Ten minutes later, he came back with a small package. Charlie grasped the trunk, and they started towards the worn stairs. As they approached the two men, one gave a low whistle and leered at Ginny. Looking into his bulging eyes, Lew thought he would like them a lot better after they had been blackened by a couple of good, stiff punches. He was walking behind Ginny and he saw her shoulders stiffen.

They climbed the stairway and entered their corner room looking down on the street. Charlie set the trunk on top of a straight chair and ran up the two cracked window shades. He turned on the ceiling light.

Lew opened his package and spread out a hacksaw, two steel punches and a mechanic's hammer. "The lock's jammed with rust," he announced, tightening the hacksaw blade in its frame. "I could smash it open, but that would hurt the trunk's antique value. So I'm going to saw the bolts and slip it loose. Then it can be put back on if you like."

Four round-head rivets held the lock in place. Lew sawed into one. It proved to be brass, and the blade bit through fast. He was cutting the last rivet when a voice said, "I'll bet George Washington used that for a sample case."

It was the man with the bulging eyes. They had left the door ajar and had been so absorbed in their work no one had heard him come in.

Charlie looked up. "You want something?" he asked.

The fellow grinned at Ginny. "After you get through with that relic come across the hall. I'll show you something swell ..."

That was as far as he got. Charlie's arm straightened, his palm striking the man square in the chest. The man staggered back, kicking frantically to keep his balance. He didn't succeed, and falling on his back, hit his head against the baseboard.

It was a hard bump, and he lay there dazed. Charlie went over, seized him by the coat collar and deftly lifted him to his feet.

"An open door doesn't mean we're having open house," he said. "This is a private room, and the lady isn't interested."

The man swayed until he put a hand back against the wall for support. His lip was bleeding, and he put his other hand against it.

"I'm going," he mumbled. "Don't hit me again."

"I didn't hit you," Charlie corrected. "I just gave you a push."

Ginny was staring with wide eyes. "What happens when he does hit somebody?" she murmured.

"Blackout," Lew grunted then continued driving the headless rivets on through the hinge with a punch.

Charlie closed the door. "Should have done that before," he explained. "Where do these fellows get the idea they're irresistible?"

"Must be the old farmer's daughter and traveling salesman myth," Lew grinned. He grasped the lock, tugged and held it up in his hand. "Everybody ready?" he asked. "I'm going to open her up."

Ginny leaned close and drew in her breath with a little gasp.

# Chapter 3 – A Secret Cache

At first, the hinges holding the rawhide trunk's lid didn't want to swing. But they broke free with a rasping sound, and Lew pulled the lid open, looked down and saw clothing filled the trunk a little more than halfway full. Something made of yellowed white silk lay on top. He motioned to Ginny Breckenfield. "You take over now."

She reached in and lifted out the silk.

"A wedding gown," she murmured. "My great-grandmother's." She held it up before her, eyes soft and misty.

Ginny held the dress so long Lew became impatient. "Don't you want to know what else is in here?" he finally said.

"Of course." She spread the gown over the bed, dug into the trunk again and came up with a pair of satin slippers. "Oh, aren't they darling! And so tiny. I wonder how she ever got her feet into them."

"They probably pinched," Lew said dryly. What he wanted to see was the lost Breckenfield family fortune Ginny believed was hidden in the trunk, and he wondered why she wasted so much time over old clothes. Still, he thought, wedding stuff always affects young women, and Ginny could hardly be more than 19. And very pretty. Her face was thin and pale but it had very nice features and her skin was clear. Lew in particular liked her jet-black hair.

"All the Breckenfield women have small feet," she said firmly, glancing at her own. Although shod in square-toed walking shoes, he could see they were almost as small as the slippers in her hand.

Ginny lifted out a leather belt with two holsters, each holding a gun. The leather was stiff and green with mold, the visible parts of the cap and ball revolvers rusted brown. She gave them to Lew. As he worked one of the guns out, the leather feel apart and part stuck to the rusted steel.

"We're getting a little closer," he said. "If these hadn't been packed in their holsters, they might be valuable. They're Colt Patersons. Collectors give real dough for them. But they aren't worth much in this condition." He placed them regretfully on the floor.

Ginny unpacked a heavy blue coat and some small items, all feminine. Her face began to show worry because she was near the bottom of the trunk. Out came a very short sword with battered hilt and rusted blade. It had been wedged diagonally in the short space. Her face lighted. "I've found some money," she exclaimed and held up a thick package of bills. "They look funny. They must be terribly old."

"That's Confederate money," Charlie said gently. "It was probably valuable when the trunk was packed, but it isn't worth much now."

Ginny thrust both hands into the trunk.

"That's all," she said, her voice choked. "No, here's something more." It was a painted portrait of a girl, hardly any older than herself. They could see the resemblance. "I don't know who she is," Ginny said, "but she's a Breckenfield."

Charlie took the picture. "This might be of some value," he suggested, "if a famous early-American artist painted it." He looked for a signature but didn't find one. The glass over the face was cracked, but the narrow, rough gold frame was in good condition.

Ginny took hold of the chair back and sank down on the seat. "I'm feeling dizzy again," she whispered.

"What you need is food," Lew declared and looked at his watch. "Those quail should be ready. Let's go." Then he patted her shoulder. "It has been a bad let-down, all right."

She glanced up, her face seeming thinner and whiter than before. "I'm sorry about your money. I can give you some of it back."

"What money?" Lew demanded. "The trunk was a present. You were to pay me the cost out of what it contained. If it doesn't contain valuables, well, we're even. The only thing that bothers me is I could have stuck the trunk on Herring. It would have been a real pleasure to see his face after he paid a couple of hundred for it and found nothing inside. Let's go and eat."

Charlie locked their room door and dropped the key in his pocket. They paused at the door of the dining room and glanced about. It contained four youngsters eating sandwiches and drinking root beer. A waitress stood near the passage that led to the kitchen. She came forward eagerly, announcing, "Your quail are ready."

She seated them with ceremony and fussed with the table service. The fine lines around her eyes indicated she would not see her 30th birthday again, but her dark red hair was well kept. She was comfortably plump yet very light on her feet.

"We're starving, Milly," Lew said. "So don't spare the horses."

"I won't," she giggled and darted into the kitchen.

Returning, she placed a platter of four roasted quail on the table. They had been wrapped in bacon, stuffed with bread and sage before roasting. "I'm keeping the rest warm for you, Mister Lew," she announced. He nodded approval and checked the other dishes she unloaded from the tray: mashed potatoes, hominy, beets, green beans, biscuits, butter and gravy.

Lew frowned. "You forgot the syrup."

"I'm sorry!" she cried and sped off for the kitchen again.

Ginny was watching with amazed eyes. "How does he do it?" she asked Charlie. "I spent half an hour here this morning trying to get a cup of coffee."

"Lew would like to think it's his manly vigor," Charlie said laughing. "But really it's the dollar tip he leaves three times a day."

Lew only grinned; he was too busy eating to talk. Ginny also made no attempt to conceal her hunger. She accepted a second quail when the platter was replenished. Yet it was in the main a rather silent meal. Lew had reached the hot biscuit and cane syrup stage of satisfying his appetite before he stopped chewing and sat with knife and fork poised above his plate. Charlie could tell his companion's extraordinarily keen hearing had caught some significant sound.

Lew put the utensils down and said, "Excuse me." Then he walked quickly towards the stairs. Five minutes later, he came back carrying the rawhide trunk. He set it on the floor between his feet.

"Somebody was in our room," he said after another mouthful of biscuit. "A little while ago I heard steps come down the stairway. They stopped halfway down, where someone could stand and watch us without being seen himself. When I left the table I heard him go back up fast. I was too late to see him, but just as I got to our room,"Frog Eyes," the guy you pushed, Charlie, came along. I doubt if he was the one in our room because he came from the wrong direction. But somebody was. I found the door unlocked. I remember you turned the key and tried the knob as you left. Whoever it was didn't have time to use his key again before I came."

"Frog Eyes, as you call him, was the lookout," Charlie suggested.

Lew nodded. "That's what I figure, too. Did you ever see either of them before, Ginny?"

"Not that I remember. Were any of my things gone?"

"I don't think so. I bundled them back in the trunk and brought it down to be safe. The lock on our door isn't any protection. A handyman could pick it with a nail file."

Dessert consisted of peach pie topped with chocolate ice cream. Lew pointed with pride. "One of my inventions," he said modestly.

Ginny tasted the concoction dubiously but then offered, "It really does taste good, better than it sounds."

Milly filled their cups with fresh coffee, and standing off a dozen paces, watched with pride as Lew wolfed down the pie.

"That was a wonderful meal," Ginny said. "Thank you."

She consulted a very small watch on her wrist.

"I should start home soon. There's a Stauton bus in half an hour. I left my coat in your room, and I want to repack the clothing."

Lew grinned. "I guess I did throw it in any old way."

Back in the room, he lashed the trunk shut with a length of canoe tracking line that had been around one of their bundles of equipment. Ginny was folding the wedding gown carefully. Charlie picked the empty trunk from the floor and said slowly, "Something is missing."

Ginny looked at him expectantly. "No letters, no papers of any kind," he explained. "Every old trunk I ever saw held some."

"That's right," Lew agreed. "Maybe it has a false bottom?"

Ginny dropped the dress and was beside them instantly. Charlie pressed on the bottom of the trunk.

"No false bottom," he announced. "There isn't enough space."

The trunk was built of thin wood panels covered with the rawhide. The lining was very light, thin leather. Charlie thought it could be buckskin sewn together in vertical seams running up each corner. He picked at one place with a fingernail. The stitches seemed slightly larger there, made with lighter-colored thread.

"I think this has been re-sewn," he said slowly. "The lining could have been ripped and needed repairing. But I think we ought to cut it loose and make sure."

"Go ahead," Ginny cried eagerly.

Charlie cut the threads carefully and pulled at the seam until it spread apart. Then he worked his hand inside over the wooden bottom. His fingers touched something that rustled, and he drew forth a folded piece of paper. It was covered with fine writing in dim, graying ink. He handed it to Ginny.

Her fingers trembled as she spread the paper flat.

"It's a letter to my great-grandfather from ..." she glanced at the back, "from my great-grandmother!"

She stepped over to a window where the sun fell directly on the letter. "Poor thing," she said a moment later. "She wasn't well and all of the slaves but two had run away to join the raiders. She apologizes to him because she couldn't get the cotton picked before the fall rains."

She turned the letter over. "Two more of their mules were stolen, which wasn't so bad because they didn't have any grain to feed them."

Then she looked at them with shining eyes. "Here it is! Here is what I wanted to know. Listen."

She began to read:

*I have been obliged to hide the jewels and gold. I did not dare wait until Amelia comes the day after tomorrow. The raiders have been seen as near as 20 miles away. Billy and Eliza went with me in the cedar boat. The moon was dark and we carried pine torches, but we did not light them until we were far inside the swamp. We saw no one, and I am sure no one saw us. I put the treasure in your iron strong box. We buried it on the end of Panther Island, at the same place you shot the big black cat. No one else knows that spot, for we were alone that day. It does not matter if somebody does see this letter, although I think you should burn it as soon as you finish reading.*

Ginny was glowing. "Isn't that wonderful? I've found the Breckenfield treasure at last."

Then she began reading again:

*I did not send the above letter* (this is the postscript, Ginny explained) *because there was no use. Word came today that my husband was killed at Manassas. The same boat that would have taken this letter brought the terrible news. The treasure must be saved for my son who was born last night. How I can do that, I do not know.*

"Poor thing," Ginny murmured softly. "What a terrible situation for her. She died only a few days later."

"That postscript explains why the letter isn't in an envelope," Charlie stated.

"Where is this swamp she talks about?" Lew asked.

"It is part of the original Breckenfield estate, on the Sharon River. At one time the family owned 30,000 acres of bottom farmland."

"Who owns it now?"

"Since my mother died, I do. That is, I own what is left of it. There is hardly anything but swamp, now. I tried to turn that over to the state for a game refuge. The big house is a ruin. No one has lived in it for a long time. All the good land save 20 acres has been sold at different times to pay taxes and support different Breckenfields. Even the 20 acres left is mortgaged.

"But I don't have to worry anymore," she added brightly. "Now I will have enough money to pay the mortgage and rebuild the old homestead. And I can pay you for buying the trunk. Isn't it grand?"

Then she saw Lew's frown. "What's the matter?" she asked.

"How big is the swamp?"

"About six miles wide."

"Is it still carried on the records in your name?"

"I believe so."

Lew's frown didn't relax. "Your claim to the jewelry and money seems sound," he began. "You can prove inheritance and that you owned the ground on which it was buried. But do you know where Panther Island is located?"

"No. But I bet Uncle Alec does. He farms the 20 acres of good land that's left. He is descended from the Breckenfield slaves and has lived on that land all his life."

"Even so, it will be a tough job," Lew declared. "Almost impossible one, I'd say. An iron box is a small object to locate in six miles of swamp, and that kind of country changes a lot in 80 years. Channels move, ground that was dry gets flooded and low places build up with rotting vegetation. Even of you do find Panther Island, it may take a lifetime to dig over that much ground."

The light faded from her eyes, leaving dark pools of tragic disappointment. "I guess I hadn't thought that far ahead," she confessed. "What am I going to do?"

# Chapter 4 – Swamp Safari

Lew wanted to help Ginny, hated to dampen her elation over discovery of what had happened to the lost Breckenfield family fortune. But he felt that it would be kinder to inject a note of caution into the project rather than to let her enthusiasm run unchecked. She had already begun forming plans to spend the money, and the more of these she made, the greater would be her disappointment if things didn't work out. Lew believed there were plenty of chances for that.

The letter from her great-grandmother to her great-grandfather that Charlie had discovered under the lining of the old trunk stated the fortune was buried in a swamp on a spot known as "Panther Island." But even if Ginny could locate the island, which looked plenty difficult, how could she find this exact place to dig for the iron chest?

"Six miles of swamp is a lot," he repeated. "The only way to get inside such a place is by boat. And then you have to follow the channels. Two-thirds of the ground is probably inaccessible."

"You make it sound hopeless," Ginny replied. Then her eyes brightened, and she smiled. "I've got the solution. Why didn't I think of it before? You come with me and help. You were clever enough to find the letter; I know you can locate the gold and jewels. I'll pay you or give you a share, whichever you want."

Lew rubbed his chin. He didn't think there was the ghost of a chance to succeed, but it was sort of hard to tell as nice a girl as Ginny. And, he reflected, it might be interesting to explore the swamp.

"I suppose we could help," he said. "But I think we have to accept that we probably won't succeed."

"I don't," Charlie said quickly. "I think we can find the money, if it is still there, as long as we can locate the island."

"You make me so happy!" Ginny declared. "Of course we can find the money. And I will give you a big share."

"Better not promise anything until you get the inheritance tax paid," Lew cautioned. "Anyway, we can work that angle out after we find the stuff." He was already unfolding a state map. "You said the Sharon River. Here it is. And I suppose this tract is the swamp?"

"Looks about 40 miles from here," Charlie said. "What about getting a boat there? Or should we take one with us?"

"Uncle Alec had a wooden skiff the last time I visited the plantation. But it leaked pretty badly."

"We better get one, then," Charlie continued. He put a finger on the map. "We can pick up the river at Millcreek. That's 18 miles due east of here. I say buy a boat there, drop it in the water, and pole up into the swamp."

Lew nodded. "We'll be bucking the current, but that shouldn't be bad. These southern rivers move slowly. Besides, we could stick on a small outboard motor. Then the cruising would be fun." He looked up, saw Ginny's anxious eyes. "What's the matter?" he asked.

"I don't have money to buy a boat, let alone a motor."

Lew grinned. "Stop worrying. We can afford it, probably rent both boat and motor if you prefer."

"When shall we start?" she brightened immediately. "But I do have to stop home first."

Charlie tapped his fingers on the map, making mental calculations. "We need a couple of days to get ready. Then a day more to reach the swamp. This is Tuesday, suppose you meet us at the plantation Friday, say a bit after noon. Okay?"

"Can do," she replied.

"This search will take time. A week, maybe two. Can we stay in the house, or will we need a tent?"

"One wing of the old house still has a good roof," Ginny replied. "The windows are all broken, but the door was alright my last visit. There's an old stove, too. I would like to bring Julie, my maid. She can clean and cook for us while we search. Is that all right?"

Charlie nodded. "Sure. I was going to suggest you bring a companion. But one thing more: take care of yourself."

"What do you mean?"

"You're the only living Breckenfield, aren't you?"

"Yes."

"If something happens to you, who inherits the money?"

"Joel, I suppose. He's next of kin."

"That's what I was afraid to hear. We only talked to Herring a couple of minutes after Lew bought the trunk. But I got the idea he can be plenty dangerous when he chooses."

Ginny nodded soberly. She looked at her watch, picked up purse and gloves and said, "I mustn't miss the bus. It's the last one tonight."

Lew lifted the trunk. "I'll carry it to the station," he offered.

Ginny held out her hand. Charlie took it in his.

"Better get that starry look out of your eyes," he told her firmly. It's a tip-off you expect to come into money. It will be safer to act disappointed when you reach the street."

Charlie wasn't in the hotel when Lew came back from the bus station. He waited almost an hour before his companion returned. "Where have you been?" he demanded.

"Down at the exchange making some phone calls."

"You tell Andy we couldn't hunt with him tomorrow?" Lew asked, walking over to a pitcher of ice water sitting on a small table. He poured a tumbler and drank it.

"I guess I got us into this business," he said. "But you didn't have to encourage Ginny so much. You practically guaranteed we would find the money. She's a swell kid. I will hate to see her disappointed, like she certainly must be."

"I didn't call Andy," Charlie replied. "We will hunt tomorrow as usual. But that's our last day. And I don't think I encouraged Ginny too much. We have a very good chance of finding her family treasure."

"In that much swamp?" Lew demanded. "Who did you call?"

"I got the state geologist, first. You've heard about the instruments prospectors use to locate metal ore in the ground? I believe they're the original radar development. They have a needle that leaps when it comes within a certain distance of metal. Just like a compass needle jumps when you lay it too close to a gun or axe."

Lew's frown had vanished. "Go on," he urged.

"I asked the geologist if he knew where I could get one in a hurry. He said the university had one in the science lab. So I called them and after liberal use of the Breckenfield name, they agreed to loan it to us if we make a suitable deposit."

"I'll be," Lew exclaimed. "I thought we were up against a needle in a haystack job. But all we have to do is find the island and carry this radar jigger around until the needle gets a jolt from the buried gold."

"I'm not sure about a reaction from gold," Charlie replied. "It might not register on the dial. But the iron box in which it is buried will. The geologist assured me about that. Either iron or steel or any ore containing iron reacts. I didn't mention gold because I didn't want to stir up any curiosity."

"There's too much already," Lew agreed.

"Somebody is interested. You almost caught him in this room, and I'm sure he came to search the trunk."

"Probably Herring," Lew grunted.

"Or someone working with him," Charlie replied, staring out the window. The sun had set and night shadows blanketed the gravel street. "I hope nothing happens to Ginny," he added.

"So do I." Lew stood up. "Well, since we hunt tomorrow, I suppose I ought to get the guns and clean them. What's the program then?"

"We hunt Wednesday. Thursday you go over to Millcreek on the river and pick up a boat and motor. Get anything else you figure we'll need. I have a date at the university to pick up the detector. I'll join you at Millcreek Thursday night. We'll leave next morning for the plantation. Ginny tell you how to recognize it when we get there?"

"Sure. We can't miss the place."

*   *   *

Charlie stepped off the bus in Millcreek at 20 minutes past five Thursday afternoon. The town was bigger than he supposed. There were about 10 blocks of stores, most of them handling hardware, feed and groceries. At the far end of the street he saw a bridge with a patch of blue water off to the side. He started in that direction, confident Lew would be on the river. He carried only two pieces of baggage, a flat cowhide bag and the case containing the ore detector. The instrument was rather small,but weighed some 20 pounds including battery. Charlie had handled it very carefully since leaving the university. He wasn't taking chances after making a security deposit of $400.

A short, rutted lane branched off from the street just ahead of the bridge. It led down to a plank dock where boats of varying sizes were moored. Charlie found Lew at the one tied farthest upstream. Boxes and sacks were scattered about, and Lew was fitting them in different parts of a trim aluminum skiff. He looked up and grinned.

"Isn't she a dandy?" he demanded, patting the gunwale fondly. "Was I lucky. The hardware store just got her in yesterday. Fourteen feet long yet only weighs just over 100 pounds. One man can lug her, and she'll slide through shallow water and grassy channels as slick as an otter. All molded aluminum, never leaks or needs calking."

"Okay," Charlie replied. "You don't have to sell me. I know something about aluminum boats. Got any money left?"

Lew's grin faded.

"Some. But I wanted this boat, and I'm going to keep it after we find her inheritance. Anyway, I came out alright on the motor. It's a secondhand three-horse job. But in good condition. I tried it out. I only paid a hundred even for it."

He reached up, grabbed Charlie's bag and wedged it beside a heavy carton. "I have our sleeping bags and air pads. My bag and now yours. The two guns and ammunition are over there. I bought a full-sized axe and a shovel. There's a coil of rope and a tarpaulin, only the guy in the store called it a wagon cover."

He picked up Charlie's bag again and fitted it in a different place. Then he went on, "I didn't check with Ginny on food. I think she will bring some, but I got more, just in case. Also, I picked up a cooking kit. I got a milk can to carry drinking water. And a gasoline lantern."

"How much gasoline?"

"Fifteen gallons, more than enough to take us there and back. We can't use the motor much inside the swamp. I got some stuff for supper, too," Lew added. "I figured we might start now and eat on the way. Then we won't have to lug all this stuff back to the hotel for safe keeping. I paid my bill so we can start anytime."

"Shove off, then," Charlie told him.

Sharon River was sluggish, and the little motor pushed them up-stream at a very satisfactory pace. Lew had taken pains in loading the craft to hold an even keel. They cruised until sunset then stopped at a small hummock that jutted out into the water, almost but not quite an island. There were small pines on the crest, but the downstream side was gravelly and without brush.

They pulled the boat up there and made it fast. Lew took cheese, liverwurst, rolls, a pie and a bottle of milk from the bundle of food. After eating, they built a fire of rich pine. The air was damp and penetrating. Charlie spread the tarpaulin out, put their sleeping bags on one half. The other half could be pulled over the beds if it rained. Lew covered the pasteboard cartons in the boat with their raincoats.

Charlie took the metal detector to bed with him, laying it close against his mattress pad. The success of their quest hinged upon the instrument, and he didn't want to run any risk of it being harmed.

Charlie awoke in the night and automatically looked at the luminous dial of his wristwatch. The hands stood at 10 minutes past 2. He lay listening, thinking some sound had aroused him. Lew was breathing regularly, and Charlie reflected over the curious circumstance that, while his companion could pick up sounds inaudible to his own ears, Lew could sleep through some pretty disturbing noises in the night.

Charlie then heard a sound so plainly he knew there was no mistake. He rose up and glanced down at their boat. It lay exactly where they had moored it earlier, but there seemed to be a patch of darker color out near the center of the stream. Charlie watched it creep away until the light mist that shrouded the water was split by a quick little breeze and he confirmed the object was a boat.

There was something familiar about the single figure sitting at the center thwart plying the oars. Charlie got up and ran down to the edge of the river. He was almost sure that man was the one from the Plumville Hotel whom Lew had dubbed "Frog Eyes."

But the boat faded from sight before he could be positive. He searched their own craft carefully. Nothing seemed to have been disturbed. He tested the stern and prow mooring ropes, both were solid. Then he got back inside his sleeping bag.

When he awoke again, Lew already had kindled up the fire and was making coffee. A thick fog hung over their camp, and the tarpaulin covering their beds was beaded with water. Charlie dressed and went over to the fire. He told Lew what had occurred in the night. "I can't shake the feeling something was tampered with," he added.

Lew tossed eight slices of bacon in a skillet.

"If Frog Eyes is working for Herring, he might want to block our trip to the plantation. So, maybe he disabled the motor, although that would only slow us rather than keep us away."

"I'll have a look," Charlie said. He went back to the boat, primed the motor and jerked the starter. It fired at once and idled smoothly. Charlie shut it off, went up to the fire and took a plate of hotcakes Lew held out. He ate hurriedly, stood and said, "Lew, I'm going to unload the boat. I still think something is wrong."

Lew grunted. His mouth was too full to talk.

Charlie pulled the boat up close and started lifting out the cargo. Every bundle seemed undisturbed. He moved the last one, a carton of grits and pushed his hand up into the open prow space. His fingers touched something silky and smooth. He knew at once he had found it.

Looking over Charlie's shoulder, Lew exclaimed, "Why, that's a raw beaver pelt. Just been skinned."

Charlie nodded. "It was planted last night," he stated. "Beaver have just been reintroduced in this state, and they are protected. Frog Eyes put that here to get us in trouble. If that's the case ..."

Lew clutched his partner's shoulder. Charlie heard it soon after, the low-pitched rhythm of a boat motor. He looked down at the half-grown pelt in his hand and said, "I'll bet a hundred bucks that's a game warden—tipped off by Frog Eyes."

# Chapter 5 – Thirty Days, One-Hundred Dollars

Standing at the edge of the river below last night's campsite and listening to the sound of an approaching motorboat, Lew would have given a lot to have a good grip on the man who had planted the illegal beaver pelt in their canoe. But he didn't lose any time in wishful thinking. He grabbed the skin from Charlie's fingers and started up the bank. "If that is a game warden coming," he said, "stall him until I get back."

Charlie glanced at the heap of supplies and equipment he had lifted from their aluminum boat before he had found the pelt hidden up in the stern. He decided to let the stuff lie as it was, for if the man they called Frog Eyes had tipped off a conservation officer, that officer would insist upon a search and there wasn't any use packing the outfit twice. So he walked up to the campfire and sat on his heels beside it. He knew Lew would dispose of the hide, and he hoped his companion would do a thorough job.

The motorboat stopped with its prow up on the low beach. A tall, bony man stepped out, glanced at Charlie and said, "Morning."

Charlie stood and acknowledged the greeting. "You're late for breakfast," he added. "But I can cook some more in a few minutes."

"No thanks. I'm Talent, game warden in this district. I want to check your license ... and your partner's. Where is he?"

Charlie wondered how the man knew he had a partner.

Lew appeared with a pail of water. He set it carefully on three rocks in the fire and pulled a heap of embers up about it. Charlie was holding out his license, and Lew produced his own without comment.

Talent studied the documents carefully. He took plenty of time. Then, lifting deep-set eyes, he asked, "Any game in your possession?"

They told him none.

"Any fur?"

They repeated the negative reply. He scrutinized them for several seconds. "Mind if I look through your stuff? Just routine, you know."

They assured him there was no objection.

Warden Talent made a thorough search. All of his movements were slow and seemingly casual, but nothing missed his long, lean fingers or sharp gaze. Finishing with the cargo, he stepped in the craft and examined it. This was easy because the hull was almost empty. Then he glanced up at their beds on top of the little ridge.

Charlie led the way up and turned back half of the tarpaulin to expose sleeping bags and the metal detector.

Talent ran his hands carefully over the bedding, raised each piece and looked beneath it. Charlie set the detector off and rolled up the tarp to expose the ground it rested on. The warden touched it with his toe and then asked, "What's that?"

"A scientific instrument," Charlie replied. "It has no connection with wildlife or conservation."

Talent looked at him, eyes plainly questioning. But Charlie did not elaborate on his explanation.

Finally, the warden said, "Open the case."

Charlie lifted the lid and disclosed the tight-fitting mechanism. Their visitor finally nodded in silent agreement that the box could not possibly contain anything else. Charlie closed the lid.

"Where you boys headed?"

"About 30 miles upstream," Lew stated.

"Going to hunt?"

"Could be," Lew replied. "Our licenses are okay."

Another slow nod. "Just be sure to get landowner permission."

Lew grinned. "The landowner will be hunting with us," he said, eyeing the warden casually. "Mind telling us what you expected to find with this routine search?"

"No, I don't mind," Talent replied. "I was looking for illegal fur. We got a tip someone had been taking beaver on the river. They're protected, and the judge throws the book at any fellow we catch."

He turned back towards his boat. "We investigate all complaints, that's our job. But you boys seem clean."

They followed him down the bank. He got in his boat, started the motor, turned and casually said, "If I were you, I'd be careful. Looks like you might have an enemy somewhere."

As the boat circled out into the river, Lew called from shore, "If you catch a trapper taking beaver, what does he get?"

"Thirty days and a hundred dollars," Talent replied. Then he poured on the gas and shot off in a cloud of spray.

"Thirty days," Charlie repeated thoughtfully. "A one-month stretch would put us out of circulation very neatly. Herring would have plenty of time to take the Breckenfield money away from Ginny. That was a real clever trick."

"He almost got away with it, too," Lew observed thoughtfully.

Then he went back to the fire, dumped the dirty breakfast dishes into the pail of hot water and churned them about. "I sure would like to meet Frog Eyes again, and real soon."

"You probably will," Charlie told him. "The fellow must be working with Herring. What did you do with the beaver pelt?"

"Weighted it with a rock and sank it in deep water. But don't forget, when we catch up with Frog Eyes, it's my turn. You had yours a couple of days ago."

Charlie nodded. He wasn't worried about the man who had cached the contraband skin in their boat. Frog Eyes was only a tool. Joel Herring had shown cunning in planning the attempt to sabotage their mission, and Charlie decided he needed plenty of thought.

The sun was well above the low hills back of the riverbank when Lew spread the cooking utensils out on top of the tarpaulin to dry. They dried fast, and he packed them back in a cardboard box and carried it to the boat. Charlie already had the rest of their gear loaded, and they shoved off without further delay.

For several hours they cruised along between low-rolling pine ridges. The river looped lazily back and forth, reaching up into broad, flat valleys and then back to pursue the same general course.

Little villages backed against the face of the hilly plateau to break the checkerboard pattern of bottomland fields covered with hay stubble and cultivated stalks of cotton and corn. They passed the occasional boat of fishermen balancing long cane poles. They passed a few small houseboats with flat, tar-paper-roofed cabins.

After awhile the hills flattened out, slowly at first, and then they disappeared in a matter of minutes. Flats of soft, wet ground covered with tall reeds and wild grass appeared along the river. There were still small settlements and plowed land, but these receded from the water-line until they lay a mile or more away. The heavy growth of wild vegetation along the waterway told them they had entered swamp country. The Breckenfield plantation could not be many hours away.

At noon they ate a quick lunch in the boat and pushed on, impatient to reach their destination and worried about Ginny.

Charlie poured a drink of water from the can. "So, how will we recognize the plantation?" he asked.

"Ginny said we can see the house from the river," Lew explained. "A short channel leads up to it, and there are two big live oak trees in the front yard. One has part of its top broken away."

They sighted the live oaks about an hour later, the outline of a roof line showing between the long, sprawled branches. The little channel was almost clear of weeds, which surprised them. They ran the boat through it to a crazy-looking structure of poles and planks that at one time had been a rather extensive loading dock. Now the timbers had rotted and twisted until they were dubious about stepping on them. But since the only alternative was to wade through a dense sea of tall weeds, Lew gingerly climbed up, testing his weight carefully on each board. Charlie handed him the guns and followed.

Once on the dock, they got a better view of the house. It wasn't a pleasing sight. What had once been an imposing mansion had fallen into ruin. Part of the roof was caved in, and only one of the giant porch pillars stood erect. The others had toppled. They looked to be a full 50 feet long and almost 4 feet through.

The weathered sides of the building were devoid of any paint. So far as they could see, not one of the big casement windows still possessed an unbroken pane of glass. They walked to the end of the dock then forced their way through the brush that overgrew the yard.

The house consisted of two wings: one two stories, the other just a single floor. The low wing seemed in better condition, its roof intact and only sagging at the ridge.

They passed within a few yards of the front entrance facing the river. It was fully 10 feet high and had once been closed by magnificent double doors. Only one still hung in place. The other lay on the ground, the open space blocked with rough boards. Lew stopped and held up one hand. When the sounds of their feet swishing through the grass ceased, Charlie heard voices from the other side of the building.

Lew started walking fast. Turning the corner, they both saw a narrow, rutted, red-clay road. In it were two autos, a very old coupe and a newer four-door sedan. The sedan was streaked with mud, but its vintage was recent. It looked speedy.

"So you see, dear cousin," a man was speaking, "you can't depend on those two Yankees for help. I'm sorry to disappoint you, but that's the way it is."

Lew's face split into a wide grin. The speaker was Joel Herring, and flanking him at each side were the men they had seen in the hotel. Lew was especially pleased to recognize Frog Eyes.

Ginny stood firmly in the open doorway of the low wing, facing the three defiantly. Her cheeks were pale but her jaw held a firm, resolute look. "I don't believe you," she said. "They said they would meet me here at two o'clock, and I know they will!"

Herring laughed unpleasantly.

"Suit yourself, cousin. But I know they won't make it."

"What makes you think that?" Lew asked. Ginny cried out happily, color flooding her face. Herring whirled, and his hand slid towards his hip pocket. Lew shook his head and swung up the muzzle of the shotgun he was carrying casually waist high.

"Don't," he cautioned. Then he stepped closer. "You didn't answer me. What made you think we weren't coming?"

Frog Eyes edged a couple of feet off to the side, then stopped shuffling his feet when Lew moved his shotgun muzzle that way. But Herring didn't flinch. "Put that gun down," he snapped. "I'll have you in jail if you threaten us with it again"

"Don't push your luck," Lew advised. Then he put the gun down on the ground and strode purposefully towards Frog Eyes.

"You and I," he said, "have a little account to settle. Get on around the corner of the house!"

Herring stepped forward, but Charlie lifted his own gun and said sharply, "Hold it." Herring froze in his tracks.

Frog Eyes backed away, eyes drawn into slits. Suddenly there was a knife in his right hand, a long, thin blade that seemed to whip out of nowhere. Holding it close to his hip, he stepped towards Lew.

Lew could tell Frog Eyes wasn't any amateur with a knife. Amateurs usually move in with the blade held forward, out of position to make a slashing upper cut. Frog Eyes' poise indicated experience.

Charlie stepped around Herring, intending to shoot the knife from Frog Eyes' fingers or stop him with a charge in the leg.

But Lew acted swiftly and decisively. He launched himself feet first at his adversary, turning sideways in the air. His left instep hooked Frog Eyes' left ankle; his right foot struck hard against the other's knee. Breaking his fall with his arms, Lew exerted a scissors move with his feet that sent Frog Eyes toppling backwards. Both hit the ground, and the look of surprise on Frog Eye's face almost made Charlie laugh. But the man still held the knife, and he made a slash at Lew's leg. Lew had already drawn his feet back, and when the slash came up short, he planted both in the pit of Frog Eyes' stomach. The man went limp, knife slipping from his fingers.

Lew got up, hooked his fingers in the man's collar and dragged him to his feet. He turned the unresisting form to the road, gave it a shove and a hard kick in the pants. Frog Eyes staggered a few yards and then began to run, feet pounding the red clay trail.

Lew dusted his hands carefully. "I don't think your pal," he said glancing at Herring, "is going to plant illegal furs in my boat again. He won't draw a knife on anybody real soon, either."

Lew picked up the shotgun. "Now, Ginny, what's going on here?"

"Joel says I have to give him half of any money we find."

"Did he say why?" Lew asked coolly

"Only that you couldn't help me because you would be in jail. Why did he say that?"

"We'll explain later," Lew told her. "Right now, it looks like Herring and his friend are trespassing. If you want to request them to leave, I'll be very glad to see they do."

"We're going," Herring said thickly, trying in vain to disguise his rage. "Come on, Ed," he said to his remaining companion.

They walked to the big sedan, Herring opened the driver's door, turned and spoke, "Don't be surprised when I come back and order you to go." Then he got in, started the engine, backed around in the yard and drove off in a thick cloud of dust.

"What did he mean by ordering us off?" Charlie asked.

Ginny's eyes were troubled. "I don't know. But I'm sure he is planning some legal trick to stop us searching for my family's fortune."

# Chapter 6 – Voodoo Hot Foot

Ginny's statement that her cousin, Joel Herring, might be planning some legal stunt to stop her searching the swamp for her family's lost fortune didn't seem to worry Lew. He only shrugged and said, "Herring was trying to scare us, and that was all he could think to say."

But Charlie had a different opinion. "I'm not so sure he's bluffing. Herring is clever. His trick with the beaver pelt proves that. We mustn't make the mistake of underestimating him. What can he do, Ginny? Can he tie the property up with an injunction?"

"Well, the taxes have been delinquent for several years. Maybe he could take title by paying them."

"We must find out," Charlie said decisively. "Do you have a lawyer you can trust?"

"Judge Catron took care of mother's affairs," she replied. "I'm sure he's honest. But ..."

Charlie didn't let her finish. "Is there a post office near here?"

"About 11 miles down the road."

"Drive there and write a letter to the judge. Tell him there may be unsuspected assets on your family plantation, and you want him to watch for any attempt to keep you from realizing them. Instruct him to take the necessary action to block any tax sale or injunction that might imperil your rights in the property. You better leave right now."

"But ..."

Charlie didn't let her finish this time, either.

He pulled out his billfold, took out $100 and pressed it into her hand. "Send this as a retainer. Buy a money order at the post office."

Tears filled Ginny's eyes. "You've already done so much."

"And we're going to see this through," Charlie assured her. Then he smiled. "I'm just protecting Lew's investment in the trunk."

He closed her reluctant fingers over the bills.

A rasping voice whirled them all around to an astounding sight. A black woman of indeterminable age stood a dozen yards away. Her features looked like they had been hacked out of hardwood. A long scar ran obliquely from one of the little eyes that glared angrily at them to connect with one side of the compressed mouth. Her short, thick body was almost dwarfish. Yet the muscles in her bare forearms were knotty like a man's. She carried a bundle of dry wild grass on her back, and as they looked, her grip loosened on the rope and let the burden drop. Then she strode forward purposefully.

"What you cryin' for, Miz Ginny?" she demanded. "If these men made you cry, honey, they gonna be mighty sorry they got born."

"It's all right, Julie," Ginny replied. "I'm only crying because I'm happy. These are my friends, Mister Charlie and Mister Lew. I want you to do everything you can to make them comfortable while they are here." She faced them and added, "This is my maid. I told you I would bring her with me."

"Howdy, Mister Charlie. Howdy, Mister Lew. Sorry if I sounded off. But I been carin' for Miz Ginny ever since she was a baby."

"That's all right, Julie," Charlie said. "I'm glad you are looking out for her. If I had met you before, I wouldn't have been as worried about her the last few days."

Julie's eyes darted towards her mistress. "He talkin' 'bout Joel, honey? That trash been botherin' you again?"

"He was here, Julie. But Mister Lew ran him off fast."

The woman gave Lew a look of grudging respect. She studied him for several seconds and then asked, "You ready for some hot biscuits and chicken gravy, Mister Lew?"

He nodded eagerly in delighted surprise.

"I'm goin' to fill you full of them tonight, then." She reached down, picked up the bale of grass and went inside.

Charlie laughed. "She picked your weak spot fast enough, Lew."

Ginny smiled. "Julie is smarter than you might think if you judged by looks alone. She's trying to make this wing of the house habitable for us. It's the only part with a good roof. There's an old stove and a table inside, but not much else. Lew told me he would bring sleeping bags and air mattresses. Julie and I have covers she will stuff with hay to lay on the floor. I brought food, and Uncle Alec, the sharecropper, has a good well. So, all we need is chairs or benches to sit on."

"Get some nails when you are in town, and we'll make them," Charlie said. "You should start right now. Lew can go along in case you run into your cousin again."

He watched them drive off in the small coupe. Then he went into the old house. Julie had a fire going in the battered stove, a big kettle of water heating on top. Satisfied that she didn't need his help, he walked back to the river dock and unloaded their boat. He carried the stuff to the house and laid it down outside the door. Julie already had swept the floor clean and was washing it with hot water and a scrub brush.

Charlie went down the red clay road to a board shack about 300 yards away. A covered well stood out in front of the building, and there was a pole barn with a straw roof in back. Behind that he saw a small pasture fenced with rails, a thin gray mule grazing in one corner. An old wagon with high wheels and narrow tires sat alongside the barn. Barred rock-chickens wandered about another small field where a tall black man was digging potatoes.

Charlie didn't say anything, just watched the man working with a steady, deliberate pace. The absence of any sign of children gave him the impression Alec, the sharecropper, was a bachelor.

He returned to the big house, found Julie had finished scrubbing the floors and was working on the tabletop and window frames. He picked up the metal detector case, opened the lid, adjusted some knobs and walked slowly towards an old wood block in which he had struck Lew's new axe.

He was still some 20 feet away when the slender needle began to quiver. The movement increased as he went closer until the pointer went absolutely wild. Charlie turned off the power and closed the case. He was well-satisfied. There would be more metal in a chest holding Ginny's family fortune than was in that axe head. It looked like they would be able to pick out its location in the swamp.

Later that afternoon, Ginny and Lew returned. Ginny reported that she had sent the letter and money order to the judge and went inside. Charlie told Lew about his test.

"What are we waiting for, then?" Lew demanded. "Why aren't we headed for the swamp?"

"We have to know where Panther Island is located, first," Charlie replied. "That's where the treasure is buried." He called Ginny back outside. "Have you spoken with Alec about the island?"

"I asked him, but he insists he doesn't know anything about any island. That's hard to believe because he has lived on the plantation all his life. He must know Panther Island."

Lew scowled. "We can't start until we get that location. There are probably a hundred islands in this swamp." He rattled some loose change in his pocket. "Suppose I go down and talk with Alec?"

Ginny shook her head. "No. I'm his landlord and a Breckenfield. He's been a part of the family his whole life. If he won't tell me, he won't tell a stranger."

Julie emerged from the door with a pail of scrub water.

"Who won't tell you what, honey?" she asked.

Ginny explained the dilemma and Julie nodded. "You leave Alec to me." She threw the water out into the woods and went back inside.

"Well, she can start working on Alec pretty soon," Charlie remarked. "He's coming up the road now."

"He's bringing us the chicken I bought for our dinner tonight," Ginny explained.

Alec shuffled into the yard. He was much older than Charlie had at first thought. His face was seamed with lines, his hair and short beard a grizzled white. He carried a big hen with its head tucked back under his arm. The chicken clucked softly when he stroked its back and held it out. "This is the fattest one I got, Miss Ginny."

Julie came through the door briskly, a long butcher knife in her hand. "Give me that bird," she ordered.

She pinned wings and legs together with one hand, struck a hard blow with the other that sent the fowl's head rolling. Then she walked swiftly around Alec, holding the neck down so it left a circle of fresh blood on the ground. When the dark, wet circle was complete, she stepped back with a grunt of satisfaction.

Alec looked alarmed. "What you doin' woman?" he faltered.

Julie eyed him grimly. "I'm puttin' the spell on you. On account of you won't tell Miss Ginny what she asked about the swamp. That's the blood circle you're standing in, and you can't break out. No matter how hard you try. Now I'm goin' to make voodoo, so your blood boils like coffee. It'll burn up your bones so you can't stand no more. Then you'll fall down like a lump of meat."

"Don't do that, woman," Alec cried. "Don't make no voodoo against me."

But Julie paid no attention. She plucked three feathers from the breast of the chicken, and leaning over, stuck them upright in the dirt. Alec shrank back, but only a few inches. He stopped abruptly when he reached the circle of blood drops. As Lew commented afterwards, it was like he had hit a solid wall.

Julie was mumbling queer gibberish under her breath, moving her arms and nodding her head in accompaniment. Lew's eyes popped. The three small feathers she had thrust in the ground started to wave. A breeze had moved them, of course. But Alec groaned in his terror. His face had turned a pasty color.

"Don't conjure on me, woman," he repeated, wringing his hands in apparent agony. "I can't tell Miss Ginny about the swamp. The ha'nts will kill me if I do."

"You're going to die anyway," Julie assured him. "My conjure is more powerful than any swamp ha'nt. Your blood is already beginning to boil. It'll start down in your left big toe. Can you feel it?"

Alec jerked his foot from the ground and yelled, "Stop it! I'm burning up, woman."

"All I got to do now is get the gizzard," Julie told him. "Then the spell is done. You'll really burn then."

She turned the body of the chicken over and flourished her knife.

"Don't use the gizzard!" Alec pleaded, sweat pouring down his seamy face. "I'll tell Miss Ginny what she wants to know."

Julie dropped the hen, stooped down and picked up the three feathers. Then she waddled slowly around the man, rubbing out the circle of blood with her shoe.

"Come on out, old man," she ordered. "And start talkin'."

Alec stepped forward, limping on his left foot.

"My toe is still burning," he complained.

"You can soak it in a bucket—after you talk," Julie replied.

"Panther Island is five miles off in the swamp. But I can't tell you exactly where. I've got to show you."

"Let's go, then," Lew said.

Terror swept back into the old man's eyes. "We can't go now. It's too late. We've got to get out of the swamp before night. If we get caught by darkness, we'll all die."

"Rubbish!" Lew exclaimed. He was a bit fed up with all this superstition. He looked at his watch. "The sun won't set for another four hours. We have plenty of time."

Julie, however, knew Alec wasn't going anywhere. "Alright," she said. "We start early in the mornin'. You be here come sunup. If you aren't ..." She left the threat to his imagination.

Alec promised he would be there early, and with relief showing in his eyes, limped down the road to his shack.

Lew watched him thoughtfully. "I wonder what made him think his big toe was burning?" he said.

Julie grunted, picked up the hen and carried it behind the house.

"He believed it," Ginny said, "and that's the same thing with these folks."

Lew nodded. "Alec spoke of ha'nts. What did he mean?"

"He meant haunts, another name for ghosts," Ginny explained.

"Ghosts in the swamp?"

Ginny nodded. "That's what lots of folks around here believe. You see, a great many people have died there. Some were lost hunters who couldn't find their way out. My uncle was one. He went into the swamp to shoot deer and nobody ever saw him again. I remember my mother telling me that 20 men searched three days for him. But mostly slaves died there. They would run away from the plantations. Then they either starved or were hunted down with dogs and killed."

"That all happened long ago," Lew suggested.

Ginny only shrugged, but Lew caught an odd look in her eyes.

"Since we aren't going to the swamp today," Charlie said, "we'd better carry our boat up from the river. We can't risk leaving it at the dock. Herring could ruin it with an axe in a couple of minutes."

After they were done, Lew walked down the narrow road to Alec's shack. He came back with a queer look on his face. "You know what the old fellow is doing?" he asked Charlie. "He's sitting on his doorstep soaking his left foot in a pail of water. I don't know how Julie did it, but she gave him a real hot foot!"

"Power of suggestion," Charlie said shortly. "How about nailing up a couple of benches to sit on when we eat?"

Lew picked up the short camp axe. "I suppose auto-suggestion could make a man think his foot was burning. But how about blisters? Alec showed me a couple on his big toe. They were soft and fresh."

Then he walked off whistling.

# Chapter 7 – The Swamp Ghost

Lew pulled a wide board from the wainscoting in the largest room of the big wing of the old mansion. Most of the trim was already gone, and he couldn't see any harm removing it to make benches for their dinner table. Anyway, he reflected, all of the old trim would come out when Ginny recovered her family's lost money and began to rebuild the place. Lew knew what he would do if the house was his. He would tear it down and start from the beginning with new lumber and stone. But he thought Ginny too sentimental for that.

Lew went down to Alec's cabin to ask the old sharecropper if he had a saw he could borrow. Alec was back in the potato patch, sullen and reticent. He mumbled that there was a bucksaw on the woodpile. Lew saw he still limped as a result of Julie's voodoo. Julie had something on the ball, he didn't know what, but it was something.

When a delicious aroma drifted from the kitchen of the old house, he remembered her promise to fill him up with chicken gravy and hot biscuits. He went to the kitchen door and looked inside.

The hen was boiling in a big black iron kettle. An uncovered saucepan was heaped with peeled potatoes, and Julie was kneading a big lump of dough on the pine table. Lew backed away, satisfied she had everything under control. Then he helped Charlie block openings in the old mansion's decrepit walls. It was a precaution they believed necessary to keep out skunks, wild hogs and other critters.

Ginny, who had been walking slowly back and forth along the clay road, came over and said, "I'm planning how to restore the place when I find my money. I'll replace the old siding boards with new ones 10 inches wide. The windows will be Colonial, and I'll build a new Colonial entrance facing both the river and road. I want a blue slate roof and a patio on the east side floored with red bricks. The low ground along the river will be leveled and seeded to grass with dozens of flower beds scattered about. Then I'll run vines over the south walls and the patio. Won't it be lovely?"

Lew started to speak, but she cut him off.

"I know what you want to say, that I should wait until I have the money before making too many plans. But planning is sometimes the nicest part of any venture. Don't you agree?"

"Sure," Lew said, glad he hadn't spoken his thoughts about how the old framework might be too rotten to hold new siding.

"The kid's enjoying this," he thought. "Why not let her dream?"

Julie came out with an empty pail and started down the road. "I'll get the water," Lew called, but she kept walking.

"I do the kitchen work here, Mister Lew," she declared.

Charlie smiled at that and said, "I want to be sure of an early start tomorrow. We should leave by sunrise."

"You want to go before someone tries to stop us," Ginny said.

"Yes. That letter you sent won't reach the judge until tomorrow. If Herring already has applied for an injunction to block our search, he may get it before the judge can act."

When they sat down around the old scrubbed pine table that night, Julie kept her promise. She heaped Lew's plate with chicken, biscuits and yellow gravy until even he had to wave her away.

The evening turned cool, and the warmth of the old stove felt good. Julie stuffed it with pine until the warped top glowed red. Watching flames streak up the rust-thinned pipe, Charlie hoped the masonry in the old chimney was tight. A single spark could set the place on fire, and then the sun-dried wood would burn like so much paper.

Still, the big room held a cheery glow. Two of the candles Ginny had brought still lit the table, and Lew had hung the gasoline lantern from a hook in the center of the ceiling.

Julie washed the dishes then sat on a bench behind the stove, listening as the others talked about tomorrow's search.

"How long do you think it will take?" Ginny asked. Her face was flushed with excitement.

"Whoa, Nelly," Charlie laughed. "I won't even try to guess. All we know is your great-grandmother wrote a letter about burying a box of treasure on one end of Panther Island. It may take hours to find the island. Then we have to locate the chest. If the place is big, there may be many small points one could call ends."

"I'll have Julie fix us some lunch," Ginny said.

"Another difficulty," Charlie continued, "is we must trust Alec's memory to take us to the right island. He acted so scared of the place I doubt if he's been there in years. I think Julie should work him a bit before we start to emphasize just how serious this business is."

Julie nodded her agreement.

Ginny yawned behind a hand, "I'm sleepy, and we must get up early. So I'm going to bed."

Lew and Charlie both started unstrapping bed rolls and blowing up air pads. When they were done, Charlie went back to the kitchen to check the stove. He turned the draft shut so sparks wouldn't shoot up the chimney during the night. The door that faced the river hung precariously on one hinge, so he wedged it tighter with a board. The night was still too hot to crawl inside a down-insulated sleeping robe, so he lay on top and used the thin lining blanket for a cover.

Charlie must have fallen asleep like that, because a dog barking aroused him in the night. He remembered seeing a yellow and white hound at Alec's place. Charlie had much respect for a dog's ability to sense intruders, so he slipped on his boots, picked up flashlight and gun, then slipped out the door. The moonless sky was black. He walked slowly down the road towards the river. When he reached the rotting dock, he looked out over the water. After a time his eyes accustomed themselves to the night, and a spot darker than the other shadows began to stand out near the middle of the sleepy river.

He thought it was a boat. He hadn't any doubts after it turned slowly and headed upstream. Charlie watched thoughtfully. The fact it turned meant the craft had been pointed downstream, that it must have come from the swamp. That made him uneasy. But with nothing else to do, he returned to the house and went back to sleep.

Again a dog's sharp yelp awoke Charlie. He sat up, heard a voice order, "Git on home, Callie," and then heard another yelp.

He decided Alec had arrived and dressed hurriedly.

The kitchen blazed with light when he entered, cool air fragrant with coffee. Ginny and Julie were placing platters of ham and eggs on the table. A steaming bowl of grits sat beside each plate.

Alec stood like a shadow just outside the door.

"Guess I overslept," Charlie said. His watch showed 4 o'clock.

Lew came in the door and announced, "I got most of the stuff carried down. You can help me with the boat after we eat. What happened last night? I heard…"

Charlie silenced him with a nod towards the door. Then he stepped over to an enamel basin and started washing his face and hands. When Lew came over, he whispered, "There was a boat on the river. But don't say anything. Alec's already shaking like a leaf."

Alec was now squatted in the doorway, resting a plate on his knees. He shook fearfully every time he glanced Julie's way. She didn't seem to notice as she took two pans of baking-powder bread from the oven, cut each sheet in quarters, split the pieces and laid slices of ham inside. She wrapped the big sandwiches in a clean dish towel and packed them in a box.

When he had finished breakfast, Lew went over to the supplies and picked out two cans of meat, two of orange juice, two of milk, a chunk of bacon and a package of coffee. He added them to the lunch box. "I got the cooking kit ready to load," he said. "I know we expect to be back tonight, but we might be delayed."

Charlie grimaced, but it was too late. Alec started to shake violently. He went over and lay a hand on the old man's shoulder. "Just take us to the island. We'll get you home on time."

"Yes, sir," Alec faltered.

Ginny looked up. "If we find the island, Uncle Alec, and everything goes good, I'm going to buy you a new mule. And a new plow and a wagon."

But Charlie doubted he even heard her because Julie was beckoning and he had started to shuffle forward. Charlie and Lew picked up the aluminum boat. Ginny said, "What can I carry?"

"Get that black box from our room," Charlie replied.

Lew was grinning. "Julie's going to put the heat on Alec again."

After they slid the boat into the river, Lew went back for the guns. Charlie began to load. Ginny handed him the metal detector case and asked, "What's in the box?"

"It's a device I borrowed from the university. It works something like radar to indicate the presence of steel or iron. It should show us where to dig on the island for the money chest."

"Why, that's wonderful," Ginny cried. "You are awfully clever."

Charlie grinned. "Trying to tease me?"

"No," she said firmly. "You know better. I am so lucky to have you helping me." She looked down, pushed several pieces of dried mud from the dock with her foot.

"Did Lew really buy the trunk to give it to me?"

Charlie's grin widened. "Lew is susceptible to feminine distress," he said. "Especially if the girl is pretty. He can't resist big, dark eyes and black hair that falls in a shiny soft cloud over a girl's shoulders."

She scraped her shoe faster. "And you?" she asked softly.

He pretended to scrutinize her closely. "Well," he said after a pause, "if you put on 10 pounds and gave your hair a henna rinse..."

"Now you are teasing me," she retorted.

Lew came up with the guns, two boxes of shells and lunch. Alec shuffled along behind, his mouth moving as if he were talking to himself. He looked at the two short oars Lew had laid on the dock, shook his head and climbed back on the ground. He walked along the riverbank, stooped over and picked up a long pole. Returning, he told Lew, "This will work better than oars."

Ginny sat in the prow, Charlie took the center seat, and Lew took the stern while Alec squatted just ahead of his feet. Julie stamped out on the dock and glared at the old sharecropper. "You remember what I told you," she threatened.

Alec bobbed his head. "Yes'm. I remember."

Julie's face softened when she glanced at Ginny. "Tell me, honey, if you have any trouble with him."

Then her eyes moved to Lew. "I'm goin' to have two chickens tonight, Mister Lew. So you be fixin' to find what Miss Ginny wants."

Lew grinned and shoved hard with the pole, sending their craft out into the river. When they reached the channel, Charlie picked up the oars.

It only took a few minutes to reach the wall of trees separating river from swamp. Live oaks stood on the higher ground, cypress in the shallows. Festoons of moss draped from branches like monstrous cobwebs. As the shallow bottom became more weedy, Charlie had to ship his oars. Then Alec stood up and began to use the pole. With short jabs he sent them straight towards the jungle.

The boat nosed between trees, pushed against tangles of wiry brush but slid across floating beds of weeds. Gradually, a narrow channel opened before them. The sun was high enough for rays to slant down into the water, but its blackness reflected the light like a mirror hiding all below. A rift in the foliage disclosed two buzzards slowly circling in a blue sky. A muskrat swam towards the boat, sensed its presence and dove with a splash.

Charlie spoke to Alec, "Sure seems to be lots of fur. Do you ever trap here?"

Alec shook his head decidedly. "No, sir!"

"Why not?" Charlie persisted. "You could make a pretty good stake with a few dozen traps."

"I'm an old man," the fellow replied. "But I still want to live some more. The ha'nts don't like for nobody to come in here."

"Doesn't anybody trap the swamp?"

"No sir, they don't."

The little channel narrowed, and when it seemed passage would be pinched off completely, another rift in the growth appeared. Alec turned the nose of the boat into it.

"Do you ever see these ha'nts?" Charlie asked.

Alec shivered and rolled his eyes. "I never saw them sure enough. But I've heard them and seen their devil fire."

Charlie let half a minute pass. He didn't want to crowd the old man too much. Then he asked, "What kind of sounds do they make?"

"A wail—like a soul in hell." Alec grasped his pole. "Listen!"

A throbbing sound reached Charlie's ears, faint at first but growing steadily louder as the boat slid ahead. There was a quality in the tone that made his neck hairs prickle. It was low-pitched but penetrating, and it filled the air all around them, seeming to come from all directions and not any certain one.

Alec's lips and face turned livid. "Lord have mercy," he groaned and shot the boat ahead with a desperate shove. The sound droned on without pause until it faded in the distance.

It was unlike anything Charlie had ever heard before.

# Chapter 8 – Panther Island

Even though the eerie sound he insisted came from "ha'nts" was well behind them, Alec still trembled and he shoved the aluminum boat ahead with his pole, displaying a surprising strength and vigor. Charlie had wanted to stop and search for the source of the noise, but he hesitated to give the order. It might make Alex hysterical with fear or sullen with anger. He might even forget or pretend to forget the course to Panther Island. That would be disastrous, because Alec alone knew its location, and they had to find it quickly before anything interfered with the search for Ginny's family fortune.

"What did you make of it?" Charlie asked.

Lew shook his head slowly. "Nothing I ever heard before."

"A bird?" Ginny suggested.

Lew shook his head again. "No bird made that sound."

Alec lifted his pole and shook a tangle of trailing weeds from the end. "It was ha'nts, Miss Ginny." His voice was gently reproachful.

"How long have you heard these ghosts?" Charlie asked.

"Always been there. My pappy told me about them just like his pappy told him."

"No, I mean the first time you actually heard them yourself."

Alec scratched his head. "Fifty years, maybe thirty," he said.

Ginny smiled at that. "Julie will expect you to tell us exactly," she suggested.

Alec doggedly pushed the pole deep into the muddy bottom of the channel. He didn't like the implication, but Ginny persisted, and after considerable evasion and stammering, Alec admitted that he had actually only begun to hear the ghost noises within the last three years.

Seeing the old fellow using the pole work as a shield against questioning, Lew announced he would handle the tool awhile. That put Alec in a more vulnerable spot. Ginny moved back to sit beside Charlie, and they both cross-examined Alec.

They learned that prior to first hearing the sound, Alec and several neighboring sharecroppers had hunted and trapped regularly in the swamp. They had not penetrated far into the morass, but they had covered the edges well. Perhaps once or twice each season, Alec had gone as far as Panther Island to shoot the wild ducks that settled down in great swarms from the sky.

"Then you stopped coming when you heard the ghosts," Charlie said. "What about the others? Did they stop, too?"

Alec nodded. "All stopped. Nobody comes anymore."

"Before that, before anything warned you away, why didn't you trap the middle of the swamp? Afraid of getting lost?"

Alec shook his head vigorously. "Nobody gonna lose me here. I did put traps near the middle, but when I came back they was gone. Something pulled the stake and took everything." He lowered his voice, "I know it was the ha'nts warnin' me."

Ginny looked at Charlie with questioning eyes. He shook his head, indicating they shouldn't pursue that angle anymore.

The aluminum boat slid easily through the sluggish black water. It rode an even keel and drew only a very shallow depth. The channel was about 6 feet wide here with a soft bottom. Lew discovered he couldn't lean his weight on the pole, for when he did, it buried itself so deeply he could hardly pull it free.

Alec called the turns of the course without hesitation. They crossed small dead-looking ponds, threaded wood-choked channels and occasionally cut across shallow water prairies, dodging the grass-covered hummocks that reared above the surface. Some of these bore scrawny trees on the high centers. They skirted bigger islands of palmettos and thick banks of impassable cane growing profusely out of the fertile mud. Trailing festoons of gray moss hung from the trees, slowly strangling their breath and life. Flocks of blackbirds gabbed noisily in the reeds and brush, and once a flock of hundreds of doves burst out over the open water, winging so close they instinctively ducked their heads. Swimming muskrats were common, and they flushed two small bucks with immature heads.

"Did you ever hear about my great-grandfather shooting a panther on the island?" Ginny asked Alec.

"No, Miss Ginny, I never did."

Lew paused to wipe the sweat from his face. The sun was almost directly overhead, and its heat had long since smothered the cooler air of morning. "I don't want to be selfish and keep this pole all to myself," he said. "You wouldn't have to twist my arm to make me hand it over."

"Okay," Charlie told him, "I'm coming." Lew steadied the craft with the pole as they changed places. "How far are we from Panther Island?" Charlie asked.

"Maybe half an hour," Alec answered.

That surprised Charlie because he had figured they must be almost there. Then he remembered the twisting course they had followed, winding along little channels, dodging hummocks and islands.

Lew opened the water can and took a drink. "Do you want to make plenty of money with this land?" he asked Ginny.

"Of course," she replied. "Who wouldn't?"

"When this business winds up okay and you get your money, pay off the taxes and rebuild the house into a hotel that caters to hunters and fishermen. Hire local guides and swamp boats to run trips back in here. People who don't hunt or fish will still come just for the wildlife and scenery. You can't miss."

"Sounds all right," she admitted.

"You've got my reservation right now for two weeks next winter," he continued. "See those ducks? Every one is a fat mallard, and there must be thousands scattered around. I'll bet Julie could do something wonderful with three or four of those birds in a roasting pan."

Ginny laughed. "There's a sure way to find out. Shoot some ducks, and give her a chance." After a pause, she added, "I am going to go out on my own for a bit after we land on the island."

Alec looked up, startled surprise showing in his face.

"I want to find something my great-grandmother left on Panther Island a long time ago," she explained.

Alec rubbed his stubby chin. "I don't know if the ha'nts are goin' to like that."

Alec sat staring out into the swamp with troubled eyes. That worried Charlie, as did the way he had taken to calling out the changes they must make in their course. His voice was faltering, and Charlie had begun to wish they had brought Julie along to bolster his dissolving courage. Alec still feared her voodoo. But Julie was miles away, and the frightening depths of the big swamp pressed close upon him.

Then Alec broke completely.

The boat had slid through a weedy bayou to a barrier of cane that split the water into right and left channels. Charlie let the boat glide to a stop. "Which way?" he asked.

"Take the ..." Alec's lips froze as the eerie, ghostly sound that had frightened him so badly before throbbed through the air. It started so low they could hardly hear it but swelled to an awful intensity that hammered painfully against their ears.

Alec groaned. "We're done for now," he muttered.

Lew grunted impatiently, grabbed an oar and with a hard shove turned the prow left. "Let's get out of here," he stated. The sound had startled Lew, although he would never admit it.

The boat shot along the split channel, then, seeing what looked like clear water on the other side of a thin fringe of cane, Lew turned the prow again, smashed through the barrier and floated out upon a little pool. Solid ground appeared beyond, and the boat ran aground with a soft jar.

Lew swung the boat broadside so he could jump ashore. He ran up the sloping bank through scattered brush and tall weeds. When he saw larger trees ahead he turned back.

"This looks like it," he declared and then looked at Alec for confirmation. He knew it was useless to ask a question that could be simply answered "yes" or "no." If he did, the answer he got would undoubtedly be "yes." So he said, "What place is this?"

He had to repeat the question twice before Alec admitted it was, indeed, Panther Island. Charlie helped Ginny out of the boat. Then they picked up their guns and started up the bank.

Lew looked at his watch. It was only 10:30, but they had eaten a very early breakfast and he was hungry. He thought, too, some hot food might put a little more life into their guide, so he said, "I'm going to build a fire and make some coffee."

He got the axe from their boat, went into the timber and found a dead stub still standing. The axe rang solidly against the hard, dry wood. But he chopped it down and dragged it back to the little beach.

Charlie carried up the carton of food and cut a pole to sling the coffeepot over the blaze. Ginny filled the pot with water from the can and measured out coffee. She and Charlie were alone now, for Lew had disappeared as soon as he had the fire going. Old Alec sat beneath a live oak with his back against the trunk.

"I never dreamed we would run into anything like these ghost noises," Ginny admitted. "They are beginning to frighten me. I'm almost ready to believe in Alec's haunts. But there has to be some other explanation, doesn't there?"

"Of course," Charlie nodded. "And a logical answer is that someone wants to frighten people away from the swamp."

"But why?" she asked. Then her eyes went big. "It's Joel! He wants to frighten us away so we won't find the money."

"No, it isn't Herring," Charlie corrected. "Remember, these sounds started at least three years ago. Herring didn't know anything about the family money then, and neither did you."

The coffee began to bubble over. Charlie raised the lid and set the pot on the ground at one side of the fire.

"I don't discount Herring's willingness to make trouble, but I think we can deal him out of this," he said.

Ginny shivered and drew her cloth jacket close around her shoulders. "It's so terribly still," she said.

Charlie, too, had noticed that as soon as they came ashore all sound seemed to cease. The birds were still. Even the breeze that had rustled the treetops and cane had died away. The quiet began to assume an ominous tone.

"I said we could deal Herring out on the ghost noises," he repeated, "but I don't mean he's out of the picture. I expect trouble from him sooner or later. He won't give up easily and let you claim your family treasure. There's bound to be a fight sometime."

"I suppose so," she agreed soberly. She took cups and plates out of the kit bag, set out sandwiches and a can of milk. "Shall I call Lew?"

"Wouldn't do any good," Charlie said. "He'll show up when he's good and ready, not before."

He went down to the boat and brought up the metal-detecting instrument. Then he showed Ginny how its needle swung about when he moved it closer to his shotgun. She took it from his hands and walked about holding it over the rough ground. Then, tiring of that, she set it down and came back to the fire.

"I saw a lot of otter sign this morning," Charlie continued. "A good trapper could really clean up in this swamp. The skins aren't worth as much as northern otter, but you can make up for that with numbers. A good trapper working on shares could pay your taxes and give you some spending money besides."

Lew came out of the timber walking very fast. "Lunch ready?"

"All ready," Ginny replied. Then she saw his eyes were shining with excitement.

"Well, put it on hold. We've got something more important to do right now."

"More important than lunch?" Charlie asked in surprise.

Lew grinned. "Come along, I've something to show you. I want Alec to see it, too. I found the ghost that makes the spooky sounds, and are you ever going to be surprised."

# Chapter 9 - Lew Lays the Ghost

Ginny and Charlie were surprised and pleased when Lew told them he had discovered the "ghost" responsible for the uncanny sound they had twice heard that morning in the swamp. As long as the mystery remained unexplained, their guide Alec would believe it had supernatural origins and be frightened so badly he would be no help in their search for the Breckenfield family treasure.

But the old man stood up unwillingly, panic filling his eyes. "I'm afraid, Mister Lew," he mumbled.

But Lew took his arm firmly. "There's nothing to fear," he said. "I guarantee it. Bring the axe with you." Then he dropped Alec's arm and led the little group around the edge of Panther Island.

"What is it?" Ginny demanded.

"Think I'm going to spoil my big moment by telling now?" Lew retorted. "I worked this out, and I am going to make the most of it."

"Should I start to applaud now?" she asked.

Lew grinned and said, "You'll know when. I heard the sound again when I went after firewood. It was faint, and since no one mentioned it, I knew you hadn't heard it. So after I dragged in the dead stub, I went back and walked until the sound was loud and marked the spot. Then I went straight ahead until it grew faint again. Next, I back-tracked until it was loud again. I marked that place and the two marks were less than 70 feet apart. I knew the source of the sound lay somewhere in between."

He glanced around to see if they were properly impressed. Ginny raised her hands, clasped them together and shook them vigorously above her head. Lew ignored that.

"I figured the sound came from a tree. Remember how there was a breeze blowing when we heard it? So I searched the treetops inside that 70-foot space. The thing had to sit high to catch the wind."

As he turned around a thicket of green briars, a rabbit bounced out of the grass almost at his feet. "Darned marsh rabbits," Lew grumbled. "Well, I found our ghost in the fifth tree I checked. Listen, and you can hear it now."

The uncanny throbbing was just audible above the rustling of grass and leaves. Lew led them another hundred yards farther, stopped and pointed to a tree with a five-inch trunk. "Look up in the top."

"All I see is a blur," Charlie said.

"That's it," Lew replied. "I climbed up as far as the trunk would hold me and then got a good look. Chop her down, Alec."

The old fellow started to obey, but his arms trembled so Charlie took the axe from his hands and sank a wide notch in the wood. When the tree quivered, he pushed it slowly over to the ground.

"There's your ghost," Lew announced.

It was a wind wheel fastened just below the tip bough. Its double blade measured some 20 inches and was formed of rough wood. From the wheel ran a wooden vertical shaft three feet in length. Little wheels with cog teeth connected the parts so the shaft would turn. At its bottom another set of sprockets revolved a small cylinder made from a section of hollow limb. Shallow notches were cut around the outside of this drum, and a short flexible shaft bore into them. Lew gave the wheel a sharp spin. The flexible shaft slid off each notch making sounds like the noise-makers at a carnival. Only the tone was entirely different.

"This contraption has two sound boxes," Lew said. "The hollow drum is one and then the slat is mounted on another, like the walnut turkey calls some hunters carry. When the wind really blows, the sound is continuous. Real clever, all right."

Charlie nodded. Then he examined the shaft, saw it was held to the limb with loose wood clips that served as bearings. Everything was whittled from wood, smoothed and darkened like it had been soaked with wax. The device looked durable enough to last for years.

Lew continued to act as master of ceremonies.

"See how the drum is camouflaged with moss to make it invisible from the ground? Even when it spins, you can't see the blades. When it is still, it hangs down like another tree limb. A fellow has to have keen eyes to spot a thing like that," he added modestly.

The most astonished in the group was old Alec. He spun the wheel carefully and then looked up at them with sheepish eyes. Instead of sharing their enthusiasm, he seemed crestfallen to see the swamp ghosts unmasked. But Alec still had a card to play. "It don't have noth-in' to do with the ha'nts' devil fire. I seen that with my own eyes."

"Tell us," Charlie invited. "Where does it appear?"

"All over the swamp. Balls of fire that float on the water."

"All right," Charlie declared. "We'll clear that up, too. If we're still here when it starts to get dark, I'll make some devil fire myself. If I do," he turned to Alec, "will you stop being afraid?

"Yes sir, I sure will."

Charlie motioned Alec over to a smooth patch of ground. "Can you draw this island to show its shape?" he asked.

Alec used a twig to make a few scratches in the sandy earth, wiped them away with his fingers and started to rough out what looked more like a big, upside down pear. When he was done he stabbed the ground near the lower pointed end. "We landed here, Mister Charlie."

Charlie nodded his satisfaction. "Since we're practically standing on the small end now, we'll search it first."

Walking back, he remembered he had left the coffeepot beside the flames of the fire and wondered if all of the drink had boiled away. But only a third was gone, so he added water and started eating.

"I've figured out a system to cover this ground without missing any," Charlie said. "The detector is sensitive up to 20 feet, so if we carry it along lines spaced 30 feet apart, it will only have to cover 15 feet either way. That provides a five-foot margin for error on each side. I'll carry the instrument; Lew will walk ahead with his compass to lay out a straight course. Alec will bring the axe to clear a path when the brambles get too thick."

"What about me?" Ginny asked.

"You break off twigs to blaze the trail so we don't search the same space twice. That won't be hard, because four of us walking through the grass should leave a plain path."

Lew finished his big ham sandwich, looked wistfully at the remaining four stacked in the paper carton, but then got resolutely on his feet. "Maybe I should have shot that rabbit," he muttered.

"Sorry, but we save the rest of the grub for supper," Charlie said.

"If I had a hook and line, I could cut a pole and catch some bream," Alec offered.

"There's a rigged line in my jacket," Lew stated. "But I think we better start to work now."

If Alec's drawing was accurate, a line running southwest would cut straight across the small end of the island. Charlie decided to run that course first. He checked the time with his watch when they started. They had to force through many low thickets of brush and briars tangled with vines, and the axe swung steadily for a time. When they reached higher ground, the brush faded and they walked easily through a stand of scattered trees.

Charlie carried the detector in front of his belt buckle, holding the case level. He paid sharp attention to the needle, because jolts from the rough trail sent it quivering. He decided to stay well behind Lew and Alec when they swung the axe. He had left his shotgun back at their little camp, tucked under the waterproof tarp. Lew, however, had insisted that Ginny carry his lighter shotgun. It weighed less than seven pounds, and she assured him it was no burden.

They passed a small spring bubbling out of the ground, the damp earth about it crisscrossed with tracks. Lew saw clear sign of coon, possum, mink and turkey.

Another belt of brush separated the timber from the other side of the island. Lew stopped at the edge and then stepped carefully off solid ground onto a crust of decayed vegetation topping the black water. It trembled under his weight and his boots slowly sank into the jelly-like surface. He scrambled back in a hurry. "If a man lost his boat here, he might never get out."

"Alligators gonna get you if you swim," Alec informed him.

Checking his watch, Charlie discovered it had taken 50 minutes to cross the end of the island. When he told Ginny she looked startled. "It is a bigger undertaking than I thought," she confessed. "I see now we would have gotten nowhere by digging blindly."

Charlie decided they should follow the edge of the island, skirting the end until they came back to their starting point. Lew agreed. "I always thought we'd find the treasure close to water," he said.

"That is a natural thought," Charlie replied. "The letter said, 'the end of the island.' But it didn't mention how Ginny's great-grandfather had taken the black cat. If it had, that might help. If the cat was taken in a trap, it could have happened at the swamp margin. But if it was treed and shot, then that probably occurred inland where the timber was bigger. No panther is going to run up a sapling."

He glanced at Ginny, saw her nodding eager agreement.

"Don't tell me again I'm clever," he said grinning. "Once today is enough." Then he leveled the instrument and started walking.

For a quarter of an hour they chopped and pushed their way through the growth. Charlie finally stopped and said, "Everybody move back. I think I've struck something."

He studied the detector needle. It was quivering like a thin-haired hound in the rain. He moved experimentally back and forth. "That's funny," he added. "The action grows stronger when I walk towards the swamp." He stepped carefully into the fringe of tall cane.

"We can't do much digging in water," Lew grumbled.

"I've found it. Seems to be a boat. Bring the axe."

"A boat?" Ginny echoed, keen disappointment in her voice.

Lew slashed at the cane, and the side of a boat gradually emerged. He stepped over into the hull. The wood felt solid, held his weight easily. He gave a low whistle. "Come and look. This boat is completely grown-in with cane. It must have laid here for 50 years."

He moved towards the center of the craft. It seemed to be about 20 feet long with a beam 5 feet. There was a square stern and only several inches of water in the bilge. That surprised him until he saw the ragged hole in the transom that drained off accumulated rain.

Lew's foot stumbled over something amidships that looked like a pile of rusted iron bars. He picked one up, saw it was an old octagonal gun barrel. A few fragments of wood stock still clung to the breech. The bore was big but almost closed by corrosion.

"What used to be a dozen or more rifles triggered the metal detector," he told his companions. He took out his knife and whittled on the gunwale. "It's cypress—that explains why it is still sound." He started towards the stern, stopped abruptly and backed away.

"Find something else?" Charlie asked.

"I just wanted to see how deep the bilge was," Lew evaded. He climbed back on solid ground. "I bet that old craft could tell some pretty good tales if it had lips."

"Suppose it belonged to pirates?" Ginny suggested.

"More likely slave hunters," Charlie said. "It's queer they would leave their guns."

When Alec went on ahead with the axe to cut trail, Lew whispered to Charlie, "There's a pile of bones back of the guns. Enough to make half a dozen human skeletons. I didn't want to get Alec up in the air again. He's jumpy enough now."

After more hard work they returned to the starting point. A faint haze climbed lazily up from the embers of the fire. Charlie checked his watch again. It had taken a little over an hour to complete the half circle. "That means we marked off at least a quarter section of the land we have to explore," he said with some satisfaction.

Lew put down his gun and went to the grub box, picked out a ham sandwich and turned around to look out over the swamp.

His hand froze halfway to his mouth and he yelled in alarm, "Our boat! It's going away!"

Charlie picked up his gun as he ran past the tarp. Their boat was moving slowly through the little channel. He started to raise the gun, then let it sink. There was nothing to shoot at; the craft was empty.

# Chapter 10 – Business as Usual

Lew stood on the bank above where they had landed on Panther Island, shaking his head in amazement. "That's the payoff," he declared. "When an empty boat starts down a channel and then makes a right-angle turn all by itself, I've seen everything."

Again becoming aware of the big sandwich clamped in his hand, he raised it and bit out a chunk.

"You got here first," Charlie said. "Did you see anybody?"

Lew swallowed hard to empty his mouth.

"Nope. The boat was only about 10 feet offshore. It was absolutely empty. Yet it glided along as nice as if a man poled from the stern. Maybe there is something to Alec's ghosts, after all."

"That's enough dumb talk," Charlie said sharply. It irritated him that Lew would encourage their guide's belief about ghosts almost as much as the loss of their boat. Charlie started running along the bank.

"Come on. The channel parallels the shore for a ways. Maybe we can see it farther down."

But they didn't. The thicket of canes was so high it blocked off any view of the outer channel. Lew climbed a tree, but that advantage didn't help. He slid down the trunk, landing in a shower of loose bark and dead leaves. They walked back to the beach.

"No more talk about ghosts," Charlie warned.

Ginny was kindling the fire when they arrived.

"I thought some fresh coffee would help us," she explained.

Charlie looked at Alec. The old man sat with hands folded on his knees, staring straight ahead. His features were resigned, calm.

"Alec," Charlie said curtly. "We need firewood. Take the axe and chop a big pile." Alec stood and got the axe. He moved like a man walking in his sleep. "Listen to me," Charlie ordered. "Ghosts didn't take our boat. And we're going home whenever we wish."

Alec looked at him doubtfully. "If you say so, Mister Charlie."

"I do say so. And after you chop some wood, cut a pole and catch a mess of fish. Lew will give you his hook and line. You know where to get some bait?"

"Yes, sir. The little worms are inside the water lily stems." The old fellow moved a little more briskly, as if the prospect of action had raised his morale. Charlie figured it would. He knew hard work makes an excellent antidote for despair.

After Alec was out of earshot, Ginny said, "Suppose he takes you at your word and asks to go home tonight? It's all right to talk him out of the dumps, but didn't you promise too much?"

Charlie grinned. "I must be slipping in your esteem or you wouldn't have even asked that. When we are ready to leave, we will use the old boat we found in the canebrake. Lew said the wood was solid, and there's only a small hole in the stern to caulk."

He turned to Lew. "When you finish your coffee, walk over and work the boat free. Then see if you can pole it around here."

"Okay," Lew replied. "I'll have to take the axe from Alec. But then he can start fishing. What are you going to do?"

"Work with the metal detector. We came here to find the Breckenfield treasure, and we're back to business as usual, right?"

"Bravo!" Ginny cried.

Lew cut a long cane for Alec to use as a fishing pole and gave him the rigged line from their emergency kit. Then he picked up his shotgun and with the axe in his other hand, started across the end of the island. Following the trail they had made two hours before was the long way around, but he was afraid if he tried a shortcut he might overshoot the location of the old boat and miss it.

A large animal crashed through the brush just before he reached the timber belt. He didn't get a clear view but he decided from the way it held close to the ground and smashed straight through dense brambles it was a wild hog. He made no attempt to shoot. He was glad, though, that he had changed from quail loads to number fours.

Lew flushed a rabbit, dropped the axe and swung the gun up with both hands. The first shot tumbled the rabbit, and after field dressing he shoved it in the pocket of his hunting coat.

Then he noticed a bright object beside the path they had made on their first trip over. He picked it up. It was a gum wrapper, and he started to throw it down. Then his fingers tightened. None of them had chewed gum that day. Someone else had passed through—recently too—for the wrapper was fresh and dry. He dropped it thoughtfully, wondering if they had been followed. "At least," he thought, "I can rule out ha'nts. Whoever heard of a ghost chewing gum?"

Another rabbit darted from a heap of leaves. Lew missed the first shot, sending the charge into a tree trunk behind which the animal had dodged. His second sent the rabbit rolling. He put the gun down, took out his knife and picked up the carcass.

"What you doin', buddy?" a rough voice came from a clump of slim trees at his right.

Lew stifled the impulse to whirl about. He slit through the rabbit's stomach and then turned deliberately. A man stood about 30 feet away. He was tall and thin with sallow skin and deep-set eyes. He held a single-barrel shotgun in one hand and wore blue denim overalls, a blue work shirt and high top leather boots laced with white rawhide. When he saw the boots Lew knew the stranger had been standing there, waiting for him. Nobody could move soundlessly through dead dry leaves and grass in that kind of footwear.

"I'm cleaning my rabbit," Lew answered coolly.

He didn't like the way the fellow watched him. The sunken eyes looked menacing, and his own gun lay on the ground about a yard from his foot. The muzzle was pointing at the stranger, and Lew was glad of that. He was also glad he had automatically reloaded both chambers before he had started for the rabbit. If the encounter led to quick shooting, he could fall to his knees, snatch the weapon and level it fast enough to hold his own.

"You're trespassin'," the stranger stated.

Lew continued shaking the rabbit's entrails out on the ground.

"I didn't know that," he answered, wiping his knife and putting it back in his pocket.

"Well, you are," the fellow stated evenly. "You're in a jam, too. Shootin' without an owner's permission is frowned on around here."

Lew slipped the rabbit in his coat, leaned over and picked up his gun. He tried to move casually, but he didn't lose any time. He saw the other begin to lift his own weapon higher, as if in protest, but that came too late. Lew already held his shotgun waist high in both hands. He felt better with his thumb pressing on the safety catch and his forefinger resting on the front trigger.

"I suppose you do have the owner's permission?" he asked.

"You bet," the stranger drawled. "Got a written lease for all huntin' and trappin' rights. That means you got to square off with me."

"Who signed your lease?" Lew asked. Ginny had not said anything about leasing the swamp.

The fellow scowled. "Who do you think? Ginny Breckenfield. Last time, it was her mother."

Conviction grew in his mind that the fellow was lying. Lew didn't like that. Still, another angle had started to clear up.

"If you have a lease why rig sound boxes in the trees?" he asked
That jolted the man. "You found them?" he asked hesitatingly.
Lew nodded.

"Those jiggers save us lots of trouble. We can't watch out for
trespassers all the time, so we put them things up and put out word that
the swamp was haunted."

"What do you mean by we?" Lew asked.

"Me and my brother," the answer came sullenly. Then the sunken
eyes gleamed. "How come you're askin' all the questions?" he snarled.
"Them things don't matter. What does is you got to pay me for huntin'
here. Either that or go to jail."

So far, they had remained separated by some 10 yards. Now Lew
walked forward to reduce the space by half. "How much you figure I
should pay?" he asked mildly.

For several seconds greedy eyes played over his new hunting
coat and engraved double gun. "'Bout a hundred dollars would fix
things," the fellow finally said.

"For a couple of rabbits?" Lew demanded.

"That's cheap compared to the fine if I go for the warden. You'll
get a jail term, too, and lose your gun. Yankees are bumped hard down
here when they break the law." He took a stick of gum from a pocket,
tore off the wrapper, dropped it and then shoved the gum in his mouth.

"You've been trapping otter, haven't you?" Lew asked.

The man scowled, but his involuntary start told Lew he had
scored. "I suppose," Lew continued, "two hustlers could trap 80 otter
in this swamp, maybe 100. Looks like a regular fur pocket to me."

"Listen," the fellow snarled. "I'm sick of your talk."

He took two steps forward. "Do I get that hundred or not?"

"The answer is not," Lew said, ignoring the bad grammar. "And
don't get any foolish ideas about using that gun. You only got one
hand on it, I've two on mine. I think you're lying about the lease. But
it doesn't make any difference what I think. We can settle it in a few
minutes. Miss Breckenfield is at the other edge of the swamp."

"Ginny Breckenfield's here?" the fellow asked in a clearly startled tone, his lantern jaw sagging.

"That's right," Lew assured him. Watching consternation grow
in the man's face opposite, Lew thought he might as well fire another
round. "You know, the state is going to take this swamp over as a game
refuge. She offered it several years ago. The deal may have already
gone through, and if it has, you're the one in a tough spot, old boy."

Lew was well pleased with himself as he watched genuine panic spread into the man's face. Then the fellow turned abruptly and dashed off into the timber. Lew could have shot him, but not a fleeing man, and not in the back. He was out of sight in five seconds, although Lew could still hear the booted feet smashing grass and brush. Lew rubbed his chin soberly. He wasn't so pleased now, and he began to think maybe he hadn't handled the interview any too well.

"An eager beaver, that's me," he muttered. "I might have learned more by holding back. I should have asked him about our boat."

That reminded Lew of his job. He went back, recovered the axe and then started briskly walking. It took only a few minutes to reach the opposite edge of the island, where he turned right and soon stood beside the old boat. His previous footmarks in the spongy soil had oozed full of water. The stuff sucked at his soles like quicksand as he walked through.

He grasped the boat's gunwale and studied the thick cane towering a good 10 feet on all sides. It would take much chopping to float the craft away. He swung up a foot to step inside but that step was never completed. His lowered eyes had seen a hole smashed through the bottom a foot wide and twice as long.

For a moment Lew felt a sensation not unlike fear. He remembered old Alec's prediction they would die in the swamp with no means of escape. Without a boat, the drowned prairies and channels would be impassable. He scrambled back to firm ground. Then the furrow between his eyes smoothed. There were at least two other avenues to freedom. The trapper he had encountered certainly had a boat. Lew felt that with Ginny backing him up on the bogus lease claim, he could put enough pressure on him to lend it to them.

Joel Herring was a possibility, also. Herring knew they were searching for the lost Breckenfield money. He would know they had entered the swamp, and when they didn't come out he would look to find the reason why. Not with any intention of rescue, Lew didn't deceive himself about that. But Herring would have to know if they had succeeded in finding the money. And if they had, he would take steps to get it into his own hands. All they had to do was wait until he appeared.

Even if these angles failed, he believed Charlie and he could build a raft that would serve. He grinned, started to whistle, but then ceased when he remembered what he must do next—that was locate the trapper who had just run off into the timber.

The best place for the man's camp would be at one side of the island, near open water. To find it, he only had to go to the place they had met and follow the fellow's trail.

The man had left plenty of sign running off so hurriedly. Some of the grass he had mashed down was still straightening up, and the little movements caught Lew's eye instantly and made trailing fast. The boot marks faded out over a patch of sun-baked muck, but Lew found something at the other side that made him grin—another gum wrapper glinting in the afternoon sun.

The trail led Lew to a shore overlooking scummed green moss and lily pads. He skirted the edge, climbed a low bank, stepped over a little spring and saw a spot of grayish white ahead. It was a tent.

Lew walked carefully now, leaving the path for places where the brush stood densest. Soon he could see the camp well. It stood above the mouth of a black-water channel that wound off through the cane, to be swallowed by the big swamp 100 yards away.

Lew's eyes touched a pile of dead limbs corded behind a chopping block. A wooden boat was tied up at the end of the channel, and several long, slim, steel fur stretchers leaned against one of the tent poles. A rope stretched between two trees held a pair of faded blue blankets. Before the tent door was a pile of dead ashes. There was a second tent in behind the first, much smaller in size. It was closed up and looked like it might be a storage cache. The smell of raw pelts hung heavily in the air.

There was no sign of the poacher Lew had trailed, so he decided to approach closer. His keen ears caught a faint sound. As he listened, a smile broke out on his face. Lew had heard the sound too often lately not to know what it was. It could only be one thing, the clunking of a wooden pole against an aluminum boat hull.

Lew was positive their missing craft was headed towards him in the narrow channel. He dropped the axe and took a tighter grip on his shotgun. The smile on his face changed to a wide grin. This was going to be some real fun!

# Chapter 11 – Looks Like We Hit the Jackpot

A few minutes after Lew first heard the bump of a pole against aluminum, their stolen boat emerged from the swamp as he expected and approached the poachers' camp. A man stood in the stern, tall and thin like the fellow Lew had encountered half an hour before. He was dressed similarly in blue overalls and shirt, but there the resemblance ceased. This one wore a wide-brim western hat, and the bottoms of his jeans were tucked inside the loose tops of cowboy boots.

Lew's eyes clung to the sleek lines of the aluminum boat; he liked that craft a lot. Edging closer to the camp, he heard a noise in the larger of the two tents and the first poacher thrust his head out the door. Then the man came outside and walked down to the edge of the water.

"Where'd you get that?" he demanded.

"I took it from those dudes on the other side of the island," the boatman replied. He poled up alongside the moored wooden skiff. "I'll bet it cost three hundred bucks."

"Nice boat, all right. What you aim to do with it?"

"Keep it a while, Ben. Then, when the dudes get worried, I'll sell it back to them or maybe return it for a reward. After they stay a night on the island and hear the noises, they'll be mighty glad to leave. And I don't reckon they'll want to come back, either."

"You're wrong, Zeke. Them fellows ain't dudes, even if they got flashy clothes. They already found your croakers in the trees. And Ginny Breckenfield is with 'em. I told one of them we had leased the swamp from her, trying to put on the bite for him hunting here without permission. That ain't gonna stand."

They were both silent for a time. Then Ben continued, "There's more, and it's worse. He said the girl offered the swamp to the state for a game refuge. If they took it, we're in a real jam."

"He was probably lyin'," Zeke replied.

He stepped out of the boat carrying a single-barrel shotgun, a mate for the weapon Ben had carried back in the woods. "But even if he wasn't, it's bad as we just got started good on the otter."

Ben nodded. "I reckon we got to figure something out."

"There's four of them," Zeke said. "The two hunters, a girl what's got to be Ginny, and an old black man."

"Four is a lot to handle."

"Not out here, not for us. It's the stink that may be kicked afterwards that bothers me."

Lew felt his heartbeat quicken. "They're willing to kill us," the thought raced through his brain.

"You said you saw them. How'd you get the boat so easy?"

"That was funny," Zeke replied, but he didn't laugh. "I landed on the island and was looking over their camp when I heard them talking in the timber. I got back in my boat and shoved off. Then I thought I could just as easy tow this one behind it, so I rigged a piece of trotline fast. Their boat dropped back a good dozen yards, and they never even seen me in mine."

He took a piece of plug tobacco from his pocket and bit off a chew. "When they saw it following without anybody inside, they thought the ghosts had come. The girl screamed, and the old man began to pray."

Lew's anger turned to disgust. "We were dopes, all right," he muttered. "We should have known somebody towed the boat off."

Zeke started up to the tent. "I left my boat in the swamp to save time. We can pick it up tomorrow. How about some chow?"

Ben stirred the ashes of the campfire. "I'll start some now."

"They found the old cypress dugout in the cane," Zeke said. "I can't figure how they knew it was there. We'd been by the place 50 times before we saw it. I put a hole in the bottom so they couldn't leave the island in it."

Ben fanned the fire with his hat and then laid on some split sticks. Zeke leaned his gun against a small tree. Lew thought this was as good a time as any to appear, so he stepped out of the brush. When Zeke started for his gun, Lew said quietly, "Not a good idea."

His own muzzle covered the man's body. Zeke dropped his hand and stepped back. Ben froze like a statue beside the fire. Lew edged around until he was by the tent door. Glancing inside, he saw the other shotgun lying on a thin mattress. He snatched it up in one hand and said, "Now, get down to the boats."

"We didn't do nothin'," Ben whined.

But Zeke remained silent, his cold eyes watching Lew like those of a rattlesnake.

"I have an idea you've done plenty," Lew retorted. "I think you're a nasty a pair of thugs. I'm going to have a nice talk with the sheriff, ask if he has any unsolved disappearances in this swamp."

He moved carefully, gathered both of their guns in one hand and walked to the edge of the trees where he had dropped the axe. The three things made a big handful, but Lew managed to keep them covered with his gun. He would have liked to look about the camp, particularly in the smaller closed tent, but he didn't dare take the risk. He walked down the bank, moving them back at a safe distance as he approached.

"I'll give your guns to the sheriff," Lew said as he stepped in the aluminum boat. "You can ask him for them when you explain about stealing this boat and trapping Miss Breckenfield's land without permission." He dropped the two guns and the axe but kept his gun pointed at them. He took up the pole with his other hand and shoved off. The boat moved away, and Lew continued the short jabs until he was about 30 feet distant. Then he laid his own gun down and pushed hard.

That was a mistake.

Zeke pounded up the bank with long leaps and dashed in the tent. He came out leveling a nickel-plated revolver. Lew gave the pole everything he had and ducked. The gun cracked and a bullet passed through the bulkhead beside his knee. He dropped the pole and brought up his shotgun. Zeke threw himself flat on the ground and shot again.

The boat was rocking from Lew's movements, and the revolver shot missed again. Then Lew fired, aiming low so the charge slammed into the ground to fling a shower of dirt into Zeke's eyes.

Lew heard him swear in a low, unhurried voice. There was a turn in the channel just ahead, so Lew put his gun down and poled for all he was worth. He decided the shooting was over for now, because he was out of sight of the camp. Then he wiped the sweat from his face and buckled down to the job of poling the boat around the end of the island so he could join his companions in the shortest possible time.

"I'm doing alright making enemies," he grinned. "These fellows added to Herring and his pair of felons makes five."

Back on the other shore of the island, Charlie hadn't lost any time getting back to work with the metal detector. He had a strong feeling they should complete the job as soon as possible, almost a premonition that they were working against time, time that was fast running out.

He couldn't explain the urge, but it was there, and he didn't waste energy fighting it. He decided to concentrate where they had landed. It was a natural approach to the island, and there was a chance it had been used long ago, too. Ginny's great-grandmother may have disembarked there when she buried the treasure. If she had, then it wouldn't be so very far away.

Alec had disappeared with his fishing pole. Ginny rinsed out the coffee cups and said, "What can I do?"

"Come with me and carry my shotgun," Charlie told her. "And bring the axe."

Starting where forest and jungle met, Charlie blazed four lines of tree trunks to enclose a rectangle of about 3 acres. Then, walking parallel along one of the long sides, he carried the instrument back and forth at 30-foot intervals.

"If you were a panther," Charlie asked suddenly. "What kind of ground would you like?"

Ginny laughed. "I don't know about panthers. But I know house cats don't like to get their feet wet. So I think I would stay on high places like this one. I would dodge thickets, too."

"I think the same way," Charlie agreed. "That's why I started here." He paused for a moment to wipe his brow.

"We're handicapped not knowing exactly what kind of cat your great-grandfather shot. The island may be named for a panther. But maybe the early settlers called all big cats panthers, which could include bobcats. Bobcats don't dislike damp places; they'll even swim to escape hunters with hounds."

"The letter said it was a big black cat," Ginny remarked.

"That does make me favor the cougar idea," Charlie replied. "Some southern cougars are quite dark with black ears and tails. It wouldn't take much imagination to think one black."

"I've seen bobcats at the zoo," Ginny said. "They're awfully smooth and slick."

"Not bad eating, either," Charlie replied. "They don't have a gamey flavor like some other wild animals."

"You have done a lot of hunting, haven't you?"

He nodded. "Hunting and trapping. For years we made our living that way. It was a good living, too. Some would think it hard, but we didn't. We had to outguess wildlife and the weather. But both are honest, not crooked like so many humans."

A distant, wistful look in his eyes made her keep silent for a second. They paused to rest at the end of one of the lines.

"What are you thinking about?" she finally asked.

Charlie's eyes left the horizon and he grinned. "Lots of things: a cabin sitting in a valley between two ranges of notched hills; snow drifted four feet deep and covering most of the windows; deer hides hanging from a pole wired between two spruces, dry enough to rattle in the wind; the wood smoke you smell when you're 50 yards away, wading through that snow with a heavy load; the glow of the fire spilling out of the stove's cracked top when you open the door; caribou steaks two inches thick, and a slab of tin pail bread spread with marrow."

"What's tin pail bread?"

"Bread made from sour dough set in a tin bucket. You keep it warm until the smell almost runs you outdoors. Then you bake it. It really tastes swell."

"What do you do when you aren't hunting and trapping?"

"Mostly make plans to go again," he replied. "We weren't able to do much of either the last few war years. After that stretch in U.S. Army special intelligence, we got roped into a couple of private investigations that we couldn't turn down."

"Tell me about them," she urged.

"There isn't much to tell," he protested. "First, we worked for a girl whose father had been murdered. She was in a tight spot. Funny, she was a brunette like you, with the same dark eyes and hair. A little taller, though, but with plenty on the ball. She paid us a thousand dollars to find some records that put her father's killers away for good. We had to take her and a friend over a wilderness canoe trail to a Northwoods hunting cabin. The girl friend turned out to be one of the crooks and almost got us killed before we found her out."

"What happened to her?"

"The crooked friend? Nothing. They couldn't prove anything on her. She had a line that made you believe she was a dizzy blonde, but actually she was smarter than a fox."

"I mean the dark-haired girl with plenty on the ball," Ginny said.

"I suppose she's married someone by now. We haven't heard from her in months."

"What was the second investigation about?"

Charlie took a thoughtful pause then replied, "A young dope named Bert went north to hunt deer. Some crooks made him think he had shot a man by mistake and talked him into concealing the accident. He paid them five thousand blackmail. Then a year later they demanded another five thousand. His father hired us to check on just what really had happened."

"Did he pay you a thousand dollars?"

"More," Charlie grinned. "We started off at $25 a day each and expenses. Then we wound up with a nice bonus. Those blackmailers would have bled the family dry if we hadn't blocked them."

"Was there a brunette mixed up in that case, too?" she said.

Charlie laughed. "Two. The girl who ran the camp and her cook."

"You make a lot of money, don't you?"

"We did all right those times. But we took some hard knocks."

"That's what Lew told me when we first talked," she said.

She looked down at her shoe, rubbed it back and forth over the ground. "If those people paid you so much, why did you offer to help me for nothing?"

"We figured we were entitled to a vacation. This isn't hard work, you know. And with very pleasing surroundings."

She flushed under his steady eyes.

"Just the same," she insisted, "I'm going to give you something very nice when we find the money."

Charlie picked up the metal detector.

"We can't do that standing around talking," he said.

They combed the marked rectangle of ground, laid off another and worked that. The sun had dropped close to the line of treetops. There weren't many hours of daylight left.

Charlie turned off course to miss some briars, plunged his foot into a grassed-over den hole and nearly fell. Straightening, he noticed the needle of the detector swinging back and forth. Thinking the fall had caused it, he leveled the box and waited for the needle to subside. But it didn't. It felt like icy water was racing down his back as he moved ahead, watching the needle's agitation grow with each step. Then the needle went wild, and he bumped into a small tree.

"I've got something," he told Ginny.

He walked past the tree, turned and approached it from the opposite direction. "This tree is the middle of the active area. The attraction must be buried underneath it. Run back and get the shovel. I'll chop the tree out of the way."

Charlie swung hard against the base of the sapling just at ground level. He was pushing it over when Ginny came with the shovel. He enlarged the sandy hole until it was 3 feet wide and then started to sink it straight down.

Ginny was strangely silent.

"Relax," he said, wiping his face.

"I'm not nervous," she calmly replied.

Charlie cut through a mass of fine roots. "Just don't be disappointed if this misfires," he warned. "Lots of different kinds of iron could be buried here."

The shovel point struck something hard. It didn't sound like a rock. He felt for an edge, cut down and got the blade underneath. Then he pried until the shovel handle cracked. But with that burst of loose dirt something raised. Charlie dropped to his knees and lifted out a square iron box.

He thought it would measure some 15 inches long and a little less high and wide. It was covered with thick flakes of rust. Two outside hinges at the back held the lid. A folding hasp lock was attached at the front. Charlie pried on the lock but it didn't yield.

"Looks like we hit the jackpot," he said.

## Chapter 12 – The Law Steps In

"Yes," Charlie said, looking down at the rusted old chest, "I think we hit the jackpot. This was buried so long ago the tree had time to grow on top of it. It must be the box your great-grandmother described in her letter."

"I know it is," Ginny asserted with complete confidence. "I've known all the time we'd find it. That's why I am not excited now. I used to think I would dance and sing when I recovered the family money. Now all I want to do is sit down."

"Legs kind of shaky?"

She nodded.

Charlie grinned. "You're still excited. Just the symptoms are different." He lifted the box. "Feels about as heavy as a small sack of flour. We'll need something to open that lock." He glanced around at the scattered tools.

"I'll carry the chest and my gun. Can you manage the metal detector and axe? The shovel handle is broken, but the blade is fine. We can come back for it later."

When they reached the landing place Ginny said, "I'll make more coffee. Lew will be hungry when he arrives."

Charlie brushed at the red stains on his hunting shirt. "I'm going to wash the loose rust from this chest. Then we can handle it without ruining our clothes."

On his way to the channel he met Alec. The old man carried a string of five small fish. He said, "Here is all I could catch, Mister Charlie. I reckon they will help on our supper."

"They look good to me," Charlie replied. "But we may not have time to eat before we leave." The assurance in his voice put vigor into the old fellow, and he walked briskly to the fire. Charlie knelt at the edge of the water and scrubbed the chest with wet leaves and grass.

When he was done the chest looked almost clean. Ginny rubbed her hand over the lid. "I can't wait until we get it home and open it. I wish Lew would hurry." Her eyes studied Charlie's bare neck. "What happened to your shirt?"

He pulled his coat closer around his throat. "I tried to wash the rust out and hung it up to dry."

"I'm sorry. It was such a nice shirt. But I'll get you another one just like it. Why doesn't Lew come?"

A minute later they heard the sound of a pole knocking against a boat hull. Ginny lifted the coffeepot lid. "It's done," she announced. "And Lew's on time. Want a cup?"

"I'll wait," Charlie replied. He moved around the fire so he faced the swamp and sat down beside his shotgun. Ginny looked up, saw his sober eyes and said, "Something wrong?"

Alec saved him answering her. "Look," the old man said. "That ain't Mister Lew."

It wasn't. The boat that emerged into the clear center of the channel contained three men. One stood in the stern with a pole, another sat up in the prow. Charlie had never seen either of them before. But he had seen the third swinging a second pole from the beam.

It was Joel Herring.

"Looks like trouble," he told Ginny.

"You knew it wasn't Lew," she declared.

"It sounded like there were two poles instead of one."

"What can we do?" There was a desperate note in her voice, and she threw a frightened glance at the iron chest.

"Sit tight and wait for Lew. I don't expect Herring will try any strong arm stuff. This looks different."

Herring jumped ashore. The man in the prow followed. He was past middle age, short with a heavy waistline and florid face. A third figure in blue overalls and a black felt hat stayed seated on the stern

Herring stepped up briskly. He didn't waste any time.

"Evening," he said curtly. "This is Deputy Bales. He has a paper to serve you, Ginny."

The deputy pulled back his coat to display a star pinned to his vest. He took a folded document from one pocket and spread it out.

"Court order and writ," he recited glibly. "Issued by Judge Henderson, Probate and Appeals. Herring vs. Breckenfield, et al. Stay of future action in the matter of search and confiscation of assets found on property claimed by plaintiff until lawful title is decided. I have authority to receive any applicable assets and deliver them into the custody of the Court."

His eyes fastened on the iron chest beside Ginny's feet.

Her eyes flashed with anger.

"Take it," Charlie said, indicating the paper Bales held out.

"Yes, take it, cousin," Herring said with a smirk. "You can't refuse. It's all legal; you have to comply."

He leaned over and poked at the lock on the chest lid.

"Leave my property alone!" Ginny cried.

Herring's smirk widened. "Did you find this in the swamp?"

"Yes, but…"

"That's all we needed to hear," he cut in. "Pick it up, Bales. It is a part of the property in dispute. I'm glad you didn't open the box, Ginny. If you had, we would have been obliged to search you."

She beat the air with frantic fists. "You louse!" she finally stormed. Then she whirled about facing Charlie.

"Do something! Are you going to let them steal my money?"

"Just a minute," Charlie said. He got up and walked over to the chest, took the document from Ginny's hand and started to read. The deputy stood quietly waiting.

"You can't buck a court order, Ginny," he finally said. "It's out of our hands now. The next move is up to your lawyer."

"I'm glad somebody has sense," Herring said. "Go on, Bales. Pick up that box. I want to get out of this place before dark."

"I'm sorry, Miss Breckenfield," the man said. "You admitted you found this chest on the property. I have to take it. Those are my orders."

"I'm not blaming you," Ginny said.

Herring was already halfway back to the boat. Bales followed with the chest in both hands. They climbed aboard, Herring picked up a pole and shoved off. The boat was swallowed up by the swamp.

Ginny's legs folded and she fell in a heap on the ground.

"It's so unfair," she wailed. "We work out a hard problem and then Joel steps in and takes the money. I'll never see the chest again."

"I think you will. The writ looked genuine. The Court will hold the chest until the case is decided. I don't see how Herring has any legal standing, but your lawyer will take care of that. Besides…"

A shout from the swamp interrupted him. It was Lew.

"Start the coffee hot. I'm hungry."

"Praise the Lord!" Alec exclaimed. "Mister Lew got his own boat back again."

Lew ran the nose of the aluminum craft aground and hopped out.

"I've been busy," he exclaimed. "I found the guys who rigged the sound makers in the trees. They're trapping your otter, Ginny, cleaning up in a big way. They said you gave them a lease on the swamp."

"That's a lie," she declared without hesitation.

"That's what I thought. One of them stole our boat. And then he chopped the bottom out of the old cypress dugout so we couldn't use that to leave the island. They planned to sell our boat back to us. Then when I told them Ginny was here, they began making plans to murder all of us. Nice neighbors you got, Ginny. You better see the sheriff and turn over the otter they already trapped."

Lew finally paused and got a good look at her sober face.

"What's up?" he said anxiously.

She put hands before her eyes and began to sob.

"Things have happened here, too," Charlie spoke. "First, we found the treasure chest."

"Was it empty?" Lew demanded. "Is that why she's crying?"

"Keep quiet and let me finish. Just five minutes ago Herring landed with a deputy sheriff and a court order that stopped any search of the swamp pending a trial to determine legal ownership. The order directed the deputy to seize anything we had found. So he took the chest away. There wasn't anything I could do. He had the law behind him."

"The dirty scum!" Lew growled.

"I want to leave quickly," Charlie said. "Load up the boat."

He went over, laid a hand on the girl's shoulder.

"Don't cry. It'll all turn out okay. I know it will."

He took her arms and helped her up, opened his lips like he was going to add something, closed them, and then walked over to kick dirt on top of the fire.

Lew piled equipment hurriedly in the boat. He took out the poachers' guns, removed the shells and laid them on the ground.

Alec got nimbly in the boat and grabbed a pole. Charlie had never seen him move so fast.

"Alec," he said. "If you know any shortcuts that other boat won't take, use them. I want to get home fast, but I don't want those fellows to see us. Understand?"

"Yes sir," the old fellow exclaimed.

Lew had brought back two poles. He took the second.

Ginny stepped in to the boat silently. Charlie came aboard last, carrying his shirt in his hands. It was wadded up in a bunch, and he shoved it under the center seat.

Moving out through the channel, Charlie glanced with troubled eyes at Ginny's hopeless expression. He seemed moody and spoke briefly, only at long intervals on the way home. Alec did know a few shortcuts, and he poled with the eagerness of a horse whose rider has at long last, finally, turned his head to face the barn.

The shadows deepened, but Alec chose their course with the sureness of a homing pigeon.

Half an hour out, Lew raised a warning hand. He had caught sounds of the other boat. They stopped to wait alongside a muddy bank edged with rank crowning grass. A little breeze hit the cane and started its tall stems rattling. A low throbbing became audible in the wind. Lew grinned. "There's one of your swamp ghosts, Alec."

"Yes sir. But I'm not scared no more. No little old whistle up in a tree goin' to scare this old man."

Then he scratched his head dubiously. "Mister Charlie, you said you'd explain the devil fire I saw on the water."

"Sure," Charlie replied. He glanced around, took a pole and shoved the boat closer to the mud bank. Then he leaned down to study the black oily edge. He pulled the boat ahead slowly a foot at a time. Then he took a match from his pocket, struck it and held it close to the water. A tiny flame licked over the surface several times and went out.

"Marsh gas," Charlie explained. "It bubbles up from the decaying vegetation buried below. This is just a trickle. I suppose the poachers found some big jets that would burn a longer time."

The kitchen of the old plantation house blazed with light when they drew along the rickety dock. Lew warmed to the sight, remembering Julie's promise to have two chickens in the pot tonight.

But he sobered quickly when he saw Ginny climb wearily out and walk with drooping shoulders.

Alec started on in a trot. "I got to feed the stock," he explained.

When they entered the kitchen a tall, thin man with white goatee was talking to Ginny. She said, "This is Judge Catron."

He offered his hand to Charlie first.

"I was just explaining to Miss Ginny about Joel Herring's suit. He filed his claim to the Breckenfield property under a very old state law that deals with male descent of heritage. I didn't get her letter in time to oppose the filing. Consequently, it went through and the county granted his stay. But Herring can't win on that. He might, however, on the matter of back taxes. He has promised to pay them promptly. They are the only cloud on your title that I worry about. If we could pay them, the other suit would be thrown out."

"I can't pay them," Ginny said wearily. "Herring took the chest with my family's money."

Catron pulled his goatee and frowned. Charlie had been standing near the door. He advanced now with something in his hands. It was his red shirt. He laid it on the table, spread the corners out carefully and exposed a good-sized heap that glinted like a myriad of suns.

"Herring took the chest," Charlie said. "But he didn't get the jewelry or the money. Here it is, Ginny."

She cried out in amazement; Charlie poked at the stuff with a forefinger. "Here's the necklace you mentioned, looks like it may be worth at least fifty thousand. Here's the brooch and the ring. They won't sell for hay, either. The rest is provincial money. I remember reading that some of the southern states minted their own gold coins in early days. There was quite a lot of the metal mined right here. Isn't that right?" he appealed to Judge Catron.

"Quite right, my boy," Catron replied.

But then he frowned, cleared his throat and asked, "How did this come into your possession?"

"Just a lucky break. When I was washing the old box, I discovered the bottom was loose. It had been a separate panel either riveted or crimped in place. I pushed it up at one side and managed to shake this stuff out. Then I stuffed mud in its place so the box would still be heavy. I had a hunch things had been going too smoothly for us. So I thought I should keep an ace up my sleeve."

"Quite clever, I'm sure," the judge rumbled. "But I wonder if it is strictly legal? I am an officer of the court, you know."

Charlie grinned.

"I didn't tell Herring we hadn't opened the box. He stated the fact himself. He didn't ask if the contents were separate. Neither did the deputy. Besides, we hadn't been served with the writ then."

"So, you just toted a fortune back in that old red shirt," Lew added, not showing the least surprise at that.

Ginny broke out in hysterical sobs. She threw herself on Charlie, flinging arms about his neck and pressing her face against his.

"Say," he protested, "this isn't any time to cry."

"I'm crying because I'm so happy! I can't help it, and I wouldn't if I could."

Julie came up and unwound her arms gently but firmly from Charlie's neck. "You come with me, Miss Ginny. I'm going to quiet you down." She led the sobbing girl away.

"You know what she meant, don't you?" Judge Catron asked. "Julie is intensely jealous. She can't bear to have anyone touch Ginny."

"Going to be tough on Julie when Ginny finally decides to get married," Lew remarked. Then he went over to the stove, lifted the pot cover and sniffed. The aroma was delicious, and he noted with pleasure that the pot was full, too.

"Alec's chicken flock won't last long at this rate," he said.

Ginny came back into the room. Her eyes glowed and her cheeks were flushed with excitement. "I forgot to thank you," she told Charlie.

"You don't have to. I'm sorry I lied to you about washing my shirt. All the way home I felt bad about your grief and disappointment. But I still wanted to play it safe. Herring might come back and ask about the chest's contents. I thought the fewer who knew the better."

"What were you going to do if he had?" Lew asked.

"Jump overboard with the bundle and hide in the swamp. You could come back for me in the morning."

Lew was stalking impatiently about the room. Finally he said, "Isn't anybody else ever going to get hungry? I'm starved. Where are those chickens, Julie?"

"Coming right up, Mister Lew," she replied. "I've made more hot biscuits with gravy, baked yams, fried hominy, dried apple pie and ..."

"Stop!" he protested. "You're making me weep."

He pushed a bench towards the table.

"I sure would like to see Herring's face when he gets that box open and finds mud in it. If I could, that would be a perfect ending!"

*The End*

# Operation Danger
## Chapter 1 – The Phantom Boat

The river twisted and turned, divided into black channels that led aimlessly through the grass flats. There was no obvious current in the brackish water, no markers to help determine a course. Charlie and Lew were sure they had missed the main channel hours ago, and the number of cabbage and sentinel palms growing in the shoulder-high grass indicated they would reach the ocean farther south than planned.

The channel forked again, and Lew hesitated. Then, shrugging, he swung the aluminum boat's prow right. "Doesn't make any difference which way we go, now," he said. "The ocean is too close to miss."

They could smell the sea in the air. Lew didn't like the salty odor because it made him think of overripe fish, and that clashed with his relish of good food. Then that reminded him how hungry he was, and he looked at his watch. The time was 4:30. It had been a long day, just like yesterday and the day before. Since leaving the Breckenfield plantation they had done nothing but ride along in their 14-foot skiff, a monotonous business for anyone liking action as much as Lew.

"I'm glad we got away from Ginny Breckenfield," he said. "She was beginning to worry me."

"How?" Charlie asked.

"The way she looked at you, like she was hearing church bells. That's why I talked up this trip to the coast to catch some striped bass and maybe shoot a deer on one of the barrier islands."

"Ginny was only grateful because we found her family jewels," Charlie replied. "I may go back in a couple of weeks. I could sure go for another of Julie's chicken dinners."

Lew grinned at that. "Uncle Alec's hen house was almost deserted by the time we left." Then his eyes glistened at the memory. "How that woman could fix chicken gravy and biscuits!"

The channel ran almost due south between sandy banks studded with dwarf oaks and palms. They suspected it followed the general course of the coast, which could be anywhere from 500 to 1,000 yards away. An hour before sunset they landed on the right bank to make camp. After the boat was unloaded, Lew shoved off in it to catch a fish for supper. He rigged the line on his casting rod with a silver spinner, added a strip of pork rind, and drifting slowly in the center of the channel, cast towards each bank and retrieved with a series of sharp jerks.

He got a solid strike on the fourth cast and brought a largemouth bass to the boat. It might go slightly over 2 pounds, a good size to eat. Lew put the fish on the stringer, but he preferred striped bass because the meat is firmer with a milder flavor. So he kept fishing. He missed the next strike by trying to set the hook too soon. Since they didn't really need another fish, and his stomach was growling, he decided to make one more cast then head back to shore.

Something grabbed the spinner and started down the channel. Lew waited a couple of seconds and then set the hook hard. The fish took off, line singing off the reel. The click drag was set light for the smaller largemouth bass in the brackish canals and bayous. Lew thumbed down hard to slow the fish, but it didn't turn, didn't even hesitate. Lew clamped on more pressure, and the line went slack. He reeled in and found the spinner and wire leader missing.

Charlie had cleared a bare place in the dry marsh grass for a campfire, had gathered a pile of dead palm stalks and oak limbs for fuel. The two sleeping robes were spread nearby, air mattress pads inflated beneath. Lew nodded his approval then cleaned the bass and fried it in bacon fat. Charlie opened a can of tomatoes, another of peaches, and made coffee. They had part of a loaf of bread left and some butter.

The sun had been down some time, but enough light remained to reveal a thin gray mist creeping in from the ocean. Charlie got up and covered their beds with a canvas tarp to keep everything dry.

Lew yawned. "In the morning I want to try for that big fellow again. We're in no hurry, are we?"

Charlie shook his head. He took off his shoes and socks and stretched his feet towards the fire. The warmth felt good in the dampness. "Take all the time you want," he replied.

Lew picked up a dead palm. Then he dropped it and pointed towards the water. Charlie turned and saw the profile of a low, slim boat cutting through the fog. A single figure sat motionless in the stern. There was no sound of an engine, no motion of oars or paddles, yet the craft slipped swiftly past their camp and disappeared into the gloom beyond. Lew picked up the stalk again and laid it on the fire.

"There wasn't any motor on that boat," he commented. "You know they can't muffle an engine so I don't hear it."

Charlie nodded agreement. He was well aware of his companion's keen ears.

"No sail," Lew continued, "and the guy wasn't rowing. There might be a tide, but it wouldn't push a boat that fast. I'd like to know how he did it."

"So would I," Charlie agreed. "I'd also like to know why."

Lew went fishing again the next morning while Charlie cooked breakfast. He caught another small bass and put it back in the water.

They packed the boat and pushed off. Lew fished the channel, cruising above and below the site of their night camp. They were about opposite it at noon, so they landed and kindled a fire on the ashes of the previous night's fire. They heated canned beans and sauerkraut and made coffee. They also had more fresh fish.

Lew had taken and released some nice bass, several going over 5 pounds. He was disappointed not to hook the big one that had got away, declaring it would go over 40. Finally, in mid-afternoon, he declared he was through and reeled in his line. They cruised down the channel hunting an outlet to the sea.

A bridge spanned the water, and since a bridge meant a road that led somewhere, they moored the boat below it. Lew emptied the gas remaining in the fuel can into the motor's tank. He poured the freshwater from their milk can into a kettle and took both containers up to the road. The highway was paved, and a couple of buildings stood some 100 yards away. One looked to be a store, its sides plastered with soft drink ads. There was a gasoline pump in front.

A man sat in a chair tilted against the wall. He rose slowly and filled the gas can. Then he showed Lew a cistern where he could get water. Lew went in the store next and looked over the stock of groceries. He winced a little when he saw the prices, but he bought eight assorted cans and a loaf of bread to maintain a safe supply. He had to make two trips down to the boat, and when he came back for the second load, he asked, "Got any ghosts around here?"

"What do you mean?" the man replied.

"Boats that move without engines or oars," Lew replied. "No sails, either."

"Trying to be funny, bud?"

"Just asking," Lew said cheerfully.

The storekeeper went back to his chair. "Might not be healthy to ask too many questions around here," he growled.

Lew stopped on the bridge and climbed on top of one of the side railings to look around. Intervening sand ridges hid the ocean, but he did see a great expanse of grassland cut into dozens of islands by a maze of channels, bayous and sloughs.

Charlie had rinsed their fish lines in the kettle of clear water and strung them along the bank to dry. He stowed them back in the boat as Lew loaded his purchases. Then they started on. A mile ahead the channel branched, and this time Lew steered into the left passage. They rounded shallow curves, looping back and forth before finally the ocean was revealed ahead. It was wide and blue, surf gently breaking on a strip of beach beside the channel outlet.

High dunes stretched out into the water, making the small inlet a natural harbor. But instead of the seaport they had hoped to find at the end of their cruise, only a dozen or so houses were strewn along the sand. A sagging pier did run a couple of hundred feet out from shore. Two fishing boats were moored on its leeward side, nets hanging to dry from posts planted above the tide line.

The houses were hardly more than shacks, ill-kept and all but abandoned. Any paint that might have covered the walls had long since been ground off by the gritty wind. The biggest building stood on a dock beside the channel.

There was a gasoline pump at one end of the platform and a ladder led down to the water. "GAS & EATS" was painted in straggling letters on the wall facing them.

Lew throttled down and steered in for a closer look, the word "EATS" catching his eye. They tied their boat to the dock. Then they climbed the splintered rungs of the ladder and paused beside the pump to look around.

A rutted sand road started in front of the store, loped off to pass between the shacks, and turning inland, disappeared into an overgrown bank of brown reeds and palmetto.

Two boys in straw hats and overalls sat on the seaward end of the pier holding cane poles. No one else was visible, but sound pouring out of the store indicated that people were congregated inside. Voices shouted and laughed over a jukebox playing a jumping dance tune. Lew could hear shoes scraping across the floor.

"Sounds like a real party going on," he grinned.

A small motor bus with faded yellow body and steaming radiator emerged from the reeds and palmetto and ground toward them in low gear. It lurched to within a dozen yards and stopped. The driver climbed out with a traveling case, set it on the sand, and held back the door while a girl in a blue suit stepped down. Then he reached in the bus for a pail and started down to the beach.

The girl looked up and caught the tail end of Lew's grin. Her mouth tightened and she turned to face the sea.

Charlie opened the screen door and then waited while Lew stood watching the driver. "I thought you were hungry," he said.

"I am. I was just wondering if that guy is going to pour cold water on top of that hot engine. She'll bust wide open if he does."

"Who do you think you're fooling?" Charlie demanded with a grin, following him through the door.

Lew also grinned. "She wasn't hard to look at," he admitted. "I wonder what she's doing in a dump like this?"

The front of the building was empty if you didn't count the shelves loaded with goods, mostly canned. The rear room, however, was crowded with at least 20 people sitting at tables or standing before a bar at the back. Most were young; both sexes equally represented. All wore T-shirts or sweaters with duck trousers or blue jeans. Two couples were dancing with a vigor that made the floor shake.

Lew and Charlie squeezed past and found an opening in the line before the bar. A bald man in a dirty white shirt with sleeves rolled up to reveal thick biceps and shoulders raised his eyes.

"Cola," Charlie said. "What have you got good to eat?"

The man eyed them sulkily. "Hamburgers, red-hots, and corned beef sandwiches."

"Corned beef," Charlie replied. He figured meat from a can should be safest. Lew nodded assent.

The bald man splashed mustard on four slices of bread, added chunks of beef, and slid the sandwiches over on two plates. He stood the colas alongside and said, "That's a dollar-ten."

Charlie dropped the money on the pine bar. They walked to an empty table against the wall. A window over it looked down into the channel, and Charlie pulled his chair closer so he could keep an eye on their loaded boat as they ate.

Lew watched the dancers. A man with bronzed skin and yellow hair stood out from the others, not just because he towered 6 inches above the rest, but because of his astonishing agility. Although slightly taller than Charlie and just as heavy through the shoulders, his feet seemed to plant no weight at all when they hit the floor.

He wore rope sandals; a sheath knife hung from a wide leather belt that rode above his hip. There was a half-sneer on his face as his bold eyes roamed the room aggressively.

"That guy is looking for trouble," Lew thought as he chewed the corned beef. "It shouldn't be too hard to find in this crowd, either."

He studied the faces of the other young men. All were lean and hard-bitten. All, curiously enough, had the same straight hair, flat features and sallow skin. But the deep, sunken eyes with heavy lids repelled him most. He shivered involuntarily when he met the dull stares turned their way. "This is one sure enough tough outfit," he murmured.

"Talking to yourself again?" Charlie asked mildly.

Lew didn't answer. He was staring at the front of the store, sandwich raised halfway to his mouth. Charlie followed the gaze and saw the girl who had arrived on the bus.

She set her traveling case on the floor beside the door and came slowly forward, scanning the room with dubious eyes. Her blue suit looked tailored. It also looked completely incongruous with the denim slacks and shirts of the other young people, and her face showed that she knew it. Her eyes touched Lew's and slid away. But he had seen enough to change his first opinion that her glance was dubious.

She was plain frightened.

## Chapter 2 – A Man Dropped Out of Sight

The girl in the blue suit, who had arrived on the bus about the same time Charlie and Lew moored their boat at the dock of the little fishing village store and tavern, surveyed the crowd with frightened eyes. Someone whistled loudly, derisively.

Her face flushed, but she gripped the top of her blue leather purse firmly, walked to the bar and spoke to the bald man in the dirty white shirt. Lew couldn't hear what she said, but he saw the fellow nod and point. She turned and looked at the two dancing couples.

The music ended; the dancers halted their fast routine, pulled down shirts and sweaters and headed for the bar. The tall man in rope sandals who had drawn Lew's eyes with his surprising agility strode ahead of the others and planted himself close beside the girl in blue. His partner shoved blonde bangs off her moist forehead and scowled. She had a short but well-developed body and a face with youthful features—save for the eyes. They were worldly, to say the least. Lew didn't know whether to peg her age as 16 or 30.

The tall man and the girl in blue were talking earnestly. Then he grabbed her arm and pulled her away from the bar. It looked like she protested, but he paid no attention and steered her to a table. Two fellows were seated at it, but they got up when he said shortly, "Beat it."

One said, "Sure, Hed. Sure."

Hed slapped the table with his open palm, making a sound like a rifle report. "I run this joint, see? "

The bartender hurried over with two bottles. Lew swung his chair around a little so he could watch as he ate without seeming to stare directly at them.

"But I don't want anything to drink," he heard the girl say.

"You drink before we talk business," her companion replied.

Lew chewed a piece of beef thoughtfully. It suddenly seemed stringy and dry. Somebody dropped money in the juke box, and chords resounded through the room. Hed jumped up and gripped the girl's arm. "We're gonna dance," he announced.

His former partner was standing at the bar with a bottle in her hand. She put it down and came over in a swaying gait, the scowl on her face changing to dark anger. She grabbed the man's arm.

"I'm your girl, Hed Litnore. You said…"

She didn't finish because he raised a hand, put it against her mouth and shoved. She staggered and fell across Lew's knees. He tried to help her, but she bounced away without seeming to notice. She trembled with rage but then went still. Her features flattened even more, and she walked listlessly towards the front of the building. A moment later the screen door banged shut behind her.

Litnore had pulled the unwilling newcomer to her feet and was dragging her from the table. "I don't want to dance," she cried.

Lew started to rise but Charlie touched his arm.

"Let me handle this."

Charlie arose, seemingly in no hurry. "This is a free country," he said slowly. Nobody has to dance unless they wish."

"Drop dead," Litnore snarled and turned back to the girl.

Charlie's hand shot out and grasped the elbow on the arm holding the girl. His fingers dug into the vulnerable spot where a big nerve passes close to the bone. Hed's hand dropped, fingers paralyzed. His face flashed with fury and his lips drew back exposing white, irregular teeth. His other hand streaked for the sheath knife at his hip, but Charlie was expecting that. He caught the hand, stepped sideways, twisted the fellow around and slid the arm he still held up across his back into a torturous hammerlock.

The man cried out sharply. Charlie tightened the lock a little and marched him to the door. "Next time you try to pull a knife on me, you'll really get hurt," Charlie told him in an expressionless voice.

Then he shoved. Bending forward with his free fingers scraping the floor, Hed kept his feet but then struck the screen door with his head, crashed it open and fell through.

Charlie didn't expect a quick return, for he had given the arm a severe wrench. He turned and faced the silent room. All stared at him, cold hate in most of those dark eyes.

Something lay against his shoe. He looked down and saw a partly filled package of cigarettes that must have fallen from Litnore's pocket. He picked it up and was going to toss it in the trash when he changed his mind and thrust it in his coat. He went back to their table. The music box still played, but the volume had been turned way down.

Charlie looked over, caught the bartender's malevolent eye, and said, "Two more colas." The man nodded sulkily and after a long interval came across the room with the order.

The girl in the blue suit had gone back to her own table. Standing beside it, she watched Charlie for almost a minute before she said, "Why don't you mind your own affairs?"

Charlie glanced up in surprise. "I thought it was my affair, or that of any decent person."

"It wasn't," she replied.

Charlie eyed her thoughtfully. Then he pulled a chair up beside his. "Come over where we can talk without raising our voices." She hesitated, flushing a little under his steady gaze, then obliged.

"I don't often apologize for doing a favor," he continued. "But if this is one of those times, I'm sorry."

She looked down at her hands nervously gripping the top of her purse. "Apologies won't help. I don't know what to do now."

"I'll tell you what you should do," Charlie replied. "Get on that bus and go home. You don't belong in a place like this."

"What's wrong with this place?" she demanded.

"I don't exactly know, but something is wrong. I can see it in the faces. Did you ever see such eyes? This may be a fishing village, but I believe there's more going on here, something dangerous."

Lew looked equally sober. He had felt the same thing, and his partner's corroboration made it real. Charlie was not prone to vivid imagining. A cold prickle tickled the back of Lew's neck.

The girl studied Charlie. Finally, she said, "You think something is wrong? That may be the reason I haven't heard from Ted."

"Who's he?" Lew asked.

"My brother. He came here two weeks ago, and I haven't heard from him since even though he promised to write me every day."

"Bet they get poor mail service here," Lew suggested dryly.

"No," she earnestly corrected. "The bus driver told me he handles mail twice a day."

Lew couldn't think of an answer for that. "Do you want some lunch?" he finally asked.

"Thanks, but I ate at Meridon."

Sensing more than seeing movement behind them, Charlie looked up quickly. A young fellow in a red and white striped T-shirt leaned down and said in a low voice, "Hed sent me for his cigarettes." Then, as Charlie made no move towards his pocket, he prompted, "You picked them up from the floor. Remember?"

"Why didn't Litnore come?" Charlie asked mildly.

"He said he didn't want to make any trouble."

Charlie stared back into hard eyes that reminded him of a snake's.

"Tell Litnore if he wants them, to come and get them himself. I want to ask him a question."

"He won't like that," the man snarled.

Charlie didn't reply, just maintained the same cool gaze. The young fellow made a sort of strangled gasp and walked back to the bar.

"What about those cigarettes?" Lew asked.

"I have a hunch about them. Let me see if I'm right."

He slid the package from his coat and examined the contents. "I was right," he said. "About half of them are hand rolled with some dark, coarse stuff, probably hemp."

Noting the girl's blank eyes, he added, "Marijuana. Addicts call it reefer."

"What made you think dope?" Lew asked.

"The dull eyes and sallow skin of these people. And the way Litnore's dancing partner went limp after being so angry a second before. Hemp smokers blow up and cool down fast."

Charlie got up and walked to the bar. Handing the cigarettes to the fellow in the striped T-shirt, he said, "Here's Litnore's smokes. I've changed my mind about asking him a question."

Back at the table he turned to the girl. "A missing man in this place is a job for the police, not a worried sister. There's a sheriff at the county seat, or you could hire a private detective—if you want to keep your brother's disappearance a secret."

He watched her closely, read the answer in her face. She didn't want any involvement with the authorities.

A motor rumbled outside. "That sounds like the bus," Charlie said. "Want me to hold it for you?"

"I can't go without finding Ted," she replied. Gears clashed then meshed in a high-pitched whine. The noise faded and finally ceased.

"What did you want with Litnore?" Charlie asked. "Why were you mad when I pulled him off your neck?"

"The man at the bar said he had a boat. I wanted to rent it."

Charlie picked up the bottle of cola that had gone ignored while they talked. His eyes swept over the room as he raised it, encountered those of the bartender. Something in the fellow's odd stare made him hold the bottle to his mouth but only pretend to drink. Then he set it back on the table. He looked quickly at Lew's cola. It was about a third gone. Lew was flexing his fingers toward the glass when he met Charlie's gaze. Charlie shook his head. Lew's hand closed, his eyes asking an unspoken question.

Charlie said softly, "Doped."

Lew looked startled then angry.

"What did you say?" the girl asked.

But Charlie didn't answer. Instead, he asked abruptly, "What's your name?"

Her face went stiff. "I don't see what difference that makes."

"None," he agreed. He was watching Lew. His companion seemed no worse for drinking the cola. His eyes were still bright and clear—and mad. That anger, Charlie thought, could help offset any effect of a sedative by increasing the adrenaline in Lew's blood.

"You have no right to question me," the girl added.

Charlie didn't reply to that. Instead, he asked, "Where are you going to stay tonight?"

That brought the fear back to her eyes. "I don't know. I guess I should have gone back on the bus."

Charlie stood up. "Let's go outside," he said quickly.

He turned to Lew. "All right?"

Lew nodded.

"Then pay for that last round, will you?" Charlie put a hand under the girl's elbow, and she accompanied him without protest.

Out on the platform he sucked his lungs full of air. It was a relief to be out of that ugly, smoky atmosphere. This girl worried him. He shot another quick glance and noted once more the quietly expensive clothing, well-kept hair showing under the small blue hat, her smoothly molded face.

Charlie looked down at their loaded boat and then out past the village to the sea. He wanted to go but could not leave this girl to fend for herself.

The sound of feet scuffing on wood brought him around. He relaxed when he saw a girl in blue jeans approaching. It was Litnore's dance partner. But her manner had changed. She was anything but listless now. Her eyes glowed and her lips parted in a vivacious smile. She came up close to him and put a hand on his arm.

"Listen, I don't know why I'm doing this, unless it's because I like to see that big ape get pushed around. But be careful. Hed isn't soft. He's snake-mean and he can throw that knife like other men shoot a gun. I hope you don't mix with him again; you're too good-looking to die young. Better get out of town, and fast."

# Chapter 3 – Peril Straight Ahead

Charlie looked down at the girl. Her breathless animation contrasted so much with the listlessness of a few minutes ago he figured she had smoked a doped cigarette like those that had fallen from Litnore's pocket in their recent scuffle. The acrid odor on her breath confirmed the thought.

She reached up suddenly and patted his cheek. "If you don't go," she added, "I'll be around. Just ask for Nan."

Then her flat-soled shoes slapped against the plank platform, and the screen door of the tavern closed behind her with a bang.

"Well," the girl in the blue suit said, "there's a character. A second after warning you to leave, she invites you to pick her up."

Charlie brushed past her, striding swiftly to the door. Lew had been gone longer than was necessary to settle for a round of colas, and Charlie realized that the sound of voices inside the building had ominously stilled. Nan stood in the doorway. Looking over her head, Charlie saw Lew backing away from a tight group of men. None gave an impression of strength, but their number alone was menacing, and so were the sunken, flickering eyes. Two others were creeping along the side wall to get between Lew and the door.

Charlie shoved Nan inside and reached the barroom entrance as the pair sidled into it. Both were so engrossed in their stalk of Lew they didn't see him. One carried a bottle. The other held an opened jackknife. Deciding that one most dangerous, Charlie seized his shoulder, jerked him around and hit him squarely on the chin.

The other raised the bottle and stepped towards Lew, but Charlie's long arm grabbed him before he could bring the bottle down. When he turned, Charlie hit him squarely on the nose. Blood began to pour before he even hit the floor.

Both had fallen directly behind Lew, and Charlie put out an arm to steady his companion so he wouldn't stumble. Lew moved clumsily.

Charlie stepped in front and said, "Go on outside, Lew. I'll finish up in here."

The group paused, feet shuffling uneasily. Charlie grabbed the bottle from the floor beside the man he had knocked down last, smashed the bottom off across a shovel leaning against the wall and lifted the jagged glass.

That stopped them cold, watching him with furtive eyes. Finally, some of the shoulders sagged. When Charlie saw that, he backed out of the building. Passing Nan, he heard her sultry whisper, "You must be some kind of Superman ..."

Once outside the door, Charlie turned to Lew and said, "Can you make it down to the boat?"

"Sure," Lew replied. "My feet feel heavy, but I can manage. That soda was doped, all right. Lucky I only drank a little of it."

He climbed down the ladder, stepped in the boat and pulled two cases from under the tarpaulin that covered the prow. Opening them, he extracted two automatic pistols wrapped in shoulder holsters. Charlie came to the edge of the dock.

"Catch," Lew said and tossed up one gun. Charlie caught it and stepped back to the tavern doorway.

The girl in the blue suit watched with astonished eyes. "Did you get in another fight?" she asked.

Lew replied with a grin. "Some guys didn't want to let me leave, but Charlie talked them out of it. They tried to dope us with that last drink. I got a notion to go back and tear the place apart."

He was starting up the ladder when Charlie said, "Untie the boat and pull it a hundred yards down the channel. Then wait for me."

He looked at the girl and said, "Get in the boat with him. I'll bring your suitcase with me."

When her mouth tightened, he added, "Do you expect this bunch to just let you sit on the beach all night?"

She scrambled down the ladder and sat on the center seat. Lew started the motor and steered the boat out into the channel. A face appeared behind the tavern door, but it disappeared when the owner saw the gun in Charlie's hand.

When he rejoined them 10 minutes later he didn't climb in over the prow of the beached boat. Instead, he stood on the sand looking at the girl with thoughtful eyes.

He reminded himself that she had intelligent features, was expensively dressed and immaculately groomed. Her poise indicated refinement and education. He decided it was time to voice his thoughts.

"You won't tell us your name. Your brother came here two weeks ago for some reason you don't want to tell us, either. You're scared because you didn't get any letters from him although he promised to write daily. So, instead of telling the police, you come here alone to find out why. Right away, you get mixed up with Litnore, the beach bully and Lothario, and he begins to maul you. I pull him off and you act mad—at me. You're stuck here until the bus comes in the morning, and there's no safe place where you can sleep tonight. That's a lot of mistakes," he concluded, "and I hope you didn't make any more."

"If I did, it's my tough luck," she said tightly. "You don't have to worry about me."

Charlie said gently, "Why don't you tell us all about it?"

"Why should I?"

"Well, for one thing you say you need a boat. We have this one; it's small, but it's seaworthy. You could use it for a small amount—or even for nothing. There will be no passes made at you, either."

Her eyes fell before his, she bent over and covered her face with her hands. Her shoulders shook with silent, wrenching sobs.

"Hey," Charlie protested, "don't do that. There isn't time. We have to start right away to get anywhere but here before dark."

She took her hands down. "I'm sorry. I have been so worried about Ted, and this place turned out so terribly different from what I expected. Litnore wouldn't tell me if Ted came here at all, and you don't know how frightened I was back in that ... that bar. When you offered your boat—and your help—I had to let go."

She took a white handkerchief from her purse and wiped her eyes. "I don't know why you want to help me, not after the way I behaved and got you in trouble with these people."

Charlie grinned reassuringly. "Maybe because I'm just a Boy Scout at heart. Or it could be because you have a nice smile—when you aren't being stubborn."

He was glad to see a little color creep up into her cheeks. It was a good sign her composure was returning.

"Trouble with Litnore and his gang doesn't worry us," Lew assured her. "We can handle their type."

"They worry me," Charlie said quickly. "Trouble always does. Where do you want us to take you?"

"To a small island off the coast called Canary Cove. My father owned a fishing camp there, and when he died last spring he willed it to Ted and me."

"What course do we set?"

"I've never been there. That's why I tried to hire Litnore."

"We can't set out blind," Charlie said. "How was the island and camp described in your dad's will?"

"Just as 'Winthrop's fishing camp on Canary Cove.' Our family name is Winthrop. Mine is Betty."

"There would have to be a deed or a lease with the legal description," Charlie suggested.

"If there was one, the executor kept it. I asked him for the papers but he refused, saying I would get them after the estate settled. Mr. Totten hasn't been very pleasant. He always thought my mother was to blame for the divorce. Ted and I lived with her and only saw Dad once or twice a year."

Charlie looked across the little bay toward the ocean. There was a lot of space out there to search with no clue to distance or direction.

"Why did you come here?" he asked Betty.

"When Dad wrote to me from camp, his letters were postmarked at Meridon, so I went there. The agent at the bus station advised me to come here, because someone would surely know where the island lay. Did you know this village is named 'Buzzard Point'?"

"Not a bad fit for this dump," Lew grunted. "Here comes an inhabitant. Let's ask her about Canary Cove."

It was the girl Nan, shuffling through the loose sand. She had pulled a scarred leather jacket over her sweater, and when she came closer Charlie saw that the recent vivacity had drained out of her face.

"Leaving already?" she asked.

Charlie nodded.

"How about taking me along?"

He nodded again. "Sure. We're a little crowded but there's room on the middle seat for two. I'm glad you came; we need a guide. Where is Canary Cove?"

She halted. "You going there?"

"That's right."

Nan stepped back. "Guess I'll stay here, then. I thought you were just cruising along the coast."

"How far out is the island?"

"Six or seven miles."

"We'll make it all right. Get in."

But Nan demurred. "I don't think your girlfriend likes me."

"You're mistaken," Betty said quickly. "I'm perfectly willing to have you come along."

Charlie looked impatiently at the sky. It was clouding over and night was close. "If you won't come, tell me the course to set."

"You could never find it. There's too many reefs and small islands to dodge. It's easy enough when you're coming in from the outside, but going from here you have to know a dozen turns."

"Look," he said. "Miss Winthrop thinks her brother is on Canary Cove and she wants to see him. Can we hire you to show the way?"

Nan dug one toe into the sand. Then she looked up.

"Okay. I'll come. But I better pick up some things. We might not get back tonight." She started back towards the group of shacks sitting on the left bank of the channel.

When she was out of hearing, Betty said, "I'll pay what she charges—but do we have to take her?"

Charlie shrugged. "You heard what she said. We might stumble on the camp or we might search for days. Besides, I think someone told her to come with us."

"Who?"

"I don't know. But if we take her, we have a chance to find out."

Lew muttered something that sounded like "too many dames."

Holding Betty's gaze with his steady eyes, Charlie said, "Tell us why your brother came here, and why you didn't go to the authorities when he didn't write. We are willing to help you, but for our own protection we have to know more of the angles down here. We won't go blindly into something that could turn out illegal."

"Ted isn't guilty of any crime," she stated clearly. "But he saw one committed and is a witness. It was a shooting at a night club. Rocky Rand, whom the papers called 'a small-time racketeer with big-time connections,' fired the shot. There was another witness besides Ted, and he has already disappeared. Ted didn't want to be killed, too, so he came down to Dad's camp to hide. Are you satisfied?"

Charlie nodded then asked, "Why didn't he stay home and ask the district attorney for protection?"

"Ted isn't brave," she admitted. "And it is difficult to protect someone if a criminal really wants to get him. Isn't that true?"

Charlie nodded again. "The only sure way is to lock a witness up in jail, and then in solitary confinement."

He glanced at the shacks. Nan was leaving one of them with a small case in her hand. He looked out toward the sea and noticed for the first time that only one of the fishing boats lay moored alongside the pier. The other had vanished.

Nan came up, gave Charlie her case and stepped aboard.

Lew started the motor. Shoving the boat clear, Charlie climbed in and sat on their bedrolls just ahead of the center thwart. The little harbor was scarcely 200 yards long. When they cleared it and reached the ocean, Lew asked, "Which way?"

"Right," Nan told him. She shifted nervously on the seat, darting furtive glances at Charlie and then out towards the horizon. After a few minutes she pointed to a distant group of islands. "Steer for them."

Charlie soon saw Nan had not exaggerated the difficulty of cruising to Canary Cove without a pilot. There were scores of little islets, some hardly more than sand reefs. The majority were long and narrow and lying broadside to the shore. They overlapped to form barriers that barred anything like a straight course. Nan told Lew how to steer, and checking their general course as well as he could by the setting sun, Charlie decided they were going more south than east.

Lew glanced up quickly, looked over the ocean and then said in surprised tones, "I hear another boat, but I can't see it."

"Could be back of any of those islands," Charlie suggested. Turning, he looked astern. The sea was calm, but he saw Nan's fingers clutching the gunwale hard.

Lew opened the gas feed cautiously. They picked up speed. The sounds grew louder. Then a dark cruiser smashed across the narrow straight between two reefs and bore down upon them. It had a high, sharp prow that plowed the water into twin cascades of foam and spray.

Betty screamed. Lew shoved the tiller to swerve left, but Charlie said sharply, "Head straight at him—with all you got."

It looked like suicide to Lew, but he didn't hesitate. He never did. He aimed their plunging skiff directly at the approaching menace and opened the throttle wide.

# Chapter 4 – A Body Overboard

There couldn't be any doubt the power cruiser that had suddenly dodged out from behind the small islands intended to ram them. Charlie knew if they turned to evade the faster craft it would quickly overtake them, so he told Lew to steer straight ahead at full speed.

Lew didn't like it, but he pointed their small aluminum skiff directly at the double walls of foam curling away from the sharp, oncoming prow. Holding the rudder with one hand, he thrust the other inside his coat and pulled out his pistol. The two speeding boats quickly ate up the intervening space.

When 50 yards separated them, Charlie said, "Hard right!" He flung his body against the opposite gunwale to prevent the boat tipping on the sharp turn. He looked at Betty and Nan, saw the frozen fear on their faces, and tried to reassure them with a grin. They missed the cruiser by less than 10 feet. Spray showered them as their boat lurched crazily. As the big cruiser rushed past, Lew whirled on his seat and started pumping bullets after it.

His aim wasn't bad, despite the water running down his face. He saw splinters jump out of the deck and rear cockpit railing. It took only a few seconds to empty the magazine. Then he straightened out of the turn and headed toward a reef several hundred yards off.

The cruiser also circled about.

"If he comes back do the same thing, Lew. He'll expect it this time, but we can turn twice as fast as he can. Go left first to fool him, and then swing right."

Lew nodded, shoving the empty gun back in its holster. The other craft came up behind them, but slowly.

"He's going to try something different," Charlie said. A movement in the pilot house window caught his eye and he yelled, "Duck!" Something whined over their heads and the report of a rifle drifted across the water.

"Sounds like a .30-30," Lew said. He pushed the rudder over to one side, then to the other, zigzagging the boat in the open water. The rifleman let off three more shots in quick succession. Bullets zipped all around them. One splashed in the water alongside. Charlie pulled the girls from their seat and pushed them down against the bottom of the boat. Lew hunkered over the stern, head almost touching his knees to make himself as small a target as possible.

There were two more shots then a pause. "Stopped to load," Lew observed. "Probably a seven-shot carbine."

A moment later a bullet plowed through the seat beside his knee and drilled through the bottom of the skiff. A little stream of water spurted up. "The son-of-a-gun is getting better," Lew said.

Charlie leaned over and plugged the leak with a finger. A bullet sang by his face. He heard a sharp cry, and whirling about, saw Nan rubbing her upper arm.

"Bad?" he asked.

Her fingers pulled at a hole in the leather jacket. "Just burned the skin," she replied.

Charlie looked at Lew. "Can we get any more speed?"

"She's wide open," Lew replied.

The rifle crashed twice more before they careened around the end of a narrow reef and were hidden by its grass and palmetto. Charlie jumped ashore and crawled up the sandy slope to the crest. "We may have to pull the boat up into the grass in order to hide it," he called.

"Okay," Lew replied. "Let me know." He shoved his handkerchief in the bottom leak, took cartridges from one of the packing cases, and reloaded his gun.

Charlie peered cautiously over the fringe of grass. The cruiser had veered off to the left. Watching it turn, he searched the broadside with his eyes for some identifying name or number, but the gray paint was unmarked. The craft finished its wide swing then started back towards the coast.

Charlie slid down to the boat. "Looks like we're safe—for a while," he said.

Lew frowned. "He gave up too easy."

"Your shooting may have discouraged him," Charlie replied.

"Did you get the boat's name?"

"No, it was covered with something."

"I'll know it again," Lew asserted. "I put several holes in the stern, and they can't hide them without leaving fresh paint marks."

Charlie emptied the sand from his pants cuffs. "I don't think there is any question about identification. It was Litnore. Wasn't it, Nan?"

"Yes!" she spit the word out angrily. Then she muttered, "The double-crossing rat."

Charlie saw she still clutched her arm, and he said, "Better find out how bad that bullet burn is."

Nan took off her jacket and rolled up the sweater. The bullet had cut just deep enough to bleed a little. Lew found their first-aid kit, and Betty cleaned and bandaged the wound.

"What did you mean by double-crossing rat?" Charlie asked.

Panic leaped into Nan's eyes. She pressed her lips tight and looked down at the bottom of the skiff.

"He knew you were in our boat, but you didn't know he was going to try to ram and sink us," Charlie said. "That right?"

She refused to meet his eyes. Struggling deeper into the leather jacket, she folded her arms tight around her body.

Charlie went back to the top of the reef. The cruiser wasn't in sight, but he knew it might be lurking among the islands a mile or two away. Approaching night and the thin streamers of fog drifting above the surface made visibility poor.

Lew scowled at the bullet holes in their boat. The opening in the floor was oozing water, so he pushed more of the cloth plug in with his knife. He said to Nan, "Nice people you play around with."

"Hed said you were Feds," she replied.

Lew's eyes went hard. "Then Hed is a bigger fool than I figured. Not for thinking we might be Federal men, but to believe he could get away with murder if we were. If we were from the narcotics detail and he killed us, this whole coast would be swarming with agents. All he had to do was ignore us while we took Miss Winthrop to Canary Cove. Now I'm not sure I want to drop this business."

"Neither am I," Charlie added as he came down to the edge of the ocean. "Two fights, doped drinks and a try at murdering four people doesn't add up to reefer smoking in my arithmetic. Litnore is mixed up in something more serious."

His glance came to rest on Nan.

"If he is, I don't know anything about it," she replied. "Honest I don't, Mister."

"Why is he trying to keep us away from the fishing camp?" Betty leaned forward, her body tense as she waited for a reply.

"Hed just told me you would make trouble about the reefers and said I should try to scare you away."

"And if we didn't scare, you were to come along and keep an eye on us?" Charlie looked until she had to meet his eyes. When she finally did, she nodded.

"He told you to bring us where he could run our boat down,"

Charlie continued.

"I didn't know about that," she cried. "You think I want to commit suicide? He said to mix you up and then act like I was lost, too, so you would stop looking for the cove."

"We're off course?"

"About a mile."

"Can you get back on it tonight?"

She looked across the water into the deepening dusk. "Not now. But if we wait until the moon comes up, I can."

"We might as well get out of the boat and walk around," Lew suggested. "How about a small fire?"

Charlie was going to say no, but then he saw Betty shiver.

The wind had scooped a shallow pit in one side of the sandy islet. They built a blaze there with dead grass and palm stalks. Lew got a kit from the boat and cleaned his pistol. Then he took a cup from the cooking kit and bailed out the water that had collected in the boat bottom. The cup reminded him he hadn't eaten dinner, and he asked hopefully, "Anybody else hungry?"

That drew incredulous stares, but Lew wasn't discouraged. "How about some coffee?" he persisted. This time the response was unanimously favorable, so he carried up the necessary supplies.

"Is that on the level, about you just passing through?" Nan asked.

"Sure," Lew told her.

"Hed is going to be surprised when he hears that," she asserted.

Lew looked at her with raised eyebrows.

The coffee was boiling, so he started to fill the cups. After a sip Betty set her cup down and pointed at a lighter spot in the cloudy sky. "If that's the moon, can we start now?"

Nan glanced at her shrewdly. "I have to have more light to find my way. What's the matter, you worried about something?"

"Of course," Betty replied. "If that man Litnore is willing to kill us to keep us away from a fishing camp, there must be something more going on there. I'm afraid Ted may be in more danger than I thought."

"We'll know soon," Charlie said and then went for more wood.

Lew used a canvas glove to lift the coffee pot from the small grate. He dumped out the grounds and put in more coffee and water.

"What do you guys really do?" Nan asked.

"Mostly private investigations since the war," Lew replied. "We were in Army Intelligence, and the work is similar."

"I bet you make a lot of dough," Nan said.

"We expect fair pay," he admitted. "But the important thing is we always work outdoors. We don't take any other kind of job."

Betty placed her cup on the ground.

"I want to hire you to find my brother. What do you charge?"

Lew hesitated. "Well, the last job we didn't charge. But a big shot who hired us to get his son out of a jam paid us twenty-five a day plus expenses. But now, there's a personal angle here," he added, scowling. "Maybe you won't have to pay us anything. I'll ask Charlie."

Betty opened her purse. "I still want to give you a retainer." She held out three bills. "Is this enough?"

Lew saw they were $100 denomination. Charlie came up with an armful of wood and asked, "What's the money for?"

After she explained, Charlie advised, "Wait until we know your brother has to be found. To pay for the boat ride, you can invite us to stay a few days at the camp."

Betty put the bills back in her purse. "You are welcome to stay as long as you like." She glanced at Nan, saw the avid eyes on her purse and added, "I'll give you twenty-five, Nan, for guiding us."

"You don't have to," Nan said shortly. "There's something personal in this for me, too." Then she walked away from the fire.

"Did I offend her?" Betty asked.

"I doubt it," Charlie replied. "She's just confused. She was friendly with Litnore, perhaps in love with him. That pulls one way while the knowledge he tried to kill her along with us pulls another. She can't decide which is stronger."

Betty considered this a moment and then said, "I don't think we should trust her."

"I don't," Charlie replied.

Nan came back, drank more of the fresh coffee and sat staring into the fire. Suddenly she jumped to her feet. "If we're going anywhere, let's get started."

The moon had cleared the cloudy horizon. It revealed the ocean as a checkerboard of bright water and black islands with equally dark shadows. At first, the course twisted between more islands. But after half an hour the reefs decreased in number and Nan changed their southerly course to due east. Lew kept his ears alert for motor sounds, sometimes shutting their own motor almost off in order to hear better.

Finally, a mass of land loomed ahead, and Nan said, "There it is."

The boat ran up into the shallows over a white shell beach. Charlie asked, "Where's the camp?"

"Straight across on the other side."

"Why not cruise around?" Lew wanted to know.

"I thought one tangle with Hed's boat enough," Nan said. Her voice sounded flat, tired.

Charlie and Lew unloaded the boat, removed the motor, carried everything inland and piled it under a stand of sea grape trees. They got out two shotguns, ammunition, flashlights, and a pair of binoculars. Lew hung the latter around his neck.

When they walked back to the beach, Betty said quickly, "There's a ship!" Following her pointing finger, they saw a slim craft slide along in front of the shadow wall that marked the limit of their vision. It moved in perfect silence parallel to the land.

Lew gripped his companion's arm.

"That's the ghost boat we saw last night," he whispered.

The boat stopped and two figures came to the gunwale with a long object that seemed to make an awkward, heavy load. Lew halted at the edge of cover and raised his binoculars. They weren't genuine night glass, but the wide exit lenses pierced the shadows effectively. He saw the figures drop their burden into the water. It landed with a soft splash. He lowered the glasses without speaking.

Charlie whispered, "See what it was?"

"It was a body," Lew replied.

# Chapter 5 – A Matter of Identity

Still moving in absolute silence, the boat that had just dumped a body overboard a few hundred feet off the island turned back in the direction from which it came. Lew whispered, "I'm glad Betty didn't see that."

"Sure it was a body?" Charlie asked.

"Couldn't have been anything else. There was a weight tied to the feet; I saw it swing when they lifted it over the side."

Charlie stared across the sea. Finally, he said, "If we don't find Ted Winthrop we may always think that was him. But we won't be sure unless the body is recovered."

Lew nodded soberly. He was thinking that the search for Betty's brother had started out decidedly dangerous and unsatisfactory. Yet there didn't seem to be much chance it would get any better.

A voice interrupted his thoughts.

"Where's the boat?" Nan asked.

"Gone," Charlie replied. Then in a low voice he said to Lew, "Keep them away until I can mark the place."

He found two dead sticks and planted them in the sandy soil so they lined up and pointed to the place the boat had deposited its gruesome cargo. He realized such markers were far from accurate, but he hoped they would roughly indicate the area of water that must be dragged to find a weighted corpse.

When he walked inland and joined the others, he heard Lew saying, "Is there a path or trail to follow across the island?"

"I don't know," Nan told him. "I never walked across. All I know is we have to go east." She frowned at Betty's skirt and nylons. "If you got any slacks in your bag, you better put them on. The greenbriers will saw your ankles off if you don't."

Charlie gave Betty his flashlight. When she came back from the boat she wore dark blue slacks and heavier walking shoes. The ground before them was furrowed with shallow gullies. Rolling sand dunes ran parallel to the coast. Walking would be tedious, at best.

They set out, and soon a sluggish tidal creek blocked their way. It was too deep to wade comfortably, so they followed the bank inland until the stream curved to one side, which permitted them to resume their original easterly course.

Several swamp rabbits darted off through the grass, and once, a larger animal that was either a deer or a wild hog crashed through stunted brush. Lew decided the hunting might be all right here, and he was glad they had brought a few slug loads for the shotguns. It took knockdown power to anchor hogs in thick cover.

"I've never been to our fishing camp," Betty said. "Can you tell me anything about it, Nan?"

"I've seen it while fishing from Hed's boat," the girl replied. "It looked like a nice joint. Be I never was inside."

"Do you know the caretaker? Dad said his name was Merchant."

"I never saw him at Buzzard Point. Guess he went up the coast to St. Jervis to buy supplies."

"I only know his name," Betty said, "and that he is left-handed. Dad was, too, and once he wrote about two southpaws fishing together. I suppose Mrs. Merchant cooks and takes care of the house."

"I heard he was single and a hired woman does the housework," Nan offered.

"How many boats belong to the camp?" Lew asked.

"I never saw more than one tied up at the pier," Nan answered.

"Did you bring some identification?" Charlie addressed Betty. "Merchant doesn't know you, either, and he may shut the door in our faces. Or did you write him that you were coming?"

"I didn't," Betty admitted. "But I have a copy of Dad's will and also my picture with the newspaper story. The photo isn't good, but you can recognize me, and it has my name printed below."

Wings flapped heavily before them. Betty gasped but then laughed uneasily when Lew said it was only an owl. Nan mumbled something and spit over her shoulder.

"What's that for?" Lew asked.

"To take the bane off. It's bad luck when an owl flies across your path—somebody dies unless you do something about it."

"Somebody dies every second," Lew replied.

"I meant one of us," Nan told him.

Charlie cheerfully interrupted, "An owl saved my life one time. I hadn't eaten for three days, and when it flew in front of me, I knocked it down and cooked it."

As he walked ahead to pick a path through the grass and reeds, he was thinking about how little Nan or Betty seemed to know about the fishing camp and its keeper. He realized, too, how little they knew about Nan, Betty, or her missing brother.

Litnore's attempt to run them down with the power cruiser wasn't the only puzzling angle to this business. He was more sure than ever that a darker evil than marijuana lurked on the island.

The timber grew thicker and taller. They skirted around small bogs of black water where cypress trees grew with swollen, deformed butts. They marched under live oaks where drooping streamers of moss softly brushed their faces. Lew shone the flashlight on his watch. Thirty minutes had elapsed since leaving the other shore, and he thought the sea could not be very far ahead.

Betty leaned against a tree and emptied the sand from her shoes. She couldn't remember if it was the fifth or 50th time. Charlie had gone on ahead, and he called back, "I can see the ocean."

When they joined him, only an empty waste of windswept beach was visible. "Where's the camp?" Betty asked in surprise.

"I didn't say we'd hit it square," Nan replied.

Charlie decided they should turn left along the shore because the bogs and bramble thickets had swung them in the opposite direction. The sand was looser and the walking harder. The wind strengthened and flung particles of grit into their faces. They were glad when the shore swept back into a little protected bay with a building standing at one end. All was dark except for the roof, which glimmered in the moonlight like aluminum or a bright metallic paint.

"There's your camp," Nan said.

"Why isn't there a light?" Betty asked uneasily. Her hand moved to the white gold watch hanging from her belt, but Lew had already checked his own and announced the time as half past eight.

As they came closer, they saw the camp had low walls and an almost flat roof. It seemed to be about as long as it was wide, if you didn't count a small right-angle wing on the rear.

Charlie led them around to the front sea side. It had a full porch, and one of the windows did glow with dim light. Several screen doors opened onto the porch, and Charlie went to the closest. It wasn't locked, so he swung it back and motioned for Betty to enter.

"It's your show, now," he said.

She crossed the floor to the solid wood door and knocked. No answer came from inside. She knocked again, and when the silence persisted, Charlie leaned his gun against the wall and then rapped the panel with a force that rattled it in the loose frame.

Only the sound of their breathing broke the disturbing quiet.

Then the door wrenched open and a huge man stood outlined in the light. Betty recoiled with a gasp then recovered and said, "I am Betty Winthrop. I want to see Mr. Merchant."

The black giant shook his head and opened his mouth in a grin that was more alarming than mirthful. He pointed to his mouth and shook his head, the gigantic body balanced on enormous feet, blocking their passage.

"I want Mr. Merchant." Betty repeated in a firm voice,

The man shook his head and grinned again.

"He's mute," Charlie said. "That's what he meant by pointing to his mouth. We'll have to get someone else." Charlie couldn't reach the in-swung door, so he struck the jamb two blows with his hand.

The black man's grin vanished and a scowl twisted his heavy features. His thick arm shot forward, but Charlie stepped sideways before it touched him. The arm dropped when its owner looked past Charlie and saw the gun in Lew's hand.

"Don't get between us," Lew warned his companions.

Nan shrank back. "Not another fight," they heard her moan.

Lew spoke to Betty without looking, "We'll go in if you say so."

He motioned with his gun to the man to step aside. But Betty was saved the decision when another man walked into the dimly lit room. He came up behind the big man and touched him on the shoulder.

The giant turned to look. The other held up a hand and manipulated the fingers swiftly. The big man nodded, moved over to a door in the opposite wall, and stood beside it.

"Put that thing away," the newcomer told Lew in a high, thin voice. "Job would break you in two with his bare hands long before a bullet could stop him."

Lew had his doubts about that, but he made the weapon safe and pushed it down into the holster under his arm.

"What do you want?" the man demanded.

The light was almost directly behind him, but Lew could see he had an average build, maybe a little heavier than usual for his height. His face was almost round with protruding eyes and a small mouth. The hairline had receded from his forehead until it was no longer visible from the front.

"I'm Betty Winthrop," Betty said sharply. "I am trying to enter my own camp."

The small mouth smiled. "I'm very sorry, Miss Winthrop. But we didn't know you were coming. We can't just open the door and invite anyone in. There are some rough people living along the coast."

After a pause the man continued, "Come in, please. I am Merchant, the caretaker."

"These men brought me from the mainland," Bette explained. "They will be staying a few days to fish."

Charlie and Lew stepped up and introduced themselves. "This is our guide, Miss Nan ..."

"Phillips," Nan supplied abruptly, her eyes surveying the room.

It was a large space furnished for lounging and dining. There were at least a dozen chairs including some softly cushioned, two couches, a small table covered with magazines and a long one that would seat eight or more. A wide fireplace with broad hearth and ceiling-high knotty pine mantel occupied most of the outside wall. Several small rugs were scattered over the wooden floor. Only one of the four metal floor lamps was burning.

Merchant's probing eyes shifted as each name was spoken and then returned to Betty. "I'm sorry you had such a rough reception. Job is a deaf mute. He couldn't hear your questions."

"How did he hear the knock?" Lew asked.

"He felt it," Merchant said. "You shook the whole house with your pounding."

Glancing at Betty again, he said, "You brought some identification? Mr. Totten didn't notify me."

Betty opened her purse. "Here's a copy of Dad's will, and here is a published photo of me with my name underneath."

Merchant examined the papers carefully. Then he handed them back. "I sent Mr. Totten a report of our fall business. But if you ..."

"That can wait," she interrupted. "I want to know if my brother came here, about two weeks ago."

Merchant's face remained expressionless. "We have had several fishermen, but no one registered as a Winthrop."

"He is a little taller than me," Betty persisted, "thin and walks slightly bent over. His hair is black."

"That doesn't fit any of the guests," Merchant shook his head.

Betty sank down in a chair. Merchant frowned. "I don't understand," he said. "Did you expect to find your brother here?"

"He started for here two weeks ago," Betty replied and then turned a helpless look toward Charlie.

"Miss Winthrop is very tired," Charlie said. "In fact, we all are. We had a rough passage. Can you show us our rooms?"

"Of course," Merchant said. "What about food? Our cook has gone to bed, but I can fix up a sort of lunch if you're hungry."

"We aren't," Charlie said, beating Lew to the draw. "What we need is sleep." But even as he uttered the word he wondered if they would get very much of it. He glanced over at the opposite doorway, saw Job had disappeared.

Following this glance, Merchant nodded and said, "That leads to the kitchen. Our guest rooms are in the other end of the house."

They followed him down a straight, narrow hall. Merchant punched a wall light switch, revealing seven doors that opened out into the corridor. "I'm afraid everything isn't in perfect order," he said. "Hattie has been sick the last two days."

"That's all right," Betty replied.

At the end of the hall Merchant paused. "We have two double rooms with twin beds made," he began.

"That'll do," Nan spoke quickly.

He opened the last pair of doors and punched more switches. The girls followed Charlie and Lew into their room, the one on the right. It was small but contained two maple beds, a dresser and mirror, and a gaudy printed curtain that partitioned off three feet of wall into a closet. A window with double-casement sash opened to the porch, another was set into the end and a third in the outside wall. A floor lamp stood beside the dresser, and Charlie realized that the steady throbbing he had been hearing was not the sound of the sea but rather a diesel engine powering the camp's electric-generating plant.

"This place gives me the willies," Nan whispered. "Thank heaven we got a double room."

Betty sat on the edge of the near bed, fingers pulling nervously at the pleats in her slacks.

"Ted didn't come here," she said. "What am I going to do?"

Charlie pushed the door shut. "How do you know he didn't?"

She raised surprised eyes. "Merchant just told us."

"I don't have a lot of confidence in what he says. He lied about his identity; why wouldn't he lie about your brother?"

"His identity?" she echoed.

"You said Merchant was left-handed like your father," Charlie said. "This fellow took the photo you offered with his right hand. He opened doors and punched light switches with his right hand, too. A southpaw might do one or two of those things, but not all of them."

# Chapter 6 – Trouble Brewing

At first hope drove the despair from Betty Winthrop's eyes when Charlie told her he was sure the man who had met them on Canary Cove wasn't the caretaker Merchant and that he probably lied when he said that her brother Ted hadn't come to the island. But then her eyes went bleak again as she realized the full import of such deception.

"That makes it worse," she faltered. "It means something has happened to both Ted and Merchant."

"We have no proof of anything," Charlie replied, so let's not make any assumptions. "Does your family have enough money to make kidnapping profitable?"

Betty considered this a moment. "We could raise several thousand dollars, but no more until Dad's estate is settled. Then we will divide about two hundred thousand. But wouldn't we have received a demand for money had Ted been kidnapped?"

Charlie nodded. "It was just an idea.

Actually, another thought was forming in the back of his mind, but he kept that one to himself. The girl was already frightened enough and he didn't want to increase her worry.

"I won't sleep a second tonight," Nan declared as she held out trembling fingers. "Let's get out of here before it's too late!"

Charlie looked at Betty.

"Whatever you think best," she told him. "I haven't managed things very well so far. I have to find out what has happened to Ted. But staying here tonight might not be the best way to do it."

"We'll stay until morning," Charlie decided. "Then we go back to land in the camp's fishing boat. Is it as big as Litnore's?"

"Bigger," Nan replied.

"Good. Then he won't try to run us over again. It shouldn't be hard to confirm the caretaker is an imposter," he added. "Somebody in St. Jervis or another coastal town can give us a description. It looks like you should call the police then."

Betty went across the hall to her room and came back carrying her purse. "I'll do what you say. And I insist on paying an advance."

She held out money, and he saw there were five bills in her fingers this time, instead of three.

"I'll find some paper to write you a receipt." Charlie said.

"I think we ought to get out now," Nan insisted. "Did you see the doors? No keys in the locks—and the bolts are on the outside! They can lock us in, but we can't keep anybody out."

Lew looked at the door and whistled softly. "She's right, and there is no rust on the screw heads. In this sea-air climate, that means they have to be new.

He shot an appreciating glance at Nan.

"I can put the bolt inside, if it will make you feel easier," Lew offered. Then he removed them from both doors with the screwdriver blade in his pocket knife, bored holes in the soft wood with the awl blade, and refastened the bolts to the inside.

Nan watched doubtfully. "That big gorilla Job could break in with one hand."

Lew agreed, but added, "Move one of your beds against the door, and if anybody bothers you, yell good and loud."

"Don't think I won't," she said.

After the girls had gone back to their room, Charlie and Lew took off their shoes, turned off the light, and lay down on the beds. The window in the rear wall had a full-length screen hooked on the inside, so they opened the sash for fresh air.

After a long silence, Lew said, "Think it was Merchant they dumped overboard?"

"Either him or Betty's brother."

"What do you figure is happening here?"

"I don't know," Charlie confessed. "If I guessed right about Merchant, someone has muscled in. But for what purpose?"

It was too dark to see, but Lew knew his companion had shrugged his shoulders and drawn his heavy brows together.

"Our best bet," Charlie continued, "is to get back to the mainland in the morning. I'd like to leave without a showdown with this fellow posing as Merchant, without making him suspicious. Maybe we can't, but I want to try."

Charlie sat up and wedged the pillow behind his back. "There are three angles to work on. We can handle two of them. We can get a description of the real Merchant, and we can convince the Coast Guard they must drag the water where you saw the body thrown. Then Ted Winthrop's movements must be traced from the time he left home. That's hard for us but routine for the police."

"Betty gave you five C's, didn't she?" Lew asked.

"Yes. I took it because paying us made her feel like she was accomplishing something. We can give it back when we leave."

"Don't be in a hurry," Lew cautioned. "We've already made a good start earning it."

"If you feel sleepy, let yourself go," Charlie said. "I'll stay awake the first few hours."

Sometime later movement in the room roused Lew and he sat up quickly. The casement window opening onto the porch was open, and Charlie's head was outlined in the dim light.

"I think I heard someone going out," Charlie whispered. "The floor on the porch creaked."

Lew walked over and stood by the window. "A boat's coming," he said. "It's still far out, but I can hear it."

"I think I'll go take a look around," Charlie replied. "You stay here and look out for the girls."

"Watch out for Job," Lew warned. "I'm not sure the judo we learned in the army can match that muscle."

"I'm bringing my gun," Charlie assured him.

Then he carried a chair to the other window, swung back the screen, and dropped out feet-first. At the corner of the building he paused to listen. The sound of a power boat was audible to him now. He knew it might be passing the island on a regular course, but the sound was getting louder like it was heading toward the fishing camp.

The shore end of the pier sat squarely before the building, perhaps 100 yards away. Coarse grass covered the lawn, too short to conceal Charlie's approach. There were clumps of red bananas and wild oranges scattered along the edges of the yard, and he ran swiftly to the nearest. It was easy to walk in these shadows without being seen from either the house or the pier.

The scattered trees ended about 20 yards from the dock. Charlie paused there to study the beach. The sky had dimmed, but enough light remained to disclose two rowboats pulled up on the white sand and a seagoing fishing craft moored on the right side of the dock. The latter looked to be 40 feet long with a stable beam. The pier was empty with only a mooring post breaking the even lines. Then the post moved, and Charlie realized it was a man.

The other boat came in slowly, minutes passing before it finally slid up on the other side of the dock. The figure moved over to it, another jumped from the deck. Rapid movements indicated they were tying up the new boat.

Charlie wanted to get closer to hopefully identify the men and possibly hear what they said. Their backs appeared to be turned towards him as they handled the ropes, and he decided this was his best opportunity to move in. He dashed to the nearest rowboat and flung himself flat on the sand behind it. He lay tense, hardly daring to breathe and wondering if he had been seen or heard.

Finally, he heard the grating of shoes on the rough planks and low voices that became a little louder as they came towards shore but were still unintelligible. Charlie wished he could hear as well as Lew.

Then he recognized the thin, high tones of the man who said he was Merchant, and words began to emerge.

"… leave Pete?"

"At the point. I came back to see if I could find them."

He knew that was Litnore, although he had only heard the man say three words yesterday in the tavern.

"That was a dumb play you made. My gosh, man, can't you use your head?"

"I thought it was all wrapped up," came the sullen reply. "It would have been, too, if they hadn't turned their boat straight at me."

"These men are smart, Hed."

The two left the dock and were walking through the short grass. Sweat broke out on Charlie's face as he waited for the conversation to begin again. Every second was carrying them farther away. He had learned a little but not enough to solve the mystery of Canary Cove.

Litnore broke the silence, something like fear in his voice. "I won't do anything again without orders. What's next?"

The answer came faintly, but every word hit like a hammer blow. "You know. There isn't any choice left."

Litnore said something, but they were too far and the words blurred back into a meaningless murmur. Charlie watched them disappear around the house. Then he ran back to the row of straggling fruit trees. There was no misunderstanding the man who posed as Merchant. They were marked for the morgue. Seconds were precious.

Swinging around the first clump of trees, Charlie almost crashed into a motionless figure. Before he could dodge, powerful fingers grasped his arm with pressure that made him wince. He recognized Job's eyes in the murky light, saw the white teeth bared in that frozen grin. Charlie pulled back with all his strength, but Job's muscles drew him relentlessly closer.

Charlie knew the end would come fast when he was close enough for both of Job's hands to fasten upon him. He stooped, grabbed a handful of sand, and threw it as hard as he could into the man's face. Job made a queer, stifled sound, but his grip didn't loosen.

Charlie stamped down hard on one of the big bare feet. The grip relaxed slightly. Charlie jerked with all his power, and his arm came free. Job clawed at his eyes with both hands then lunged forward. Charlie doubted if he would get anywhere hitting the man's granite jaw. So he struck hard, planting his fist solidly in Job's throat. Job rocked on his feet, and his arms came down. But when Charlie moved in for another blow, Job's head had sagged enough to cover the vulnerable Adam's apple. Charlie instead chopped down on the side of the bull neck. He heard the collarbone break with a snap, and the enormous hulk sank slowly on the sand.

Charlie put his hand over the prostrate man's heart. It was beating slowly, and he figured he would be out for a while.

When Charlie reached the open window of the room, Lew was already climbing through it. He said, "Sounded like a fight."

"It was," Charlie motioned him back into the room. "Job surprised me, but I handled it."

"Did he hurt you?" Lew asked.

"No. But we're lined up for plenty of trouble."

He repeated the conversation he had heard on the beach.

"Okay," Lew said briskly. "We know where we stand. Let's go take them while there's only two to handle." When his companion remained silent, he added, "A good offense is often the best defense. This looks like one of those times."

"The logic is sound," Charlie admitted. "But it won't help us find Betty's brother."

"Maybe he didn't come here."

Charlie had little faith in that possibility. Ted likely did reach Canary Cove; it seemed to be in the cards.

"Job got anything broken?" Lew asked.

"Collarbone. He can't use his arm."

"Now is the time," Lew insisted. "We'll never have a better one."

Charlie sighed. "Okay. Maybe you're right."

He took off his shoes and picked up a flashlight. Then he opened the door. The hall was dark. "Merchant was wearing a coat when he let us in," Charlie whispered. "So he probably packs a gun."

They moved along the corridor, walking close to the walls to reduce the chance of boards squeaking under their weight. The shades in the room beyond were pulled shut, but enough light leaked in to show it was empty. Lew clutched his companion's shoulder. The door leading to the porch swung open, and a dark figure was outlined for a moment. Then the door closed and the figure crossed the floor and went into the kitchen.

There was no mistaking Job's bulk or flat-footed stride. He moved slowly, painfully, one hand clutching his shoulder.

Lew released his companion's arm and stepped forward. "Better wait until we know where the others went," Charlie whispered.

Lew squirmed uneasily. A door closed softly somewhere. They waited what seemed like minutes, and then Charlie started towards the porch. Lew pushed past him at the door.

"We're too late," he growled. "They're already going."

The low rhythm of a boat motor rolled up from the beach. They ran outside in time to see a dim shape stealing away from the pier.

"There goes Litnore's boat," Lew said. "We might as well go back to our room and stand watch there."

# Chapter 7 – Trapped is the Word

Lew was badly disappointed when he saw the cruiser leave the fishing camp pier. "We had a perfect deal," he whispered. "Job laid up with a busted collarbone and only Litnore and the fellow who says he is Merchant. But you took so long to make up your mind they got away. I can't figure why you hesitated. You overheard them plan to kill us."

"Maybe I slipped up," Charlie admitted as they walked back into the house. "But I tried to think about the long-range angle. A show-down now wouldn't necessarily locate Betty's brother. Our job is to find him, remember? Besides," Charlie continued, "what were you going to do with Litnore and Merchant after we jumped them?"

Lew rubbed his chin doubtfully. "I hadn't figured that far ahead. But I would have worked something out."

After they entered their room, Charlie bolted the door.

"Almost midnight," he said as he lay down on one of the beds. "I'll get some sleep if you can take over the watch. I think Litnore went off alone and Merchant is still around."

"You wouldn't settle for putting at least Merchant on ice so he can't murder us?"

"No," Charlie said firmly. "You could get hurt jumping an armed man in the dark. And if you did have to kill him, that might look a lot more like murder than self-defense, no matter what I say I overheard. I know it won't be any fun waiting for a bullet through the window, always watching to see that no one gets behind us. But we'll have to live with that until the deal ripens."

"Okay," Lew agreed reluctantly and then went to the window. The sky was so dark and clear the stars seemed to hang just above the tops of the tall palms behind camp. "What do we tell Merchant in the morning? What a nice sleep we had?'"

"Probably," Charlie said calmly. "It depends on him. If he wants to ignore what happened to Job, we'll play along."

Charlie closed his eyes but didn't fall asleep. Finally, he got up, dragged the mattress from the bed and put it on the floor where he would be less in line with the windows should one of their enemies try to shoot into the room.

A pounding on the door awakened him. He sat up and saw Lew

sliding the bolt back then admitting Betty.

"What's the matter?" Charlie asked.

"Nan's gone! Her bed is empty."

"Maybe she's in the bathroom," Charlie suggested.

"She isn't. I looked. Something has happened to her."

Lew grunted. "I'd as soon try to kidnap a bobcat as that girl. Nobody could take her away without a racket."

He picked up his flashlight and crossed the hall into the other bedroom. He came back in less than 60 seconds. "No secret doors," he announced. "Just an unhooked screen. She took off through the window. I saw the prints of her feet where she landed on the sand."

"Where would she go?"

"Probably home," Charlie said. "And she has two ways to get there. Litnore was here with his cruiser, and she may have gone with him. Or maybe she walked across the island and took our boat."

"That's it!" Lew declared. "The little schmoe stole our boat. She'll probably pile it up on the rocks," he added gloomily.

Lew pulled his coat over his shoulders. "What are we waiting for?" he demanded. "We're planning to go to the mainland in the camp's fishing boat, aren't we? If we start now we can overtake Nan before she gets very far."

"All right," Charlie agreed. "We need to check on Merchant's identity as soon as possible. But maybe Miss Winthrop wants to search the camp for her brother before we go?"

"You don't think Ted is here, do you?" she asked.

"I think he did come to the camp, but that will be hard to prove. These people have had plenty of time to cover up any evidence showing he arrived. And if they are hiding him for any reason, they aren't dumb enough to keep him in the house."

"Where would they hide him?"

"Out on the island, back on the coast, or even on Litnore's boat."

"You don't think they have Ted," she said. "You believe they killed him, don't you?"

"There's a good reason for not killing Ted," Charlie assured her. "You said Ted saw a killing and that his testimony will send the gunman to the chair. Suppose Litnore and Merchant learned about it and have been dealing with the gunman to sell Ted out? In that case, he must be kept alive until the deal is completed."

Charlie smiled crookedly. "Sounds wacky, I know. But it's the best I can figure—and it does fit the facts we do have."

"How would they know about Ted being a witness?"

"Does he drink?"

She nodded. "More than he should."

"Is he apt to brag and talk importantly?"

"I'm afraid so."

"Talk, talk, talk," Lew said impatiently. "Can't you save it until we're aboard the boat?" He tucked his shotgun under his arm and started out the door.

"I'll get my jacket," Betty said quickly.

Outdoors, the air was warm and soft with a promise of rain. They followed the white shell path down to the pier and went aboard the cruiser. It was a standard ocean fishing boat with long, open cockpit aft and trunk-roof cabin ahead. Maybe a bit outdated, but the hull and deck were thoroughly painted and the rope rigging almost new.

Lew climbed up to the small bridge and studied the controls. The ignition switch wasn't locked, so he shoved it over and pressed the starter button. He could hear the engine turning over under the deck but it didn't fire. He jockeyed the throttle without result.

Charlie lifted the hatch cover out of the floor and stepped down beside the power plant. It was a 6-cylinder job: big, husky and clean. The brass was polished and the steel free from oil or grease. Everything looked fine—with one exception. The feed pipe connecting gasoline tank and carburetor wasn't there.

"Hold it, Lew," Charlie called. Lew released the starter button and jumped down. Charlie showed him the gap in the fuel line. Then they climbed up from the pit and Charlie slid the hatch back in place.

They walked slowly past the galley. The space ahead was partitioned off to make two cabins, each fitted with double tier bunks. Betty's head was thrust through a small door in the last bulkhead. Looking over her shoulder, Charlie saw the space held a galvanized tank and several coils of anchor rope.

"I'm crazy about this boat," she said. "It will be fun to cruise the coast when we … when we find Ted."

"She's a good solid craft," Charlie agreed. "But the cruise is on hold for now. The engine fuel line is missing."

"Was it taken to disable the boat?" Betty asked after a pause.

"I don't know all the answers, but probably, yes."

"Then if Nan took your boat, we can't leave," Betty said.

"Trapped is the word," Charlie said soberly.

Betty walked back to the cockpit. She stopped, stared at the house for several seconds, then jumped over onto the pier and started off with a determined stride. Charlie and Lew followed silently.

The man who claimed to be Merchant, the caretaker, met them in the combination living and dining room. He smiled affably and said, "Good morning. You got up early."

Betty walked up to him and demanded, "What's the matter with our boat? We want to take a cruise—today."

"I'm sorry," he replied. "I forgot to tell you last night. The fuel line broke and I ordered a new one from the yard at St. Jervis. Hed Litnore promised to bring it over as soon as it was ready."

"Can the old one be repaired?" Betty asked. "Can we see it?"

"I think the pieces fell under the engine," Merchant replied slowly. "I'll have Job look. The repair won't be expensive, Miss Winthrop. If you think I have been negligent, I'll pay for it myself."

"I do think you have been negligent," Betty said firmly. "Maybe not with the boat but in picking your friends. Did you know this man Litnore tried to run us over with his cruiser last night?"

Merchant's face registered concern and surprise.

"You must be mistaken," he exclaimed. "Litnore is irresponsible and has a queer sense of humor. I've seen him run close to small boats to rock them with his wake. But he wouldn't actually harm you. Don't take his practical joking too seriously."

The little eyes slid across Charlie's face as if trying to gauge his reaction in addition to Betty's.

"It didn't look like a joke to me," she replied. "Especially when he shot a rifle at us."

Merchant wagged his head as if bewildered. "I can't believe it," he said. "Litnore does carry a rifle in his cruiser. But only to shoot sharks or frighten people on the water."

He paused as though thinking and then continued, "There is one explanation. Litnore has a serious fault. I don't like to mention it because he is trying to cure himself. But he has smoked doped cigarettes for the thrill they give. I wonder if he smoked one last night and was more irresponsible than usual?"

Again the small eyes swung to Charlie, but the face they met revealed nothing.

Betty swung about and looked at Charlie, her eyes asking him to back up her accusation. But Charlie remained expressionless.

Merchant began talking again. "Litnore has been very helpful. When we have more guests than our boat will handle, I charter his. He passes the island twice a day when he fishes for himself and does a lot of errands for us on the mainland. But if he is irresponsible enough to shoot at you, I'll end our relationship at once."

"I think you should," Betty replied.

Merchant cleared his throat. "Last night seems to have been unfortunate all around." He again glanced at Charlie. "Job told me you attacked him and broke his collarbone."

"He jumped me," Charlie replied shortly.

"Job was only doing what he considers his duty," Merchant continued. "We have trouble with trespassers, and he often walks the camp at night to see if everything is safe. There wasn't any need for you to be so rough with him."

"Sounds like his habit of prowling in the dark could be the problem," Lew interposed. "Why don't you give him a flashlight?"

Merchant ignored Lew. Still eyeing Charlie, he said, "It's a good thing Job didn't lose his head. He might have hurt you badly."

Lew laughed shortly. But Charlie only said, "Have him keep his hands off me, and there won't be any trouble."

Lew tilted his nose higher. "I smell bacon," he announced.

Merchant's small mouth again smiled. "I told Hattie to start breakfast as soon as I saw you on the pier. If you'll excuse me, I'll hurry her along." He moved off with the short, light footsteps so many heavily built men employ and disappeared into the kitchen.

"Why didn't you tell me you fought with Job?" Betty demanded.

Charlie beckoned her to the other end of the room. "Talk low," he warned. "I wanted Merchant, not you, to mention it first."

She thought that over. "Did I do wrong to tell him Litnore attacked us?"

"No. It was the natural thing to do, and Merchant might have been suspicious and thought we know more than we do if you hadn't."

"Did you really break Job's collarbone?"

Charlie only nodded, but Lew couldn't restrain the urge to supply the details. "Charlie laid him out cold," he said. "And when he came wobbling back to the house, he was a whipped man."

"You like to fight, don't you?" she asked Charlie. There was a note of reproof in her voice—perhaps to balance the admiration in the eyes she turned upon him.

"It has nothing to do with liking," Charlie said. Then he added, "Merchant told Litnore to kill us, finish the job he started. I overheard him say it last night."

Betty shook her head. "He seems so plausible. I almost believed what he said excusing Litnore."

"He is clever," Charlie admitted. "He carried it off very well."

The kitchen door swung open and a tall, light-skinned black woman came in with a stack of dishes. She said, "Good morning," in a low voice and then distributed her load.

Betty went over to her. "You're Hattie, aren't you?"

"Yes, Miss Winthrop."

"I'm so glad to meet you, Hattie. Please call me Betty. Have you been here long?"

"Five years."

Watching closely, Charlie saw Hattie raise her face for a brief glance at Betty. He saw her features only momentarily, but the look of fear and anxiety shocked him.

"What ..." Betty started to ask, but the woman turned pleading eyes upon her and laid a finger to her lips. Betty finished the sentence, "... are we having for breakfast?"

"Fried fish and corn bread."

Hattie went back into the kitchen, closing the door behind her.

"Did you see her face?" Betty whispered.

Lew clutched Charlie's arm and pointed out through the window. "See what I see?" he demanded. A figure was tramping over the sand towards them. It was Nan, moving wearily like each foot weighed dozens of pounds. A travel case dangled from each arm.

Nan crossed the grass yard, came up on the porch and entered the room. Standing by the door, she surveyed them. Her face was smudged with dirt; a three-inch scratch crossed one cheek. Burrs covered the legs of her denim jeans, and one sleeve of her sweater was torn. She came a few steps closer and set the cases on the floor. One hand went up automatically to fluff her hair and straighten the blonde bangs, but it didn't do much good.

"You look a wreck," Lew said. "Like you had a date with an octopus and got pawed. Where have you been?"

"I went around the island to get your boat. I was going to borrow it and go home." Her voice was husky with fatigue. "But it was gone. So I came back. I brought our suitcases since it looks like we're going to be staying awhile."

# Chapter 8 – You Saved Our Lives

Lew's spirits had soared when he saw Nan coming across the beach. Her return meant that she hadn't gone home in the boat they had hidden on the opposite side of the island, and he thought they could use it to escape. But when Nan said the boat and motor were missing, Lew's cheerfulness vanished.

He surveyed Nan's disheveled appearance again. "You sure are a wreck," he repeated. "How does the other party look?"

She tried to register disdain, but was too tired to pull it off. "I got lost in a dozen bogs and thickets going over," she told him. "So, coming back, I took the long way around. I bet I walked twenty miles."

She dropped down in the nearest chair. "I'm hungry enough to eat that owl we saw the other night."

"Sure you looked in the right place?" Charlie asked.

"Your other stuff was there," she said. "And I got the suitcases."

The cook came from the kitchen and said, "Breakfast is ready."

Betty smiled, "Thank you, Hattie."

The orange juice was dark with the pungent flavor of wild fruit. Hattie made more trips bringing coffee, sugar, butter, and steaming bowls of grits. Lew watched her face at every opportunity. She tried to keep it turned away, but on occasion, he caught a glimpse of fear-ridden features that disturbed him as much as they had Charlie. It made the woman look old, though her upright carriage and springy step indicated she could hardly be past 30 years.

Lew noticed that she swung the kitchen door shut as quickly as she could, sometimes hardly leaving enough room to squeeze through. He leaned back in his chair a little, trying to see back into the kitchen. He caught a glimpse of Job hunched over in a chair beside the stove.

Nan emptied her coffee cup with a couple of gulps and loaded her grits with butter and sugar. The hands raising food to her mouth were far from steady, and her eyes darted around the table uneasily.

She jumped when Charlie spoke to her.

"You heard me say last night we would go back to the mainland in the camp's cruiser, didn't you?"

Her eyes dropped. "I know I should have waited. But I was scared and got so jittery I couldn't stand it anymore, so I climbed out the window. But I wasn't stealing your boat, honest. I would have had somebody bring it back."

"Forget it," Charlie said. Then, catching Lew's glance, he added, "You said you brought your suitcase and Miss Winthrop's because it looked like we were going to stay awhile. How did you know that?"

"I found the boat gone, didn't I?" she demanded.

Charlie shook his head. "Not good enough. We were going in the cruiser, remember?"

Nan gulped a big spoonful of grits and raised her eyes defiantly. "All right, I'll talk. Hed Litnore was here last night."

"We already knew that," Charlie told her.

Her defiance melted.

"I heard voices when I left the house, so I went down to the beach to see who was there. Hed was leaving, and he said something about making sure you wouldn't get away in the big boat. This Merchant guy said there wasn't any chance—that it was all taken care of. So I knew we were stuck here for a while."

Lew whistled softly. "You got nerve," he told Nan. "Job was prowling last night, and you could have bumped into him instead."

Her face went white under the smudge of dirt.

He eyed Nan critically. "You ought to wash your face before you eat," he concluded.

She flushed. "I guess I'm a regular sight."

"You look fine," Betty stated. "Food comes first. You can fix up after breakfast; I'll help to mend your torn blouse."

"Thanks, Miss Winthrop. You're swell."

The kitchen door swung open to admit Hattie with two big platters. Fried fish was piled on one, corn bread on the other. Charlie said, "Could we have more coffee?" Then, as soon as she left, he whispered to Betty, "When she comes back, ask her where Merchant eats."

Betty nodded, and when Hattie returned with the coffee she asked, "Isn't Mr. Merchant going to eat with us?"

"He ate this morning, miss." When she moved around to fill Betty's cup, she turned her back to the kitchen door and whispered, "This food is all right, don't you worry." Then she went swiftly out before Betty could reply, leaving the pot on the table.

Charlie looked thoughtfully at Betty. "Better have an intimate talk with her, and soon," he advised.

"When she comes back," Betty promised. But Hattie did not come back. Finally, Betty got up and went into the kitchen. There were two doors besides the one behind her, one leading to the porch, the other framed in the center of the opposite wall. This door opened and Merchant appeared. "Did you have enough breakfast?" he asked.

"Plenty. Everything was fine. I want to see Hattie."

"She went to her room with a headache. I told you last night she isn't well. It's migraine, and the only help is to be quiet in the dark and wear the attack out. She said she would clean up later."

"Which is her room?" Betty asked.

He pointed behind him.

"But I don't think she wants to be disturbed."

"I'll only be a moment," Betty promised.

Merchant started to bar the way, but then thought better of it and stepped aside. Betty passed into a short hall with three doors, all on the same side. Merchant spoke from behind her, "Hattie's room is the center one." Then he added, "The first is mine and the last is Job's."

Betty knocked. Listening, she heard a faint rustling inside. She knocked again and said, "Hattie?"

"Yes?"

"I want to speak with you."

Another pause. Then, "I'm awfully sick. I can't talk now."

Betty turned the knob, but the door held fast. She heard the rustling sound again and another like floorboards creaking. Waves of fear seemed to radiate through the locked door. She called, "Hattie!" and rattled the knob. Then she leaned against the door, knees shaking.

A short silence ensued; then feet shuffled behind the door. A bolt rasped and a narrow crack split the frame. Hattie's face appeared in the opening. "Don't make me," she begged, and there was so much misery in her eyes Betty's hand dropped from the knob.

"Of course I won't," she said gently.

The door closed; the bolt grated again, and Betty walked numbly past Merchant, through the kitchen and into the dining room. She caught Charlie's eyes, and he followed her into the other hallway.

"Maybe you should have made her let you in," he said gravely.

"I couldn't. I never saw one so stricken with terror. Someone had to be in the room with her."

Charlie nodded. He agreed they definitely didn't want to make Hattie suffer anymore than could be helped. He was thinking she might hold the solution to this mystery, and he felt more keenly than ever the loss of their boat and the crippling of the camp cruiser. Either craft would have permitted them to take Hattie away where she could talk safely and freely.

When they went back into the large room, Lew said, "We ought to bring our equipment over before it rains."

"Come out on the beach with me," Charlie replied.

Betty and Nan followed, neither one willing to remain alone in the house. Charlie walked to the two rowboats pulled up on the sand. He and Lew turned them right side up and slid them into the water. Their hulls looked tight, and each had a pair of oarlocks.

"I'll ask Merchant if there are oars," Charlie said.

"Look under the pier," Nan said. He did and found two pairs.

"How many miles did you actually walk this morning?" he asked.

"About three," she admitted.

"It will be easier to bring our stuff back in a boat than carrying it," he said. "Coming with me, Lew?"

Lew said he would rather use the other boat to try to jump-shoot some ducks along the edge of the island. Charlie looked at the girls.

"I just got back from the other side," Nan said, "So I'll take the ducks. I can row a boat just as good as you can," she added when Lew opened his mouth like he was going to protest.

Betty stepped in Charlie's boat. "Could this reach the mainland?"

"Not today," Lew answered. "And if we met Litnore again we'd be as helpless as a winged coot. But it might work after dark."

Charlie didn't say anything. He had already decided to try to make the crossing that evening.

Lew brought both shotguns out of the house, watched the other boat slip around the end of the pier and then told Nan to row in the opposite direction. The sky was overcast enough to be perfect for shooting, but he didn't put a single fowl down. Most of the ducks swam in big rafts too far offshore to approach. They jumped a few pairs and singles along the beach, but all got up beyond shotgun range.

Nan rowed without noise, and he couldn't find any fault with the way she handled the boat, either. They had been out about an hour when she pointed across the water to a dark line of rock.

"That's Sharks Reef," she said. "You can hook 50 of the devils if you want to waste bait on them."

"Litnore fish for them?"

"Some. But he likes shooting them even better."

Lew eyed her speculatively. "You're in a real jam, aren't you?"

"You mean with Hed? Oh, he'll get over it."

Her voice didn't sound very convincing.

"When you were down at the beach last night, did you hear Merchant say what he had planned for us?"

She shook her head.

"Charlie did. Merchant was riding Litnore because he laid an egg when he tried to run us down. He said he had to finish it. That means four murders. Betty, Charlie, me—and you."

"I don't believe it! You're trying to scare me!" she cried.

"I wish I was," he said soberly. "You might coax Litnore not to slit your throat along with ours, but five will get you fifty you can't."

Nan dropped the oars. "Stop it!" she screamed. "What are you trying to do to me?"

"Massage a little sense through that thick skull of yours," Lew growled. "Only Charlie and I can get you out of this alive. There's no one else, and you know it. Maybe we will fail, but we'll try. A little more talk from you might save all of our necks."

"I don't know anything," she sobbed.

"What kind of a racket is Merchant running, anyway?"

"Hed never told me. All I know is that every Thursday they make a long trip somewhere in the boat at night."

"Today's Thursday," Lew repeated thoughtfully.

Nan picked up the oars and tried to row, but her arms were too shaky. "I shouldn't have told you," she muttered. "I don't want to get Hed into trouble."

"Still like the guy?"

She nodded, crying softly.

Lew shook his head in disbelief. Then he spoke briskly, "Stop worrying about Hed. What you should worry about is how to stay alive. If we had our boat or could make the cruiser back at camp work, we could leave and take you along."

"I don't know what happened to your boat."

He watched her carefully. "When we go, we will take you anyplace you like. You don't have to stay in Buzzard Point. You're young and good-looking. You could find a job. And you could break that reefer habit when you get away from the gang."

She didn't reply, but he could see she was thinking.

"You didn't happen to hear Merchant say where he put the fuel pipe from the cruiser," Lew asked, "did you?"

Nan rowed silently for a minute and then said, "It's wired back of the rudder shaft, about three feet deep."

"Thatta girl," Lew said. "Change places. I want to row."

He broke the shotgun, unloaded the chambers and put it on the boat's bottom. When Nan slid past him he patted her shoulder. "I think you just saved four lives, including your own."

"Remember you promised to take me away," she said quietly.

"I keep my promises," Lew assured her. "I only wish you had told me this morning."

Nan was silent for a long time. Then she said in a flat voice, "The pipe is jammed full of rags. You gotta punch 'em out before it'll work."

Lew grinned at her. "Thanks again, baby."

He swung the oars with long, powerful strokes. It didn't take long to get back to camp. But when they were still several hundred yards out Lew became uneasy. In a brief glimpse of the pier over intervening ridges of sand, grass and palmetto, the place didn't look right. Then they rounded the side of the little harbor, and his fears jelled.

The empty pier pointed like a naked finger towards the rising sun. The cruiser was gone.

## Chapter 9 – Lew Finds a Fugitive

Resting on the oars, Lew surveyed the empty pier with bitter eyes. The seagoing craft that had been moored there ever since they arrived on the island was gone. He shifted his gaze to Nan.

"I may have spoke too soon about you saving four lives when you told me where Merchant hid the fuel line."

When Nan's frightened glance crossed his, he added, "If you know anything else that might help keep us from getting murdered, spill it, and spill it now."

"I don't," she said in a shaky voice.

Lew ran the rowboat up on the beach, picked up the shotgun and started towards the house. Nan followed a few steps behind. Halfway across the yard, Lew broke the gun and slipped shells in the chambers.

"I'd have told you sooner about the fuel pipe," Nan said, "but I couldn't make up my mind to go against Hed. But I don't want to get mixed up in murder."

"Especially when you're on the receiving end," Lew retorted.

Keeping up with his long strides had her gasping for breath. "You going to keep your promise about taking me someplace away from here where I can get a job?" she asked.

"I don't break promises," Lew said brusquely. "We'll take you with us if we get away."

He was thinking that the disappearance of the boat might not be a total loss, after all, and that something could be salvaged. It looked like Merchant had gone off in the ship, and if he had, then only Job remained to guard Hattie and keep her from telling what she knew. Lew believed the cook would tell once she was safe. She had assured Betty the breakfast food was safe to eat.

He entered the dining and living room of the camp, started for the hall that led to the maid's quarters. But before he had gone far, Nan said, "Here's a letter for Betty."

Lew picked up the envelope. It was unsealed, and without hesitating, he pulled out the letter. The message clinched his foreboding:

*Dear Miss Winthrop,*
*Litnore brought the new fuel pipe for the cruiser this morning*

*and I have taken Hattie to the doctor at St. Jervis. I wanted to wait until you returned, but she was so bad I couldn't risk the delay. I will try to get back tonight, though if she goes into the hospital I may not return until tomorrow morning.*

*—A.L. Merchant*

Lew tossed the note onto the table and exclaimed angrily.

"What's wrong?" Nan asked.

"Merchant says he took Hattie to a doctor at St. Jervis. What he probably did was drop her overboard with a weight tied to her feet."

"He wouldn't!"

"No? Remember last night when a boat came by after we landed on the island? You girls hid in the grass but I watched it with binoculars. The men in it dumped a body into the sea."

"Betty's brother?" Nan gasped.

"Him or the real Merchant. Baby, you better get straight on this: The gang you're palling around with plays for keeps."

Lew went into the kitchen, looked over the shelves and took down a can of sliced pineapple. He thought it as good as anything to help dull his disappointment. Nan refused the fruit, so he ate it all.

Then he went down the short hall and shoved on the door to Hattie's room. It was locked; so were the doors to those occupied by the bogus Merchant and Job. He wondered if the giant was sitting behind his door, nursing the broken collarbone he had received from Charlie.

Lew saw no advantage to confronting him, so he went back to the big room and sat drumming his fingers on a small reading table. Nan watched with anxious eyes. They were both glad when Charlie and Betty stepped through the door.

"All gone?" Charlie asked.

"Job may still be here," Lew replied. Then he picked up the note and held it out. Charlie read then passed it to Betty.

"No chance of getting information from Hattie," he said and exchanged a quick glance with Lew.

"Chatterbox, here," Lew began, "told me where the fuel pipe was hidden—after it was too late to do us any good. She also said Litnore made a long cruise somewhere every Thursday night. That's today."

"Something has to break soon," Charlie replied. "It could come tonight. We've been in their hair too long."

Betty walked over to the fireplace.

"Years ago, Dad wrote me that he had a wall safe hidden in the mantel and kept a book of traveler's checks there for emergencies. Suppose it would help if we opened the safe?"

"Do you know the combination?" Lew asked quickly.

"Yes. I couldn't forget because it's my birth date: 11-14-29."

"Now all we have to do is find the safe," Lew said. The knotty pine mantel extended to the ceiling. About two-thirds of the way up, the boards had been framed with ornamental molding to form four squares set in a rectangle. He pounded each with his fist. Three gave back hollow tones; the fourth was backed by something solid.

"This is it," he said confidently. "The panel must slide sideways." He wet the palm of his hand and shoved the wood. It slid easily to reveal the door of a small safe cemented into the chimney.

Lew stepped back, but Betty told him to finish. When he dialed in the combination, the door swung open. He looked into the space behind. "I don't know if this stuff will help—but there's a lot of it."

He took out a stack of what looked like paper tablets.

"I'll be darned," he said. "They're not checks. They're blank birth certificates from six different states on the East Coast. And here's a pad of nonresident hunting licenses, two more for residents."

He glanced up at Betty. "Could this stuff belong to your father?"

She shook her head firmly.

"Then Merchant put it here. I'd like to know what sort of queer racket he is running."

Charlie picked up the forms. "Must be something that requires fake identification," he said.

Lew was poking in the safe again. He whistled softly.

"Something that pays pretty good, too. Look at this." He held out a bundle of paper money. "All hundred dollar bills, jammed in here like hay in a barn. I could hardly pry this stack loose."

They crowded around as he extracted package after package. "That's a total of ninety thousand bucks," he calculated. "These guys don't work for peanuts, do they?"

He glanced at Betty. "Maybe it belongs to your dad?"

"I don't think so," she said firmly.

Lew patted the money affectionately. "Well, it's yours now. We found it in your safe on your property. Nobody has any business stashing money here."

He looked inside the safe again. "No traveler's checks, though. Maybe Merchant swiped them."

Nan stared at the stacks of currency.

"You're rich, Miss Winthrop," she said. "Can I hold one of them in my hand?"

Lew frowned. "Don't get any ideas about borrowing some."

"Don't tease her," Betty rejoined quickly. "Pick up a bundle, Nan, if you wish. Then put it back in the safe. I don't want to touch any of it until I know where it came from."

After Nan was done Lew replaced the money and took a little extra time closing the door. "I reset the combination," he told them. "That will keep Merchant from cleaning it out on short notice. I used my birth date—nobody but Charlie knows that, besides me."

Charlie smiled. "It's Betty's safe; maybe you should tell her?"

"There's no hurry," Betty replied.

Nan jumped up. "I'm not going to steal your dirty money," she cried and stamped out of the room.

"You were a little rude," Betty said, after a short silence.

"I don't trust her—not $90,000 worth," Lew said simply. He shoved a magazine back from the tabletop and marked figures on the wood with his finger. "Okay?"

Betty nodded, and he rubbed over the marks with his hand.

The wind was rising. Dead leaves showered on the aluminum roof and slid off with scraping rustles. "I'll bring our duffle in before it gets wet," Charlie said.

"Was it all there?" Lew asked. His companion nodded. Abruptly, Lew struck the table with his fist. "We've got to do something, Charlie, and quick. We can't keep on like this."

"If you got a plan," Charlie said, "let's have it."

"First," Lew replied, "we search the house. I don't think Betty's brother is here, but we need to make sure."

They began with the guest wing. The work went fast because the absence of closets let them sweep each room with a few quick glances. They found Nan in her room putting on makeup. She followed as they went into the kitchen and then the second hall. There were no complications there, either. The shelves and cupboards were too shallow for any secret hiding areas.

The ceiling contained two hatches. Lew got up on a chair under each, pushed the lid back and climbed in. A minute later he dropped back to say, "Attic empty."

Three locked doors in the servant wing remained. When Lew slanted a glance at Betty, she said promptly, "Break them open."

It was easy to do, for the locks were cast iron and the wood holding them soft. Each chamber contained furniture similar to the guest rooms: a maple bed and dresser. A careful search revealed nothing in Merchant's room or Hattie's that would help. When they reached the last door they moved cautiously, but their caution proved unnecessary. Job's room was empty, too.

Charlie went outside to search the shed that housed the electric-generating plant. As he expected, it held only generator, fuel, engine, batteries and charging switches.

Betty could not hide her disappointment. Although realizing the heavy odds against such a discovery, she had still hoped to find her missing brother.

Lew checked his watch. "I want a quick lunch," he said. "Then I'm going to search the island."

"I'll cook," Betty said. "I think I can manage an oil stove."

"I'll help," Nan offered. She seemed to have recovered from her recent pique.

Betty asked the guys if ham and eggs with a lettuce and tomato salad would be all right. Lew assured her it would, then advised her to cook four eggs for him if they were big and five if small.

When the food appeared on the table Lew eyed it with approval. The eggs were nicely crisp at the edges; the ham hadn't been burned. But when he took a huge swallow from his coffee cup, he gasped and choked. When he could talk again, he sputtered, "What did you make it out of, sulfuric acid?"

"Just coffee," Nan replied innocently. "We like a man's drink in the Tideland Country. Can't you take it?"

Lew went out in the kitchen for some hot water to dilute his coffee. After eating, he got his shotgun and started for the door.

"See you before nightfall," he said. "And don't forget dinner."

Betty watched him cross the porch and turn the corner of the house. "Does he expect to search the whole island in a few hours?" she asked incredulously.

"Lew knows what he is doing," Charlie assured her.

Lew had no intention of hunting blindly through all of the grass, brush, vines and trees that covered Canary Cove. He knew if Ted Winthrop was hidden in that jungle, there would be evidence of the fact, and the evidence would start near camp. A prisoner would need fairly regular attention, would have to be fed and checked at intervals. So Lew began looking for a trail leading inland.

Circling behind the house, he studied the ground closely. There were shoe prints and lots of mashed-down grass close to the building. They thinned as he moved farther away. Finally, they disappeared altogether. There was no sign of any traffic headed towards the center of the island. Lew concluded that Betty's brother was not hidden back in the brush, or if he was, a clever mind had planned the business.

Next he went to the beach and walked along it, staying close to the edge of the grass. He had to go almost half a mile before he found footprints heading inland. Lew grinned.

He kept walking along the water, however, until he discovered a second trail. There was the mark of a boat prow at the water end of this one, and Lew grinned more widely than before.

He followed these footprints, thinking that while the man who had made them used canny caution in coming part of the way with a boat this time, he still wasn't that smart. Lew wasn't surprised to find the two trails converging some distance back in the brush.

He moved cautiously then, making as little noise as possible. It seemed reasonable that if Ted was imprisoned up ahead, a guard might be watching the trail.

Three quail rocketed up from the grass. Lew half-raised his gun then dropped it. He didn't like that noisy rise. A smart enemy might easily read a warning in it.

A few minutes later, Lew caught the odor of tobacco. He left the trail and made a wide detour. Something brown caught his eye. Coming closer, he saw it was canvas. The odor of tobacco grew stronger as he came sideways up to a squat wall tent, stooped and looked inside.

A young fellow needing a shave lay in a heap of grass at the back, reading a magazine. He was unguarded; his hands and feet weren't tied as a prisoner's should be.

"I'll be darned!" Lew said,

The fellow looked up. Fear widened his eyes, and he cried out in a frightened voice.

# Chapter 10 – Death Drops from the Sky

Lew looked closely at the young fellow and could plainly see the resemblance to Betty Winthrop in his even features. This was without a doubt Ted, the brother she was so anxious to find and for whom she had hired them to search.

The ease with which he had discovered Ted didn't surprise Lew as much as the fact that the young man was free and unguarded. So far as Lew could see, there was nothing whatsoever to prevent him returning to the camp anytime he chose. That suddenly made him angry, and he said, "You're a real character, aren't you?"

"Who are you?" the other demanded. "What do you want?"

"I came for you," Lew said. "I am …"

"Don't kill me!" the boy cried. Then he beat the heap of grass on which he sat with frenzied fists.

"Stop!" Lew growled, lifting a menacing hand. "One more yelp and you get slapped. I didn't come to kill you. I came to take you back to your sister."

"You're just playing with me. I won't testify at the trial; I swear I won't. I'll stay here the rest of my life …" His voice faltered into a quaver, his face twisted with fear.

"For Pete's sake, stop sniveling," Lew said in disgust. "How many times do I have to say it? I came to take you to your sister Betty."

The boy's face smoothed a little as the name clicked in his confused mind. "Betty? What's she doing here? Doesn't she know Rand's gang could follow her and get me?"

"She got worried when those letters you promised didn't arrive," Lew replied. "That's why she hired me."

"I can take care of myself," he replied petulantly.

Lew pointedly glanced around the interior of the hovel and said, "You sure about that?"

"Sure I can. I didn't write because Litnore said he'd mail a card from up the coast saying I was OK. That way it couldn't be traced."

"You told Litnore you came down here to hide out so you couldn't be called as a witness at Rand's trial?"

"Why not? He puts over some pretty slick deals down here. But Hed's a swell guy, and sometimes he has to lay low, too."

Lew shook his head. It was hard to believe what he was hearing. The boy's confidence was growing fast in the face of Lew's increasing indifference. "Listen," he said, "how did you happen to get mixed up with Betty? Where did you meet her?"

Something in his voice gave the impression that such a meeting was socially impossible.

"She had some trouble over on the coast. We helped her. Then she paid us five hundred dollars to bring her here to search for you."

"Five hundred? Well, you can hand it back. I don't want to be found. You might as well give it to me. I'll see she gets her share."

Lew made a queer noise in his throat before he found his normal voice. "We made our deal with your sister," he said softly. "If she wants a refund, we'll give it to her. Maybe we do owe her something," Lew added reflectively. "Say, four hundred and ninety-nine. You can't be worth more than a buck on any market."

Ted flushed. "Talking smart won't get you anyplace," he said.

"I don't want to get anyplace, not with you," Lew replied. Then he fixed Ted with a cold stare. "How long you been hiding out here like a swamp rabbit?"

"I came last night, after Merchant said a boat was due. I only hide when there's strangers on the island. They take pretty good care of me. Look," he went on as he pulled up a fifth of liquor. "Want a drink?"

Lew shook his head. "Listen, bird brain. I hate to shatter this dream world you're living in, but do you want to know why Merchant and Litnore are taking such good care of you, helping you hide? That's to keep you safe until they can sell you to Rand.

"Of course they don't want you to be seen by strangers. They don't want anybody to know you're here. But when the right guy happens along and hands them the dough, you'll be wiped out like a country school blackboard."

Ted surveyed him scornfully. "You can't scare me that way. Litnore is a pal of mine; we're just like this." He held up two crossed fingers. "Merchant worked for my dad for years. They'll take care of me—and do anything I say."

"Anything you say," Lew said wearily. "OK. Only you're coming back to camp now. Let's go."

"Sure, I'll come," Ted replied. "I want to see Betty's face when she learns the joke is on her. Wait until I get my coat on. I better take the rest of the whiskey along, too."

Lew watched him struggle into a short corduroy coat. When Ted came stooping towards the door, Lew didn't wait. He turned around and started back along the trail leading to the coast.

Even as he did so, he realized he had made a mistake. But it was too late. He heard something whistle through the air but he couldn't avoid the blow. The bottle clenched in Ted's fingers caught him on the back of the head and toppled him over on the ground.

Lew didn't know what a prophet he was. For at the exact time he told Ted that Litnore and Merchant were scheming to sell him out, a small seaplane with a two-seater cabin was circling in the sky above the fishing camp. After a few loops it put out to sea, turned, and losing altitude fast, came down on the water with a smack then taxied up to the beach. It halted in shallow water and a man wearing a golf jacket and cap climbed out of the cockpit and waded in.

Betty and Charlie heard the plane and were watching from the yard. Betty said, "Thank heaven somebody has come. I'll hire them to fly us to the mainland. If they won't, they will surely carry a message."

The man approaching them was still 50 feet away when Charlie said quietly, "Go in the house. Watch through a window if you want to, but keep out of sight."

When she hesitated he snapped. "Do it!"

The porch door slammed behind him, but he didn't look around. Instead, he kept his eyes fixed on the thin cheeks and almost color-less eyes of the stranger. The man came up to within a dozen feet and stopped, hands hanging loosely down and relaxed.

"You Blare?" he asked, speaking with only a slight movement of his lips. He seemed a little more tense than Charlie at first thought, and he worked his shoes into the loose soil as if trying for firm footing.

"Blare's away," Charlie said. "I'm in charge now."

"We had a time finding this place," the other said. "When will Blare get back?"

"Sometime tonight."

The man scowled. "I don't want to wait that long. We got to start back soon." He eyed Charlie cautiously.

"You come for Winthrop?" Charlie asked.

"You know the deal, don't you?" the words came quickly.

Charlie nodded. If he didn't know the details, they were becoming clearer by the minute.

The man relaxed, and a thin smile warped his lips.

"We aren't going to take him. After we finish with him, you take over then. You can play undertaker, if you like."

Charlie nodded. "Brought the dough?"

"Sure. It's in the plane. But we got to see the kid, first. Rocky'd be real sore if we happened to get the wrong guy."

"You know Winthrop?" Charlie asked.

"I got a picture." He slid his left hand into a coat pocket and brought out a square of cardboard. "He's got to look just like this."

Charlie stepped forward. "Let's see. I can tell if it's the guy."

"Hold it, bud." The voice was solidly hard. "Don't crowd me. This has to be done my way. First, I identify the kid. Then I do the job. Then you get the cash."

"Blare told me to see the dough before I hand Winthrop over."

The eyes got colder. "Blare knows how we do business. We laid the deal out for him. What are you trying to pull?"

Charlie leaped forward when he saw the man's hand dip under his coat. He slipped in the sand but still managed to get there before the pistol cleared. He struck the muzzle and almost simultaneously felt the tug of a bullet ripping through the bunched folds of his shirt to the side just above his belt.

Charlie gripped the gun in his left hand before it could discharge again. Then he hit the gunman's jaw with his right fist. The man's fingers slipped off the pistol and he began to sag. Charlie thought that all of the gun-toters he tangled with seemed to have glass chins.

He grabbed the limp form before it fell and jerked the man up against his own body. Something thudded into this human shield, and a gun report drifted across from the water.

A second bullet cut a beeline uncomfortably near Charlie's cheek, and remembering he was inches taller than the man he hid behind, he bent his knees and stooped.

He had his own gun out now, and aiming past the other's shoulder snapped three fast shots toward the plane. At least one hit something solid for he heard the plunk of impact.

His shield was dead weight—perhaps in every sense of the words. Charlie edged backwards, dragging it with him and trying to get around a corner of the house. A rattle of reports filled the air, and Charlie replied by pumping more bullets across the yard, aiming at the plane's nose in an attempt to hit the whirling propeller. Then he realized the sounds were not gunshots but engine explosions.

The plane cut along the beach and then out to sea. It gathered speed, climbed off the water and sped swiftly into the northern sky.

Charlie let the body slip from his fingers. A cursory examination was enough to show the man was dead. The first bullet had struck him squarely in the heart.

Betty came out of the house on shaky legs. "Are you all right?"

Charlie wiped his forehead. It was beaded with sweat despite the chilly sea wind. "I'm okay," he said a little stiffly.

She looked down at the body beside his feet. "Is ... is he ..."

Charlie nodded and then looked up into the sky. The seaplane had already disappeared among the clouds.

"I heard you talking," Betty said. "How did you know they were hoodlums come to murder Ted?"

"It added up so neatly. And this fellow looked like a killer. I stalled him enough to let him prove it. What I said earlier is true, all right. Ted is still alive. Merchant—or I should say Blare—and Litnore wouldn't pass up such an easy way to make money."

"You are fearless in a fight," Betty said, eyes glowing.

"I was scared," Charlie replied in a dry voice.

Then he regarded the corpse distastefully. "We can't leave him out here. Open the screen door."

Charlie deposited the dead gunman on the porch floor and covered him with a blanket from one of the bedrooms. He got more ammunition from his suitcase and filled his pistol magazine. Then he sat down in the living room trying to shake off the feeling of ill will that enveloped him.

He stared moodily into the cold fireplace. Such sudden death, with prospects of more coming. And they had made practically no progress in finding the missing Winthrop or in unraveling the web of mystery spun about the island.

"Where's Nan?" he asked.

"She ran in our room and bolted the door when the shooting began. Here she is now."

Nan came in slowly, licking her lips nervously. She stared in frank wonderment at Charlie. "Don't you ever lose?"

Charlie tried to smile.

"What can I do?" she asked. "I wish I was home."

Charlie hadn't any doubt about that. He looked at her reflectively, wondering about her secret thoughts. Like Lew, he didn't fully trust the girl. Yes, she had told Lew how to repair the sabotaged cruiser, although the information had come too late to help. Charlie wondered if her loyalty still lay with Litnore, and he hoped the next test of it wouldn't add to their peril.

130

"If Lew finds Ted," Betty declared, "everything will be all right."

"He will have a chance," Charlie replied. Then he stopped talking to listen as footsteps sounded near the porch. "That may be Lew."

Nan went to the window and looked out. "No, it isn't. I never saw this guy before."

Charlie stood up, fingers on his pistol's butt.

"Hi, Sis," a voice rang out. "Where are you?"

Betty gasped then cried, "It's Ted!"

She ran swiftly out the door, and Charlie's hand came away from the holstered gun. He heard Betty laughing and crying at the same time, and a man's voice protesting her display of emotion.

"Take it easy," the voice said. "Don't go squishy on me."

The two came across the porch and into the room. Ted was trying to loosen the arms his sister pressed about him. Nan caught his eye, and he started to swagger. "Hi yah, beautiful," he said.

Then his eyes fell on Charlie and he stiffened. "Who's that, Sis?"

"One of the men who helped me find you. I would never have been able to without them. I'm so glad to see you. You look so well and strong." She stepped back to survey him with admiring eyes.

Charlie walked towards him. Something in the purposeful tread and in Charlie's grim eyes sent a flicker of fear across young Winthrop's face. He stepped sideways, partly behind his sister.

"Where did you get that gun?" Charlie asked him.

Ted was really frightened. He tried to answer confidently, but could only stammer. "Why ...why ... I took it from some guy."

Charlie jerked the shotgun out of his hands.

"What do you mean, took it?" he demanded.

"The guy was messing with my business, said Sis had paid him to find me. I wasn't lost and I didn't want to be found. So I ... I hit him on the head with my whiskey bottle and brought his gun along."

Betty cried out, "Oh, Ted, you didn't!"

"Where is he?" Charlie said.

"I left him there. He isn't hurt bad, I didn't hit him very hard. He'll be all right..."

"He'd better be," Charlie replied coldly. "If he isn't, you're going to wish you had never been born."

# Chapter 11 – Contraband Comes Aboard

Charlie turned grim eyes on Betty's cringing brother. "You're quite a prize," he said, sarcasm dripping. "When Lew finds you hiding in the brush so he can help you out of a jam, you hit him over the head with a bottle and leave him lying on the ground."

"I'm not in a jam," Ted blustered.

Charlie picked up his hat and coat. Then he grasped the youth's arm. "Come with me," he ordered and shoved him out on the porch. "Lift up that blanket."

Ted obeyed then recoiled with a moan when he saw the body of the dead gunman.

"Take a good look," Charlie said. "There were two of them; the other got away. They came in a seaplane to kill you. Merchant and Litnore sold you out. I don't know how much they planned to collect, but before this fellow died he told me the money was in the plane. They were told not to turn it over until they made you ready for the morgue."

"I ... I don't believe you," Ted faltered. The pasty hue of his face and his twitching mouth, however, gave the lie to the words.

Charlie wasted no more time with him. He shoved him roughly towards the door. "Take me to Lew, now," he ordered. "We've lost too much time already."

"Did you kill him?" Ted stammered, turning his eyes on the body.

"His companion shot him," Charlie said shortly.

Betty and Nan came out of the house.

"We're going, too." Nan said.

"We'll be running most of the way," Charlie warned.

"Nobody is going anywhere," a new voice announced. Charlie whirled around and saw Blare, the man who had posed as Merchant, at the corner of the house. He held a gun in his right hand, and the barrel pointed squarely at Charlie's stomach. Charlie decided not to swing up the shotgun he held and let his arm drop lower.

"Put it all the way down," Blare ordered. Charlie glanced at the loose sand around his feet. Even now, he was thinking he should prevent grit clogging up the lock of such a fine weapon. He compromised by leaning it against the side of the porch. Then he stepped back.

"This is really too easy," Blare said with a smile.

"Where did you come from?" Charlie asked.

"We anchored the boat on the other side of the island and walked across. I heard the plane and the shots. That was Rand's men?" Blare's voice was almost pleasant.

Charlie nodded.

"And you ran them off, I suppose?" the man continued.

Charlie nodded again.

"You would, of course," Blare replied. "I tried hard to get here soon enough to stop you. You spoiled a very nice deal for me. But you won't spoil any more." He held up his left hand and beckoned.

Job slouched around the side of the house. Charlie noted with some relief that the big man's arm hung straight down, and he walked carefully so as not to jostle his painfully broken collarbone.

"You know my name isn't Merchant?"

"We knew that last night," Charlie told him. "The real Merchant was left-handed, and you aren't."

"And you didn't do anything about it? Maybe I overrated you." Then his eyes narrowed. "You said Merchant was left-handed. Don't you mean is?"

"We saw you dump his body in the ocean last night," Charlie replied. His brain was working nimbly, trying to devise a plan to escape the menace of the gun.

"Where's your partner?" Blare asked.

Ted spoke promptly, "I slugged him back at my camp. Don't forget I took care of him for you."

Blare shot him a distasteful glance. Even a snake like Blare couldn't hide his disgust for a worm like Ted Winthrop.

Blare motioned, and Job stepped forward, picked up the shotgun, jerked the pistol from Charlie's underarm holster, and walked back towards the beach.

"You didn't help," Blare said, slanting his eyes at Ted then snapping them back almost instantaneously to Charlie. "I would rather have him here. But Job will bring him in, dead or alive. It doesn't make any difference, not now. All of you go inside."

"What are you going to do with us?" Nan asked fearfully.

Blare raised his thin eyebrows. "What do you think? But it won't happen until Litnore comes back. He started this job last night and bungled it. He will have to finish it. Only I will be here this time to see that he doesn't fumble the ball again."

They walked single file across the porch and into the living room.

Charlie was last in line. He walked slowly, hoping Blare would come close and poke the gun into his back. Charlie knew a way to handle a situation like that. But Blare stayed back and didn't take the bait.

He ordered them to sit on the floor with their backs against the fireplace wall. Then he shoved the furniture away to leave a clear space before them and sat in a chair against the opposite wall.

The open hearth of the fireplace was at Charlie's left and he began to move his hand back towards it to discover if it held ashes he could fling into the face of their captor. But Blare said sharply, "Keep your hands in your lap where I can see them."

Betty stared straight ahead. Her hands were clasped rigidly against the sides of her hips. Ted slumped in a corner, his shoulders sagging, his face a frozen mask of terror. On the other side of Charlie, Nan crouched with feet drawn under her knees, darting short glances at their captor and nervously licking her lips with the tip of her tongue.

Charlie glanced Blare's way and calculated the odds. Twenty feet of space separated them, far too much. The prospects didn't look good, but Charlie relaxed, resting his head back against the wall.

*   *   *

Lew groaned and then rolled over. He sat up with some difficulty and rubbed the sand from his face. He put a hand to his head and winced when he touched a lump that was bigger than any of the eggs he had eaten for lunch.

He looked about. Winthrop was gone, of course, and so was his shotgun. He shoved one hand under his coat and let his breath go out in relief. The pistol was still there.

"Wait until I get my hands on that whelp," he muttered.

He rubbed his head again. His fingers came away without a trace of blood on them. He guessed his felt hat had cushioned the blow from Ted's bottle enough to prevent a gash.

Then Lew got up on his feet, swayed, and when the dizziness abated, started walking. He moved doggedly through the grass and brush. Presently, he tried to grin. "I hope Charlie hasn't given Betty's five hundred bucks back. I've earned my part, alright."

He checked his watch, was surprised at the lateness of the day. He must have lain unconscious for a rather long time. His dizziness increased as he covered a half-mile of the sandy trail. He sat down to rest but first turned off the path and went 20 yards inside the brush.

Twice more he stopped to wait until the giddiness permitted him to travel. The last time, he was so close to the ocean he could hear waves breaking gently upon the shore. A steep dune crowned with brown grass and cabbage palms intervened, and he rested longer than before to gain enough strength to climb it.

His eyes finally cleared the crest of the bank and he saw the water. Then he ducked, fast. A cabin cruiser was anchored a few hundred feet away, a yacht tender containing two men pulling away.

Lew stumbled along the side of the dune to a safe distance off the trail. Then he crawled back to the top and peeped over again. He was able to recognize the men in the tender just as it beached.

The one in the prow with the yellow hair was Hed Litnore, and the other handling the oars and wearing a striped T-shirt was the fellow who had asked for Litnore's marijuana cigarettes after he dropped them during his scuffle with Charlie.

They jumped ashore, pulled the boat up out of the water, climbed the bank, and swung along the trail leading to Winthrop's hideout. When he was sure they were back in the brush, Lew ran down to the ocean. They had to have some way to leave the island, and the cruiser looked like a windfall.

Lew didn't stop to consider if someone was still on board the boat. It would have made no difference if he had. He floated the dinghy and then rowed out until its nose bumped the craft. Then he tied it fast and climbed into the cockpit.

Another dizzy spell seized him, and he leaned against the rail, trying to clear his head. He made a move towards the bridge to start the engine. Then he thought a drink of water might help steady his faculties and lurched into the narrow passage to find one. He noted from the arrangement of cabins and galley that this wasn't Litnore's boat, as he had believed at first, but the larger, wider boat belonging to the Winthrop fishing camp.

Lew pushed the right-hand door and found it locked. That struck him as queer, but he merely rubbed his aching head, slid the bolt back, and went in. Curtains were drawn over two portholes, and for a moment he saw nothing in the semidarkness.

Then his eyes made out a form stretched upon the lower bunk. He jerked one of the shades away and stared into the terrorized eyes of Hattie, the camp cook. The fear in them abated a little when she recognized Lew. Her mouth was crammed with a gag, and her arms and ankles were lashed solidly to the metal frame.

He untied the handkerchief holding the wad of cloth between her jaws. Then he took out his knife and slashed the cords. Her lips worked silently. It was some time before she could speak.

She finally gasped, "I thought you were Job come to finish me."

Lew leaned back against the wall and closed his eyes for a moment. Then he said, "What's going on here, Hattie? What kind of racket are they working?"

"I don't know," she replied truthfully, "only it's bad. The man who told you he was Mr. Merchant came here last year. Then, three weeks ago, he returned with Job. They kept the real Mr. Merchant and me locked in the house all day. Yesterday, they took him away and I haven't seen him since."

She stood up, balancing her weight against the bunk until her knees stopped trembling. "That Job sits in the kitchen with me all the time. He has a razor in his pocket, and he keeps motioning like he'll cut my throat if I talk to anybody."

"Have you had any other guests since they muscled in?"

"No regular folks. Sometimes they bring a crowd of people, but they don't stay long, and they don't go fishing."

"OK, Hattie. Let me figure something out."

Lew closed his eyes again, hoping the dizziness would go. He remembered what Nan had said about Litnore taking a long trip in the cruiser each Thursday night. That was today, and these trips had to tie in with the mystery of the island.

Lew wished he could think more clearly. The only way to find out where Litnore went was to go along. He could hide on board somewhere, he thought. On the other hand, the cruiser had been dropped in his lap. They needed a boat to escape Canary Cove, and when they got back to land they could start the machinery of the law in operation. If he ran the boat around to the pier, they could all leave.

He made his decision. "Hattie. I want you to go ashore. Take the little boat and pull it up on the beach when you land. Don't forget that—it's important. Then run back to camp. Stay off the path because Litnore is coming back and you mustn't let him see you."

He stopped, rubbed his eyes again. "I think it's all right at camp, but you better stay outside for awhile and make sure. When you do go in, tell Miss Winthrop and Charlie that I have stowed away on the boat to find out where it goes at night. Understand?"

She nodded.

"Better hurry," Lew said. Standing in the cockpit he watched her row ashore, drag the boat up high in the sand, and then dart off into the brush. He sighed wearily, wondering if he had made another mistake.

He went back to the cabin to devise some way to make them believe Hattie had freed herself. Finally, he brought a knife from the galley and laid it on the bunk. That was the only device he could call to mind, and he hoped it would head off a thorough search of the boat.

There was only one place he could hide with a fair chance of success. That was the little compartment up ahead that contained the water tank and anchor rope. Lew opened the bulkhead door, assured himself he could manipulate the latch from inside, and crawled through. Two small ventilators admitted light and air. He shoved the rope aside and crouched down behind the door.

The ache in his head was better, but he still felt drowsy and confused, and in spite of his cramped position, presently fell asleep. An agitated voice woke him.

"We got to find her. Blare will blow his top if we don't."

"Let's go, then," another replied.

Following hard, fast footsteps in the cockpit he heard the splash of oars. He moved his legs a little to ease the cramping muscles, and then he fell asleep again. Lew was suffering from a concussion, though he didn't realize it at the time.

The next time he opened his eyes the little hold was dark. Voices were audible again, but less clearly.

"Don't you think we better go back?" He recognized the deep tones of Hed Litnore. "Blare won't be nearly so mad if we bring in a good load."

"But it's too early ..." Lew's keen ears missed the rest of that sentence, but he heard part of the reply. "Eat first, and take it slow."

Soon the smell of frying food added to his discomfort. His legs were almost paralyzed from squatting, but the second nap had cleared his head. He guessed the pair killed an hour cooking and eating.

Finally, the boat moved away from its anchorage, slowly at first, and then when the louder smack of waves against the bow told they were well out to sea, it settled into a steady gait. Lew's hunger and impatience made the voyage seem interminable. He dozed a little but not much because his brain was too busy figuring out what sort of load Litnore expected to bring back.

The trips paid well. He knew that from the amount of cash they had found in the wall safe back at camp. The cargo had to be fairly light because the ship was too small to handle any heavy or bulky material.

It could be diamonds, or it could be opium, maybe refined morphine. Since Litnore and Nan were both obviously addicted to marijuana cigarettes, he was inclined to favor the dope angle.

Hours later—he didn't know how many but the number must have been considerable—the boat slowed to trolling speed. It began turning in wide circles as if trying to pick up a marker in open water. Lew could tell when the direction shifted by the way the waves smacking against the hull. The men on the bridge talked softly, but only a low hum reached his ears.

A dazzling light glared over the sea and the boat, enough of it filtering in through the ventilators to show his watch marked a few minutes after midnight. A second flare followed a few seconds after the first died away. The boat stopped. Engine sounds told him another craft was approaching. There was a low hail and answer; then the boat moved again, very slowly as if jockeying for position.

Hulls bumped together, muffled voices spoke fast, then footsteps sounded in the cockpit and flowed towards him. Voices whispered, giggled, and he suddenly realized that the latter were feminine.

Understanding broke over him when he realized that women were on board. The blank identification forms in the safe confirmed it. "They're smuggling in illegal aliens," Lew thought. "No wonder the safe was crammed with cash."

He suddenly remembered the smallness of the two cabins. "Hope they don't plan to put any of them in here with me."

# Chapter 12 – Questions Answered

Sitting on the floor, Charlie studied the face of the gunman who occupied a chair across the room, covering him with a revolver. No flight of imagination could read mercy in the thin mouth and colorless eyes. The round face was cold and ruthless. Charlie didn't doubt that as soon as Litnore returned, this man Blare, who had taken over the Winthrop fishing camp to run some mysterious but lucrative racket, would have them slain.

What puzzled Charlie was the fact that he still lived.

He glanced at his three companions. Betty still stared straight ahead with tense face and clenched fingers. Nan was watching their captor with the fascinated terror one displays when watching a dangerous snake. Betty's brother Ted seemed shocked into a stupor. His mouth worked at times, like he was trying to persuade himself the bad news about impending death wasn't really true.

Charlie's eyes dropped to the floor that separated him from Blare. It was covered with a dark, self-figured rug that had been pushed back against the opposite wall to leave a clear space before the fireplace hearth. A little tingle of excitement gripped him. The near edge of the rug lay under his outstretched feet. The other edge was pinned down by the rear legs of the chair in which Blare leaned back against the wall. He half closed his eyes to prevent any gleam warning their enemy.

"Litnore going to use a gun or knife on us when he comes?" he asked as casually as if he was asking if it was going to rain.

Blair's face was expressionless when he replied.

"What difference does it make?"

Charlie shrugged. "I was just curious. Nan said he was good at throwing a knife, and I wondered if he would stand us up for targets or just slash our throats."

That did it. His words shattered Nan's frozen terror and she screamed in a cracked voice that shocked his ears and brain. Charlie was already drawing his feet up under him when Blare's eyes turned towards Nan. As he started to rock his tilted chair down, Charlie flung himself forward, and crouching close to the floor, grabbed the edge of the rug and yanked.

The gun exploded and a bullet fanned the hair on top of his head.

The man shot again, but that ball hit the ceiling because the pulling rug had pitched the chair and him over backwards.

Charlie lunged across the room. Blare was handy with a gun; there wasn't any question of that. Lying on his back, sprawled over the flattened chair, he swung the muzzle of the revolver up and started to press the trigger. Charlie's shoe lashed out and kicked the weapon from his fingers. It slid across the floor and bumped against the wall.

Blare rolled lithely over on hands and knees and scrambled like a crab after the weapon. He had one hand stretched out to grab it when Charlie instead scooped the gun up in his right hand. Face and eyes still expressionless, Blare sprang up from the floor. Charlie stepped back to miss the clawing hands. A new sound intruded upon his eardrums. Somebody was walking across the porch.

Charlie brought the revolver down twice on the gunman's head, striking with the part where cylinder joins barrel. Blare's eyes had already started to glaze before the second blow landed, and he fell in a heap on the floor.

"Get the gun from my room," Charlie ordered. Then he pulled two shells from his pocket and tossed them towards Betty.

He stepped back out of line with the porch door. He didn't know how many were coming through the door or how many loads were left in Blare's revolver.

The door swung open slowly. Job appeared in the opening. His eyes flashed about the room and he swung up Lew's shotgun. Charlie dropped to one knee just as a blast tore through the air. Something stung his cheek. He shot the huge man's legs out from under him, one at a time, before the man could fire again.

Job dropped the shotgun, clutching instinctively at his knees. Charlie jumped forward and kicked the shotgun out of reach. He pointed the revolver at the big man, hoping it still held an unfired load.

But all of the fight was gone from Job. He flattened on the floor and didn't resist when Charlie reached cautiously down with his left hand and recovered his own pistol.

The pistol was fully charged, so Charlie tossed the revolver on a chair. He went back to examine Blare. The man was still unconscious. Charlie took a deep breath. His fingers were shaking a little, and when he saw them, he frowned. "I must be getting old," he muttered.

He put a hand up to his cheek. The fingers came away bloody, and he knew one of the pellets had struck. Betty came in with the other shotgun. Charlie unloaded it, unloaded Lew's, and picked up Blare's revolver again. He was thinking that one charged firearm was enough in that suspect crowd. Charlie glanced at Nan.

"Thanks for the scream," he said. "It was a dandy."

She gulped, staring at him with amazed eyes.

"You're a one-man army!"

Charlie sighed. Every muscle in his body felt tired.

"Get some rope and something to bandage up Job's legs. I don't want him to bleed to death."

Job watched while Charlie bound up the holes in his legs and then tied them and his hands together. His hateful eyes glowed, but he made no attempt to protest.

"You did a pretty fair job," Ted finally spoke. "I was getting ready to jerk the rug myself when..."

"Shut up, Ted," Betty interrupted.

He flushed, bit his lip and walked out on the porch.

After tying Blare, Charlie said, "I've got to find Lew."

He remembered that Ted had struck Lew on the head with a bottle and left him unconscious, and Job had gone to find him. It was possible that Job had murdered Lew, and he had to discover the truth.

"You all better come along," he said.

Out on the porch, Ted pointed to the lowering sun and said he wasn't sure he could find the place. "You'll find it," Charlie said quietly. He led the group across the yard with long strides. A figure stepped out from behind some wild orange trees and ran towards them.

It was Hattie. "Praise the Lord you all right," she cried. "I been hiding here ever since the shooting." Tears streamed down her face. She came and clasped one of Betty's hands in her own.

Charlie motioned impatiently. "Not now, Hattie. Come along."

"I got a message for you," Hattie told him.

"From Lew?" he asked quickly.

"Yes. He said to tell you he was hid on the boat to find out where it went tonight."

"Was he all right?"

"He looked good to me. He cut the ropes off my hands and feet so I could get away."

A feeling of relief eased Charlie's mind. Lew was still in danger, of course, but he had chosen to face it willingly and with full realization of what it meant. Apparently, he was none the worse for Ted's blow. If things broke right, it looked like Lew might even clear the mystery of Canary Cove.

Charlie realized that he had reached some clarity, himself, and he felt that he could trust Lew to handle the rest.

\*   \*   \*

Lew felt disgruntled with himself for not having solved the island riddle before. There had been enough clues that the man who posed as the camp caretaker and his partner Litnore were smuggling aliens into the country, things like the big bundle of cash in the safe and the pads of blank birth certificates. The birth certificates, forged with signatures and seals, were exactly what someone needed to prove he had not entered the United States illegally.

Crouching in the forward bulkhead storage compartment of the cruiser, Lew could understand why the safe had also held hunting and fishing license blanks. They, too, could come in handy when putting aliens on shore. Should a game warden stop the boat, the foreigners could be represented as hunters or anglers, and they would have the permits to support the claim.

As Lew listened to the men and women out in the passage, light dawned upon another part of the mystery: the strange boat that moved so fast and silently in the night with no visible means of propulsion. Such a craft would be ideal for stealthily carrying aliens upriver.

Lew pressed his ear against the door of the little hold trying to hear what the voices said. Some of them seemed to be admonishing, others apparently acquiesced to the warnings.

Footsteps proceeded along the short corridor. The boat began to move, and Lew felt it heel over as it made a sharp turn. When it straightened, the power was poured on and it leaped ahead. The timber about him trembled from the vibrations of engine and screw.

Lew began to speculate about the people packed in the cabins. He wondered what they were like, if they were unfortunates who through the disaster of war lacked necessary credentials to make legal entry or if they were subversives, buying their way in to carry on propaganda or sabotage. He wondered how much each had been obliged to pay.

Lew's curiosity finally overcame his caution. He slowly opened the bulkhead door and looked out. The passage was empty and dimly lit by one small bulb set into the rear ceiling. He opened the door wider. His keen ears caught a murmur of voices well astern, and deciding that Litnore and the young fellow in the gaudy T-shirt were both on the bridge, he stepped boldly outside.

Lew saw something that had escaped his eyes before. Both cabin doors were secured with bolts on the outside. He shoved the bolt back on the left door, opened the panel quickly and slipped inside. He closed the door and put his back against it.

A startled voice said, "What do you want?" Four people confronted him, their faces blurred patches of white. But he could see well enough to know that three were men, the fourth a woman. It was the latter who had spoken.

"Take it easy," Lew whispered. "I'm just checking on you."

"Why? We were already checked. Our passage is paid in full." Her voice had a husky accent, and she hesitated over some of the words like she wasn't sure of them.

"How much did you pay?" Lew asked.

"You don't know? It was $6,000 American dollars. Why do you ask such a question?"

Lew felt like whistling, but he didn't. He thought if there were eight people aboard, that made a very nice haul. Then he remembered that this was only the receiving end of the game. Racketeers on the other end, which could be Cuba, would also take a share. But even if the money was halved, it made nice pickings.

On a sudden impulse Lew took out some wooden matches and lit one. Holding it up, he saw the woman's high cheeks and Slavic features. Heavy black hair was piled on top of her head. The next face was thin and long and blonde; the third was round and flat before the little flame. Before he could cast it upon the last face, that man leaned forward quickly and blew it out. Lew had a brief glimpse of deep-set eyes below tousled red hair. The man pounded on the cabin wall with his fist and yelled, "Spy! Help!" The he rushed Lew.

Feet pounded across the cockpit and entered the corridor. Lew slashed out with his fist and silenced the red-haired fellow with a stiff jolt in the mouth. Then he pulled out his pistol and flattened against the wall beside the hinge side of the door. It burst open and Litnore's companion dashed into the compartment.

Lew whipped him over the head with the gun, being careful not to hit too hard in case he had a thin skull.

Lew felt through the man's pockets and found a small-bore revolver. Then he saw the fingers of the man's right hand held a blackjack. Lew slipped that in his pocket, too. The action had been so fast the aliens could only watch with open mouths.

"Don't make a sound!" Lew warned fiercely.

He pushed the fellow on the floor back so he could open the door, darted outside, shut the door and bolted it.

Litnore called down, "What is it, Pete?"

Lew made a gurgling sound in his throat. He didn't know how the man on the bridge would interpret it, but he hoped it would bring him down to investigate. It did. Litnore's tall frame filled the corridor a second after Lew had dodged into the galley niche. Lew struck a little harder this time, figuring Litnore was the hard-headed type.

Then Lew found a hank of trolling line and tied the man in a web of loops and knots.

He considered the other smuggler safe enough locked up in the cabin, so he went on the bridge, unlashed the wheel, and after checking the course on the compass, held steady hoping it would bring them back to the fishing camp on Canary Cove.

Daylight was breaking when he sighted the island. Charlie, Betty, her brother and Nan stood waiting on the pier as he pulled the boat alongside. Charlie and Lew grinned at each other; that was about as near as either ever came to an emotional demonstration.

Lew jumped down on the dock with a mooring line. Ted ducked back and stood behind his sister. Lew ignored him as he wrapped the line around a timber cleat.

"All tied up?" Charlie asked.

Obviously, he wasn't referring to just the ship's line.

"Tight," Lew replied confidently. "They were smuggling aliens. Both cabins are packed. We'll need to find a Coast Guard station."

"Want some breakfast first?" Betty asked with a grin of her own, remembering his prodigious appetite.

It was tough to turn down food, but Lew did it.

"We can't risk a delay. Some of the people locked in the cabin are tough enough to break out and cause trouble. They aren't going to like being turned over to the law. Get your bag, and we'll start."

"What about the money in the safe?"

"Bring that, too."

Ted followed the girls back to the house. He had been very careful not to meet Lew's eyes on the pier. Lew glanced at his back and said to Charlie, "You now, he actually helped by cracking me on the head. But don't ever let him know that. He's a big enough pain."

They talked earnestly then, bringing each other up to date on their individual experiences.

"We'll leave Blare and Job here," Charlie decided. "Our cargo will be difficult enough without them in the mix."

"Only one thing still puzzles me," Lew said. "How did they run that small boat without it making any sound?"

"I asked Blare about it," Charlie replied. "He said it carried an electric prop and a big warehouse hoist battery that could supply juice for hours. They recharged the battery with the island's plant."

"I should have guessed," Lew replied. Then his eyes turned serious. "What's going to happen to Nan? I feel sorry for the kid; she isn't a bad sort."

"We don't have to say anything about her relationship with Litnore," Charlie told him. "She's going home with Betty. They have a deal cooked up so Nan can work for Betty while she goes to night school and learns stenography."

"That's swell," Lew agreed happily

Then he glanced down the beach. "This white sand looks enough like snow to make me homesick. I sure would like to see the real stuff."

"No reason why not," Charlie grinned again. "We know where there's plenty of it."

*The End*

# Caribou Claim
## Chapter 1 – An Old Friend is Afraid

Lew and Charlie found the bush pilot Jeff in the field office writing reports. The building was only slightly larger than a big packing crate, but it served as headquarters for a tight little group of airmen who could be hired to deliver anything flyable anywhere there was room to set the landing wheels of their small planes. The room also contained a large wooden desk and chair, metal file, phone, bulletin board, stove and two nail kegs for stools. It was pretty crowded.

Jeff looked up and scowled. "You're early this year," he observed. "I wasn't expecting you for another month."

"We got homesick for that ugly mug of yours," Lew said as he brushed off the top of a stool and lowered himself upon it. "Everything looks the same as last year," he added cheerfully. "Dust may be a little thicker, and the window needs washing, but that's the only difference."

Jeff surveyed them, still scowling. "I need business, but you're always bad luck. Twice I had fuel leaks when I chartered you two. I suppose this time we'll crash. Well, my insurance is paid."

He finally grinned and thrust out a hand, "Glad to see you!"

"We're only going partway." Charlie said, taking the outstretched hand. "Remember that emergency landing last year at Brown Grizzly Project? We want to go back; we've some unfinished business."

"Sure, I remember. That was the place the army had just abandoned. I got you a guiding job that day with the two cheechakos Chuck Anderson flew in. It was a good job. Plenty of pay but all you did was gripe. There was a girl … a girl and her brother."

"Dirk and Dorina Driscoll," Lew prompted him.

"Sure. She was a real dish, but snooty. You going to see her?"

"Why we're going back is none of your business," Lew said. "But I'll tell you so you won't get insomnia worrying over it. Before we left we staked out a couple of gold claims next to theirs. We want to find out if they made anything of theirs. If they did, we'll nail ours down tight, provided, of course, the claims are worth keeping."

"Gold?" Jeff asked. "People are always hoping to find a million dollars back in the mountains, and I guess a few do. But I sure didn't figure the Driscolls for gold prospectors."

"They had an uncle who was," Charlie said.

Jeff frowned. "I've heard some things about Brown Grizzly. First, the army came again, but they didn't stay long this time. And it seems somebody from there died or got himself bumped off."

"The storekeeper Woolman had a heart attack," Charlie said. "It was bad, and I doubt he lived long after."

Jeff mulled that over. "Maybe, but the name doesn't ring any bells. There was another guy, too, asking about Brown Grizzly. Some of the boys told me."

"You know if the Driscolls came out last fall?"

"No. But they'd have had to, wouldn't they? Nobody could mine then without dynamite, and that pair didn't strike me as having enough savvy to use the stuff, nor to survive a winter in the North."

Charlie and Lew nodded.

"Chuck Anderson's on the field," Jeff said. "Maybe he knows. I'll ask him." Anderson was a short, wiry man like Jeff and wore the same kind of patched, leather-trimmed suit and high-top boots.

"Do I remember that pair?" he echoed. "Who could forget them? It was yakity-yak all the way up. There was nothing they didn't argue over. Her mink coat cost five grand, easy, but I had a heck of a time getting my full fare. And when we put down at Brown Grizzly, she thought I'd hit the wrong strip. Sure, I remember."

"Seen or heard anything since?"

Anderson shook his head. "Not of them. But I heard things about Brown Grizzly. Some Indians are supposed to have brought in chunks of pure gold. Not the rounded nuggets washed out of a gravel bed. These had sharp edges like they'd been chopped out of bigger rock. But you know how it is—some wild rumor is always floating around."

Pulling a sheaf of papers from his coat, Anderson continued, "Bill Tucker told me he flew a man up there last month and then went back to get him three days later. He says the place has grown some with new shacks going up. Bill thought his fare was a government man, although the fellow didn't say so."

He held up the papers. "Jeff, I got to figure rates on these. How about a turn at the desk, or did you plan to rest your feet all day?"

Jeff slid off the swivel chair and motioned Charlie and Lew outside. "When do you want to start for Grizzly?"

"How about now?"

Jeff looked at his watch. "Guess we can make it in time for me to get back before night. Got much stuff?"

"We're going light, 50 pounds each."

"OK. It'll take thirty minutes to gas up and file a schedule."

When Jeff saw their luggage—two pack boards with a sleeping bag lashed to the top of each and two cased rifles—he whistled. "You two are traveling light. Throw it on the scales."

"You going to weigh that little pile?" Lew demanded.

"You know the rules," Jeff grinned. "Forty pounds on each ticket; anything more costs extra."

He stared at the scales in disbelief. "Wow! What's in that sack, gold to salt your claims so you can sell them?"

He figured on an old envelope. "It'll be a hundred bucks."

"We're only going one way," Lew protested.

Charlie started counting money. He knew Lew was equally aware of the expense of operating a plane where both gasoline prices and the risks encountered are tremendous.

"Thanks," Jeff stuffed the bills in his wallet. "About eating at Brown Grizzly, they might have a restaurant, but I doubt it."

"That isn't important," Lew assured him. "We're all set. The pack you thought was filled with gold holds concentrated food. And this bag is full of sandwiches. They cost us 80 cents apiece, but if you get hungry, I'll sell you a sandwich—for a dollar."

"What kind?" Jeff asked.

"Smoked salmon on brown bread."

"Never eat the stuff," Jeff growled. "Let's go."

Once airborne, Jeff straightened the ship out on a course approximately north by northeast. Two hours later, they were passing over some of the least known country on the continent. It had the same wild look they remembered from a year ago: nameless peaks and unmapped valleys with dense timber shading from lighter birch and willow into the darker green of spruce and dwarf cedar. An unnamed stream traced a silver thread along the bottom of every draw and canyon.

Jeff slid around granite peaks with a deft nonchalance acquired from countless hours flying through such hazards. Lew said, "I had thought of mentioning you in my will when I strike gold. But I'll have to get there first."

"Save it," Jeff told him. "No bush pilot lives long enough to inherit from a greenhorn like you."

Lew opened the paper bag and took out a sandwich. He didn't enjoy flying, but eating always took his mind off discomforts.

When Jeff dropped down on the narrow airstrip at Brown Grizzly, they agreed the place had changed less than they had been led to believe. The runway was still rough, although some of the worst breaks were tamped level with gravel. And the big store up on the hill overlooking the landing field did have a new roof of split shingles. The walls of three of the smaller structures were unseasoned enough to indicate they had been built a very short time ago.

"Want me to come and get you?" Jeff asked.

"We do, but we don't when," Charlie replied. "I see a radio tower behind the store. We'll try to get word to you if we can."

"Yeah, it'll be a long walk," Jeff agreed. Then he glanced at Lew, grinned, and said, "My middle name's Aloysius—if you still want to mention me in your will."

They shouldered their packs and rifles and walked slowly towards a double row of low houses. Three boys and a shaggy brown dog had come down to watch the plane land. Two men stood beside the door of the big store, a third wearing a gray and red stag shirt leaned against the first house on the left.

Lew nodded at a shack made of rain-stained lumber. It bore a sign that read: *United States Post Office, Caribou.*

"A post office means mail service," he said. "Let's go in."

It was a small room with a short counter backed by three shelves bearing a few heaps of goods. Two kegs stood in one corner. A swarthy woman got up from a rocking chair. She was short, with graying hair and two chins. She nodded and then waited for them to speak.

"How often do you send out mail?" Lew asked. He was looking around for a letter drop, letter box, or pigeonhole, but none was visible.

"This is not a post office anymore," she replied. "The government started one when the army men came back. But they said it did not pay. I have not had time to take down the sign."

"Sign reads Caribou," Charlie said. "We thought this was the Brown Grizzly Project."

"The army used that name. But before it was Caribou, and that is what the post office people used."

"Then we can't send a letter out?" Charlie asked.

"You can. But you must wait until a plane comes. Then you pay the pilot a dollar to take the letter out and put on a stamp."

"Did you handle much mail when you were open?" Lew asked.

She nodded. "I still have two letters that were never called for."

Lew winked at Charlie. "Maybe they're for us."

He spoke their names carefully, and the woman moved silently on moccasined feet to the end of the counter, opened a drawer and took out two grimy envelopes. She held them close to her eyes, nodded and walked back. "They're both for you," she said.

Lew's eyes widened. "Thanks," he said. "Thanks very much."

Outside he stared at his companion. "Can you beat that?"

"Aren't you going to read yours?" Charlie asked. "You came a long way to get it. I'm going to read mine now, so hand it over."

The envelopes were addressed in pencil, properly stamped and postmarked locally. The date, however, was illegible. Charlie tore the envelope open and took out a small piece of paper. It read:

*You said you might come back to your mining claims, and if you do you will get this note. Please hurry, but be careful. There is danger. I think someone is watching us, and I am afraid — D.D.*

"D.D.," Charlie repeated. "The writing is small and feminine, so Dorina Driscoll and not her brother wrote this. What does yours say?"

"Same thing, word for word. What can she be talking about?"

"I wish I knew," Charlie said soberly.

"She could have written a little more," Lew growled. "There's room left on the paper. How dizzy can a dame get?"

Charlie folded his note and put it in a pocket. "I'm going back to ask the lady some questions."

Inside the little store he asked, "Do you have any tea?"

She nodded. "How much?"

"I know it costs a lot of money up here, better give me five dollars worth." She produced a small packet that scarcely weighed four ounces. He laid a bill on the counter. "Would you remember who mailed these letters to us?"

"No. We had a box fastened to the door so they could be dropped in from outdoors."

"How long have you had them?"

"I don't remember. A long time."

"Perhaps you remember two friends of ours, a tall young man and his sister. She was very thin; both had light hair. They came here last fall. They may have left before winter and then returned in the spring. Did you see them?"

"I was not here in the fall. I came in March when the army men moved back. But I have not seen your friends."

"Does Woolman, the heavy-set man, run the store on the hill?"

"He is dead. The store now belongs to his son."

Charlie thanked her, and they left.

"That tea was expensive," Lew said.

"Think so? I don't. By saving these letters," he touched the one in his pocket, "she may have saved our lives."

"I'm surprised she didn't send them to the dead letter office."

"If this was the States she would have. But up here people will come in eventually to ask for mail, even if it's a year later."

They walked between the two rows of buildings that comprised the little settlement of Caribou. Some were empty, the tenants out on traplines or cutting timber. People were working in back of the nearest shack, and obeying a sudden impulse, Charlie stopped.

"Maybe they know of Dirk and Dorina," he said. "You try across the street, I'll ask here."

Walking around the building, Charlie found an old Indian man and woman. She was scraping the hide of a half-grown timber wolf laced inside a pole frame; he stood watching.

Charlie described the Driscolls. He knew even a sketchy picture would suffice, because the Driscolls were so different from Caribou's usual visitors. "Have you seen them?" he asked.

The man smiled and nodded, "Sure."

"Where?" Charlie asked.

The man shrugged. "In the woods."

"When?" Charlie asked.

"Last month ... maybe yesterday," the man said vaguely.

Charlie knew his first question had been a mistake. He should have phrased it so a "yes" or "no" answer was not possible. He doubted the old man had actually seen the Driscolls, but he made a final test. "There was a little boy with them this big," he said, holding his hand about a yard above the ground. "Did you see him?"

"Sure."

Charlie thanked the man and rejoined Lew in the street.

"No luck," Lew said. "They didn't speak English, or if they did, they wouldn't admit it." He glanced back. "We seem to have stirred up some interest. The man in the gray and red shirt is following us."

"Maybe Woolman's son can help," Charlie suggested. Approaching the big store, they saw its weather-beaten sign still carried the family name, only the initial "C" had been changed to "J."

And then they had their second great surprise of the day. A young woman in fur-trimmed parka, skirt and white tan mukluks came around the building so suddenly she almost bumped into them.

Lew dropped the pack he had slung over one shoulder. "Rena!" he cried. "What are you doing here? I thought you left last fall?"

The girl's eyes grew frightened and she backed away. "I am not Rena," she stammered. "I do not know you."

"What's the matter, you got amnesia? Why ..."

"Don't talk to me!" she said and then ran behind the store.

Lew started to follow, but then stopped. Maybe he had made a mistake, but it didn't seem possible. They had shared many dangerous days together the year before, and every detail of Rena's good-humored face was indelibly impressed upon his memory, the bronzed skin and neatly combed black hair. She looked a little thinner, but it was definitely her.

He turned a baffled face to Charlie.

"That was Rena," Charlie nodded. "I'd know her anywhere."

Lew stooped to pick up his pack. "But why would the sight of us scare her? It isn't like Rena to become frightened."

"She must have a good reason for not recognizing us," Charlie said, "and we better go along with her until we know what it is."

## Chapter 2 – It Isn't Santa Claus!

The Woolman store had also changed, the merchandise less varied and more suited to the needs of Native people. A man uncrating galvanized tubs straightened and said, "Can I help you?"

"Mr. Woolman?" Charlie asked.

He nodded.

"I saw a radio tower behind the store. Can we send out a short wave message?"

"Set's broke, and it may be a month before the parts come."

"We want to contact our pilot when we're ready to leave."

"You can get a message out in six days. A plane's arriving with freight for the store."

"That's fine. We're also looking for a young man and his sister. They're both blonde and they came in last fall. Their name is Driscoll."

Charlie thought the man's eyes might have flickered. But his voice was even when he replied, "I couldn't say about that. I didn't come until January of this year."

"Thanks anyway," Charlie said. "Is there someplace we can get a meal and perhaps a bed tonight?"

Woolman nodded. "Baptiste's rooming house, third building south. Would you like a drink? I have some cola, also ginger ale."

"Cola will be fine," Charlie replied.

"I have to get a dollar a bottle, but you know about air costs."

"We know," Lew agreed.

Woolman called, "Rena!" There was no reply. "My girl must have gone out," he said. "But I can serve you."

They followed him to the bar and dropped packs and guns on the floor. When Rena came in from a room behind the shelves, her face paled again when she saw them.

"These men want a cola," Woolman said sharply.

She brought two bottles, and when Charlie laid money on the counter, she lifted her eyes and whispered, "Don't talk to me."

The cola was cold, and that reminded Lew that it was only necessary to dig a few inches to find frozen ground that never thawed during summer, and this supplied ideal storage for anything perishable.

"I don't like it," Lew said in a low voice. "Dirk and Dorina

Driscoll flew here last fall, and now, nobody has even heard of them. Maybe Rena knows something, if we can get her to talk."

The man in the gray and red stag shirt who had followed them up from the airstrip came in and walked up to Woolman. Talking, he gestured rapidly with his hands. Woolman glanced at Charlie and Lew then walked into the room behind the counter. After a moment, he called, "Rena! Come here!"

The girl hesitated but obeyed.

Lew tilted his head towards the man who remained in the center of the store. "I don't like that guy's looks, and Woolman didn't appear especially benign when he went by. I smell trouble in the air."

Then they heard the sound of a slap and a startled cry. Lew didn't waste any time getting into the rear room. He jumped over the bar.

There wasn't a door, just a curtain cut from patched canvas, which he swept back with one hand while he reached out the other to grab Woolman, who was raising his hand to hit the girl again.

Woolman shoved the girl into Lew. Before he could recover, Woolman jerked a pistol from his coat and leveled it. Charlie, who had gone around the bar, halted just inside the curtain.

The storekeeper's features were taut. But he managed to speak evenly. "This is a private room. So leave."

Lew was watching the pistol, a Walther 9mm. Its hammer was down, but Lew knew the gun had a double-action hammer you cocked by simply pressing the trigger, same as a double-action revolver. Lew also looked down at his hand, the one that had pushed aside the curtain, and saw with surprise it still clutched the bottle of cola.

Woolman motioned impatiently with the gun. "You heard me. Get out!" His voice had raised to more nearly match his anger.

Lew raised the bottle a little, like he was going to take a swig. Then, slipping his thumb off the mouth, he directed a stream of lively froth into Woolman's sallow face.

Ducking sideways, he yelled, "Get him, Charlie!"

If Woolman's pistol had been cocked, he might have fired an aimed shot, but before the hammer could fall, Charlie had gripped the man's wrist and twisted it so the muzzle of the gun pointed up. That was where the bullet went. Then, wrenching the weapon free, Charlie slammed the man against the wall with a stiff jab to the jaw, jerked him forward again to slap his pockets and the space below each armpit to see if there was another gun or perhaps a knife. With an easy uppercut to the chin, he drove him back against the wall.

Lew stepped out to the bar to check on the man who had given Woolman reason to beat Rena. But the fellow was gone. When he returned to the little storage room, Charlie was saying, "If anybody bothers her again, they'll get really hurt."

Woolman's eyes were glazed, but Charlie knew he understood. He unloaded the Walther, slid out the magazine, and stripped off the top cartridge. Then he dropped everything on the floor and said to Lew and Rena, "Let's get out of here."

Lew swallowed the rest of his cola before picking up his pack and rifle and stepping towards the door.

Charlie had no regrets about helping Rena. But if the short notes they had received from Dorina Driscoll meant anything, and he was pretty sure they did, then they already had been exposed to danger. Now there was the added menace of Woolman's anger. Men of the North Country do not forget let alone forgive such treatment.

"Looks like we can count on getting into trouble here, Rena," Lew said. "Last year, I had to twist that guy Pete's arm when he stole your money. What's become of Pete? He still around?"

Rena shook her head. "I have not seen him since I came back."

"What was that all about?" Charlie asked.

"Until today he has been nice. Pays me good money."

"Then why did he hit you?"

"Because Wolf said I spoke to you. Mr. Woolman says I must not talk with anyone from the outside. If I do, I will lose my job."

"But you gave us a real brush-off," Lew said. "Who's Wolf?"

"He does not like me because I will not let him be my friend."

Lew gave her an approving glance, and Rena added slowly, "I am sorry. But I never thought I'd see you again, and when I did, I was afraid Mr. Woolman would not let me work anymore if I talked."

"It's all right," Charlie told her, "we understand." He didn't, not really. But he thought they might soon find out what was going on.

"We do know one thing," Charlie continued. "Woolman doesn't want you to talk, so he must be tied up in some shady deal. Does he do anything besides run the store?"

"He is in the mining business," Rena said.

"Do any of your customers ever get sleepy after they drink?" Charlie asked suddenly.

Rena nodded. "It happens. But the men work hard in the timber and travel long trails. They are always tired when they come."

"Maybe Woolman helps them home when they fall asleep?"

"Yes. He takes them to Baptiste's rooming house."

"Slips the poor devil a Mickey and then rolls him," Lew grunted. "No wonder he doesn't want Rena talking to anyone."

"Maybe," Charlie said. "But I think there is more to it. Rena, you said you had some money. Where is it?"

"It is invested," she said proudly. "Soon, I will be rich."

Lew stared at her. "Invested?" he repeated. "How?"

She reached inside the wolverine-trimmed parka and pulled out a bundle of papers. She opened one and held out a handsome piece of art, printed in two colors on a coated bond that crackled. Across the top, it read: "CARIBOU GOLD & MINING COMPANY, LTD."

"This is ten shares," Rena continued. "It is worth fifty dollars."

"Who says so?" Lew asked.

"Mr. Woolman. He is president of the company. He gives one to me each week for my work, also five dollars on which I live."

"What a crook!" Lew exclaimed.

"Now wait, Lew," Charlie said. "You know uranium has been found near here. And there's gold. That's why we came, isn't it?"

"Sure," Lew admitted, "but that doesn't mean Woolman hasn't stacked the deck. I bet he deals off the bottom, too."

"I do not understand," Rena said. "My stock will be worth more every year. If I buy more each week, I can go back to my village and build a school for the children."

"You poor kid," Lew muttered.

Charlie said, "Have you heard anything about the Driscolls?"

"No," she replied, still looking puzzled.

"We can't stand here talking all afternoon," Lew interrupted. "Where do you live, Rena?"

"At my sister's, the same as last year. You can stay there now." When he hesitated, she added, "It is cleaner than the rooming house."

As they walked, Lew asked, "Why did you come back, Rena?"

"Because the army came. There is always work and money where they stay. Then I got work with Mr. Woolman and Mr. Breed."

"Who's he?"

"Mr. Woolman's partner. He and Wolf's brother make many trips into the mountains to look for gold."

The two-room structure was exactly as it had been before. The furniture consisted of a whaling boat stove, two wood benches, and a shelf acting as sink and cupboard. The shelf held an enameled pail that served as a sourdough keg, judging from the yeasty odor.

Lew surveyed the otherwise empty shelf with a gloomy eye. One of their packs was filled with dry trail foods, but he wanted to save it, so he said, "I'll walk back to the store and pick up some stuff."

"Mr. Woolman will be mad," Rena said doubtfully.

"He won't refuse my money," Lew told her confidently.

But Woolman was not there, and a man who looked like he might be Wolf's brother filled Lew's order. He bought a can of beans, tomatoes and peas, a strip of bacon, a pound of rice, a small sack of flour, and thinking of the next morning's breakfast, a pail of syrup and a carton of dried peaches. It knocked a big hole in a $10 bill.

Rena made a pan of sourdough biscuits and set them on the back of the stove to rise. Lew thought he saw a hungry gleam in her eyes when he spread out his purchases, and that touched him because it confirmed his suspicion that she had been depriving herself to buy Woolman's stock. "Don't you eat anything besides biscuits?" he asked.

"Not much," she confessed. "I snare rabbits, but I do not have one now. I am out of tea, too. But tomorrow I will be paid."

That reminded Charlie of the tea he had bought at the former post office; he took it from his coat.

Rena's small kerosene lamp was almost dry of oil, so after dinner they opened the stove door and threw in small twigs to supply light. The girl was yawning before she finished washing the cups and plates.

"I will sleep now because I must get up early for work," she said.

Later, as he and Charlie spread their sleeping bags in the front room beside the stove, he said, "Can you tie that? She's going without grub to buy that worthless stock. How could she fall for such a deal?"

"Because she wants to believe," Charlie replied. "The situation now is just the same as last year," he added.

"What do you mean?"

"Rena's in trouble. It's with a different Woolman, but the overall picture hasn't changed. He'll finish the beating we interrupted as soon as we leave tomorrow morning."

Lew folded his sleeping bag back so he could pull it over him without awakening when the room cooled. "OK," he said, "You don't have to spell it out. She goes with us if she wants. She's too good a kid to be abused by that crook. She's a good cook, too."

The panels of the old stove buckled and snapped as they cooled in the night, and the rough, battened wall boards creaked with the wind. It may have been one sound or it may have been the other that aroused Charlie hours later. He lay quietly listening. Then the sound of footsteps in the dirt street outside reached his ears.

He got up and peered out the door. The northern lights were bright enough to print dark blocks of shadow behind each building, and to reveal two men striding towards the store. Each carried a pack, and Charlie watched until they reached the store door, either opened it or had it opened for them, and stepped inside. Rena had said Woolman's mining partner often went into the bush searching for ore. He felt sure he had witnessed his return.

It was creaking floorboards that aroused him the second time, and this time he saw Lew tiptoe in socked feet to the door. Lew opened it and went outside. When Charlie joined him, he pointed to the roof and whispered, "Somebody's up there, and it isn't Santa Claus."

Hugging the wall to stay under the projecting eaves, they moved to the corner of the house. This gave a better view of the bulky shadow above. Without any question, a man was standing up there.

Lew whispered, "I'll get my rifle."

"Bring both," Charlie replied.

The upright shadow moved a little, and though Charlie knew it was risky, he edged out away from the wall until he could see the man and not just the shadow. The fellow took something from his pocket and held it over the stove pipe.

"Get out, Lew!" Charlie yelled. "Get out fast!"

# Chapter 3 – Charlie Invests in Stock

Lew had barely leaped out through the door with a rifle in each hand when flames burst from the stove and filled the room in which they had been sleeping. The flames accounted for most of the explosion's force, but not all, because a column of fire also shot up the short chimney and enveloped the figure beside it. The man screamed and flung both hands over his face, lost his balance, rolled down the slope and tumbled to the ground. Struggling to his feet, he ran towards the lower end of the one-street settlement.

"See if Rena is alright," Charlie said. "I'll get the packs and sleeping bags."

The flames died fast, but the air was thick with smoke and ash. Lew ran towards the girl's room and stepped on something hot that burned through his wool sock. He gave a yell and jumped back, hoping the foot wasn't injured because they had a lot of hard tramping to do. Before he reached her room, Rena ran out clutching two skin blankets.

Charlie tossed their own gear outside and grabbed the water pail. So far nothing in the room had started to burn. Little tongues of flame flickered up from the floor near the stove, but Charlie doused them.

But the stove and pipe were twisted. Ash covered everything, and more was settling from the air. The Eskimo girl picked up a shaved birch broom and began to sweep. Charlie and Lew went outside.

"Gunpowder?" Lew asked.

"Or blasting powder. He must have thought the stove was cold and the stuff would lay in it until we built a fire in the morning."

"I don't think it was Woolman himself," Lew declared. "But I'll bet he engineered the deal."

Rena had the house cleaned by breakfast time. After they had eaten fried sourdough biscuits with bacon, stewed peaches and tea cooked on an outdoor fire, Charlie said, "Rena, I want you to sell me one share of your stock."

It was hard to tell if she or Lew was more surprised. She produced the bundle of certificates and said doubtfully, "If you say so."

"I'll give you five dollars, which is what Woolman said it was worth." He turned the paper over so its transfer form was up. "Put your name here." She signed with a hard pencil. Lew signed as witness.

"I'll be back in a few minutes," Charlie said. "Better pack up so we can leave in a hurry."

Entering the Woolman store, Charlie saw two men. One was saying, "... the danged fool got himself burned so he's no use to us now."

"I know that, Breed, but I didn't ..." this was Woolman, and he stopped abruptly when he saw Charlie.

"Good morning," Charlie said.

"What do you want?" Woolman snapped.

"To do some business. You're a businessman, aren't you?"

"What do you want?" Woolman repeated in a milder tone.

"I want to buy stock in your gold and uranium mining company."

The eyes of the man Woolman had addressed as Breed turned wary. He was not as tall as the store owner, but he was heavy-set with thick shoulders that suggested considerable strength. He had pale eyes and a thin mustache. His face and hands were tan, but they lacked the sallow bronze of a Native. The man, Charlie decided, could be trouble.

"What do you want the stock for?" he asked.

"It's a good investment, isn't it?" Charlie countered.

"Sure. But it may be some time before we operate profitably."

"I can wait."

The two stared at each other. Then Woolman said crisply, "Sorry. No stock is available now."

Charlie glanced at the thick-shouldered man. "Your name Breed? Winthrop R. Breed?"

He hesitated, and then nodded. "Yes, I'm Breed."

"Then," Charlie said, "you can enter this transfer in the company books and issue my new certificate." He held out the share he had purchased from Rena. Breed took the paper reluctantly.

"What's your game?" he demanded.

"Game?" Charlie echoed. "I don't know what you mean. I bought a share of stock, and it's up to the secretary to transfer it in my name. And according to this," he pointed, "that's you, Winthrop R. Breed."

"Suppose I don't?" Breed asked.

Charlie sighed. "I was hoping you wouldn't make trouble. But if you're a genuine corporation, you are registered with the Securities Commission. That entails certain obligations to your stockholders and to those who buy stock. It's a long ways up here, but I think they would investigate if I complained."

"Why did you buy it?" Breed asked.

"Not because of the pretty ink," Charlie replied. "Share owners have rights, too. Even a minority shareholder can demand to see the books, check the list of stockholders, and do other interesting things."

Woolman took a step forward, but Breed blocked him with a thick arm. "I'll handle this," he said. "You've bungled enough."

Breed dug up what he thought was a friendly smile. "Suppose I buy this from you? Would $10 be OK?"

"That sounds all right," Charlie said. "Only it isn't quite that simple. You see, I can get more where this came from, and if I sell I'd want to sell all."

"You're talking about Rena's stock?" Breed asked.

Charlie nodded.

The man made a quick decision. "Bring it here and I'll give you $3 for every share."

"Woolman charged her five," Charlie replied.

Breed thought fast, and the look he directed at his partner was murderous. "All right," he said. "Bring it all here and I'll pay you."

Back in the little cabin, Charlie had some trouble making Rena understand the situation. But the thought of having all of her money in the form of cash helped him convince her she should sell.

She inscribed her name on each transfer form, and watching, Charlie suddenly wondered what he would do if the Caribou Mining and Prospecting Company really did uncover some rich deposit of ore. But he reassured himself with the thought if it did, Breed and Woolman would manage to cheat her out of any returns, anyway.

Charlie carefully counted the money Breed gave him.

"Thanks," he said. "I don't know if this is a sucker game or not. Fact is, I don't care. But you know as well as I you shouldn't have taken all of the girl's money. That was just too raw."

His companions had finished packing when he rejoined them. Rena had loaded her few garments, tableware, skin blankets and sewing kit in a canvas bag. She tied a rope around it to form a tumpline and laid out a fur mitten for a pad to cushion her forehead.

The trail that would take them back into the mountains to the Driscoll claim skirted one end of the landing strip. Before they reached it, they heard a plane and stopped when the craft shot out into view over the treetops. It was flying so low they knew it was going to land.

"That's Jeff," Lew said. "We didn't forget anything, did we?"

"Hope not," Charlie replied. "Not at the rates he charges."

Jeff grounded with his customary deftness, the ship bumping over the cracked runway until coming to a rest some 50 yards away. A solidly built girl who seemed scarcely taller than Rena jumped to the ground. A man followed. Then he turned to take some packages Jeff handed down, but the girl approached them briskly.

"I thought we would never get here," she swept them with determined eyes then fixed her gaze on Lew. "You took Dirk and Dorina into the mountains last fall and left them there alone."

Lew nodded.

"You had no right to do that. If something has happened to them, I'll hold you responsible."

"Now wait, Miss ..." Lew began.

"Nash. Elma Nash." Her tone erased any reason for doubting it.

"The Driscolls asked to be left alone," Lew said. "You ever try to argue with them?"

Her gray eyes blinked, but she persisted. "Well, I'm glad you finally decided to come back for them. We'll go together."

"That is one reason we came back," Lew admitted. "But we're going into some hard country. Why don't you wait here until we get back? Then, if the Driscolls are in trouble ..."

"Of course they're in trouble," she replied. Or Dorina would have written like she promised. I'm so worried I haven't eaten in weeks."

Lew wasn't sure about that, but he let it pass.

"I'm a good hiker," she continued, "and I brought a cold-weather outfit. Mr. Bell helped me pick it out in Fairbanks."

The plane was moving now, and they stepped aside to let it pass. Jeff waved and yelled, "Looks like I got you another job." He grinned at Lew's scowling face and added, "Don't forget my commission."

Charlie walked to the pile of gear. The man beside it held out a hand. "I'm T.C. Bell," he said. "Your partner might as well stop arguing. He'll never get anywhere with her. Miss Nash is a close friend of the Driscolls, and I'm a private investigator she hired in Fairbanks."

Bell was a little taller than Charlie and about the same weight. His features were white, but the straight black hair suggested he, like so many territorial residents, could claim at least one native ancestor.

"I came up here last month, but nobody had seen the Driscolls. One old fellow thought they had gone back into the mountains with two men and an Eskimo girl. That was you?"

Charlie nodded.

Bell continued, "The old fellow didn't know in which direction, so I came back and wrote Miss Nash. It was my only lead, and not a good one. I asked what she wanted to do. Next thing, she's walking into my office telling me I must have slipped up somewhere, that there had to be more leads, and she'd uncover them. She did, too. Found the pilot who flew the Driscolls in last year. He told her about the one who brought you up yesterday, and she hired him on the spot."

He glanced at Charlie and added, "I know I should have checked with every bush pilot in the district. Guess I didn't have much faith in the job, didn't know how far she was willing to take it. But she's going the limit to find her friends. Must be loaded, too. Told me not to worry about expenses. I wanted her to stay in Fairbanks and let me handle this end. But no go—and I don't blame her much after my boner."

Elma Nash strode up. "Your partner can't make up his mind. I hope you can. I want you to help find the Driscolls."

"What if we don't?" Charlie asked. He didn't mean to sound brusque, but he found her irritating. Looking over his shoulder, he saw Lew throw up both hands in a baffled gesture.

"I will hire men in Caribou. I think six packers and hunters will be about right. But why won't you go? I'll pay you the same."

It was evident that whatever irritating traits she had, Elma Nash was passionately loyal to her friends, and Charlie thought later this was what made his decision. He nodded and said, "For the record, let's say you have joined *us*. You understand, of course, the more people the slower we travel. We don't know if the Driscolls are in trouble, but if they are, Lew and I could get there a day sooner going alone."

She shook her head. "I am going. This job must be done right." She shot a glance at Bell, who winced visibly.

"Now, what wages do you want?"

"Since we are going anyway, they can be nominal, just enough to cover the extra work you make for us. Say eight dollars apiece for the three of us; we include Rena," he glanced at the girl sitting on her pack and watching with grave interest, "and she'll earn every penny."

"That's all right," Elma replied quickly. "Dorina wrote and told me about her. Now, let's get started."

"I want to check your gear, first," Charlie replied. She and Bell each had a pack, and Bell had brought a rifle. Their clothing was wool, the style outfitters sell for big-game hunting and warm enough for any weather they could expect this month. Each also owned a down sleeping bag and short air mattress, a mess kit, and Bell said his pack also contained 15 pounds of emergency rations, mostly candy bars.

Elma offered to buy more food at the store, but Charlie thought everyone had as much as he or she could carry over the trail ahead. It might mean more time hunting, but he couldn't see any other course. Arranging shelter would not be difficult, because Bell's duffel, like their own, was wrapped in a waterproof sheet and then roped to his pack board, making three tarps for the party. One would serve for Elma and Rena, the other two could be pitched as an open tent for the men.

"I broke my pipe," Bell said. "I'll go to the store and get one."

"Would you really have gone on this trip with a party of native hunters?" Charlie asked Elma.

"Definitely," she replied. "I am very worried. Dorina wrote me they had found their uncle's mine and were working hard. She said they would soon have as much money as they ever possessed, and she would write again before they left. That letter never came."

"When did you get the first letter?"

"Last November."

"Can you remember where it was postmarked?"

"No. Is that important?"

"Could be. You see, we don't know if they came out last fall or if they stayed the winter. They weren't really outfitted for a winter up here, and I thought they would leave. But if they did, nobody in Caribou saw them or saw them return this spring, either."

"Dorina would have written me if they had left," Elma declared. "Time went so fast it was summer before I realized I hadn't heard from her again. So I contacted Mr. Bell and hired him to investigate. I still think we need more men."

"We can handle it," Charlie assured her. "We know exactly where we left them. What we find there will determine our next move."

Bell returned with a cheap corn cob pipe. "It's all they had," he said with a wry grin.

They shouldered the packs, walked past the airstrip and entered the edge of the timber. A little later, Lew moved up beside Charlie. "When we were in Woolman's store yesterday," he said in a low voice, "I saw a dozen pipes. And there were several different kinds."

"Maybe he wanted an alibi for a cheap one," Charlie replied.

"Cheap?" Lew echoed. "He said Woolman charged him five bucks for that gimcrack."

"Think what a good one might have cost," Charlie replied.

## Chapter 4 – Chunks of Virgin Gold

The first few miles of trail passed timber slashings with piles of decaying brush and cull logs where the army people had cut timber for their buildings. They glimpsed, too, occasional huts where native children peeked out half-open doors to watch their little party pass. They passed deserted cabins with tumbled-in pole and dirt roofs.

They made a noon stop to brew tea, and while the water heated, Charlie took the rimfire rifle from his pack and circled around in search of game. But wildlife proved scarce, and he wondered if it had been a bad year for the ptarmigan and rabbits, both of which are subject to cycles of abundance and scarcity. When slight movement caught his eye, he stopped and imitated a rabbit scream. A fox stepped out from a clump of moosewood. Charlie didn't shoot. Having eaten fox, he wasn't eager to repeat the experience unless necessary.

Before they started on, Charlie picked up Elma's pack, and despite her protests, carried it with his own. An extra 20 pounds meant little to his solid shoulders, and he didn't want her to wear down on the first day. It had taken four days to reach the Driscoll cabin before, and he hoped to make the same good time.

By late afternoon, the great expanse of timber looked so alike Charlie had to consult his compass to pick a course. Before, they had followed a map. The second time he paused, at a fork in a stream, Rena asked, "Are we going to the same cabin as last year?"

Charlie looked at her in surprise. "Yes, we are."

"Then this way is wrong."

"How do you know?" Lew asked.

"I always know how to go if I have been there before."

People with photographic memory recall physical details automatically. Rena apparently had this skill.

"OK," Charlie said. "You pick the trail."

Rena turned to the fork and followed the other branch.

"You sure she knows what she's doing?" Bell asked.

"I'm very sure," Charlie replied. "If she didn't, she would have kept silent. Rena can do things you and I can't."

He had an idea Bell would have liked to question him more on this, but he quickened his gait, and the man finally fell back in line.

Charlie's watch showed almost 4 o'clock, and he knew they would have to camp soon. Elma was very tired.

They were following another small stream, which like the others formed a series of frozen pools that cut back and forth across a narrow valley hemmed in by hills. "Rest a few minutes," Charlie told Lew. "Then camp not more than a mile ahead. I'll hunt for supper meat. Maybe," he added, looking at Bell, "you would like to hunt, too?"

Bell agreed, and Charlie gave Lew his rifle, planning to use the handgun. The report would be less apt to frighten bigger game out of the vicinity, and if the small stuff continued to be scarce, they might have to shoot and pack something bigger. The food in the packs had to be supplemented with fresh meat to last in and back out again.

When he separated from Bell, Charlie turned from the water. The valley contained plenty of brush and piles of rock with an occasional stand of taller trees. It looked like good cover for all kinds of game.

Upon hearing a dry rattling noise, he stopped, looked up and saw a porcupine in the top of a 10-foot aspen. Charlie grasped the little tree trunk and shook hard. The porcupine tumbled out, landed on its feet, and swinging around, faced him with spine-barbed tail waving.

Charlie picked up a stone and killed the porcupine with a solid hit on the nose. He tied a leather thong to the rear legs so he could carry the carcass without the quills jabbing his leg.

The ground was starting to rise into the hills, and he had about decided to turn around and return to the stream when a snowshoe hare jumped from its bed of caribou moss. The animal disappeared behind a rock ledge. He followed cautiously. Looking from behind a boulder, he saw the hare standing 60 feet away, watching its back trail. He aimed carefully at the base of the neck and fired. The hollow-point bullet hit with a solid thump that knocked the rabbit sprawling.

On his way back to the creek, Charlie saw another porcupine in a taller tree but didn't stop. One was enough, especially since he didn't know how well Elma and Bell would like the meat. But he was pleased to find small game, and this pleasure only grew when he reached the water course and saw two ptarmigan in a birch. He moved up slowly until the birds began to duck their heads nervously. Then he shot.

One fell, tumbling end over end so there was no question of it being stone dead. The other flew. Charlie didn't attempt the wing shot because they already had meat for supper and breakfast in the morning.

He didn't hear a shot from Bell's rifle, so he wasn't surprised to learn the man had returned empty-handed. But Bell said he had flushed a large animal of some kind, and that was good news, too.

Lew had felled several small spruces with the folding saw; Rena had trimmed them with the axe, and they were working together erecting shelters. Rena also had kindled a fire, and Elma sat before it on her sleeping roll, head propped on elbows that rested on knees.

"Stand up and move around," Charlie suggested. When she gave no response, he raised her by the arms. She shook his hands off angrily.

"You can only sit a few minutes at a time," he explained. "Then you must walk. Otherwise, you'll be too stiff to travel in the morning."

Elma hobbled slowly in front of the fire.

"I remember a fellow who sat too long after a hard day hunting elk," Lew said. "The next morning the guides found him doubled up in his blankets, head almost touching knees, just as he had sat at the fire the night before. He tried but couldn't unbend. So they cut a long pole, shoved it through his suspenders, and packed him home that way."

"What happened then," Bell asked with a grin.

"He couldn't go back to his old job. So he hired out to help women find the shoes they kicked off in the theater when they saw a movie."

"Very funny," Elma said. Then she hobbled down to the creek where Charlie was cleaning the rabbit and ptarmigan.

"What do you think of my friends, the Driscolls?" she asked. "Dirk give you any trouble?"

"We got along all right," Charlie replied. "They were afraid they wouldn't find their uncle, that he hadn't actually discovered gold."

"Had he?"

"We left before they did any real work on the claim. But it looked good enough for us to stake our own claims and make this trip back to check on them." He laid the cleaned bird on a clean stone.

Elma walked back and forth several times then spoke again. "Which of them would act best in an emergency, Dirk or Dorina?"

"I'd bet on the sister."

Elma sighed, "And you'd be right. When Dirk gets in a jam, Dorina usually has to get him out. I've known them all my life. I guess I told you they were my best friends. I like Dirk—a lot. But to him, I guess I will always be the dumpy girl who lives next door." She pressed her lips firmly together. "I don't know why I'm telling you this."

"Because you're worried," Charlie said, "and it helps to talk one's troubles over with another."

"What do you think happened to them?" she continued.

Charlie regarded her gravely. "I'll give it to you straight," he said. "If they stayed on, they may have died from exposure or starvation. They would have had to depend on game meat, and we've traveled three days out of a winter camp to find caribou, moose or bear. If Dirk and Dorina had tried that, they might have never returned."

He slit open the belly of the skinned rabbit, grasped the legs and swung the carcass about his head. The entrails flew out.

"Clever," Elma commented shortly.

"Takes practice," Charlie replied.

Rena came and took the rabbit and ptarmigan back to the fire. Charlie washed his hands in the icy water then flipped them dry.

"There's something else we can't ignore," he continued. "Men will murder for gold. I suppose Dorina wrote you we had trouble last fall. We came out all right, because the leader of that gang died. But he had three hard men working for him who knew about the Driscoll claim. They may have left the country; they may still be around. All we know is they aren't in Caribou now, because we asked Rena."

Charlie rolled down the sleeves of his shirt, picked up his coat and pulled it about his shoulders. "I don't trust the man running the store in Caribou or his partner, a fellow named Breed." He studied her face, decided she might as well have the whole story. "There were two identical letters from Dorina in the old post office."

"Letters?" she repeated. "Why didn't you tell me?"

"Here's mine," he said and handed her the brief note.

She read the scrap of paper carefully and then read it again. "What does Dorina mean, somebody is watching them?"

"Just that, I suppose. She mentions danger for us, too. I can't explain that either, but we must be very careful."

She glanced at the trees encircling their camp. "It doesn't look good, does it? I mean for my friends."

"I haven't finished," Charlie said. "I thought you should hear the bad part first. Now for the good. It is possible Dirk and his sister came through the winter OK. They're young and strong. Also, they could get help from a prospector friend of the uncle who lives a day's journey away. Maybe she only imagined they were being watched. The loneliness and solitude up here does queer things to people. So let's not worry too much until we find out just what has happened."

Lew rolled the porcupine around in the campfire coals until the sharp quills burned away. Then he removed the entrails, shoved a pole through the carcass and staked it before the fire to roast. Rena fried the rabbit and bird so they could be heated quickly in the morning and made three loaves of bannock bread. She cooked each partly stiff with a little fat in the spare skillet, then propped them before the fire on sticks to finish baking. Charlie put rice with dehydrated tomatoes and onions in a kettle of boiling water and simmered it into a thick stew.

Bell had kept working on the shelters, filling the open ends with brush to block drafts. He covered the hard ground with twigs.

The porcupine was the larger species found in timbered parts of the North. Its dry flesh tasted of pine, but they cleaned off every bone. The stew and bread disappeared more quickly.

After supper, Rena washed the dishes then washed everyone's socks and hung them on a short line behind the fire.

Charlie rolled stones around to serve as seats. The air was chilly, so they draped coats about their shoulders and sat down.

"The pilot told me you have gold claims, too," Bell said.

Charlie nodded. "So far they're just prospects, never been worked. But we plan to check them out."

"You think the Driscolls are still back there?" Bell asked.

Charlie nodded.

"Are they near your claims?"

"Fairly close," Charlie said. He knew Bell was smart enough to have connected gold and their last year's trip. He put two pieces of wood on the fire and leaned over to untie his boot laces.

Rena pointed into the night and said softly, "There are men."

"Coming here?" he asked quickly.

"I think they just watch."

She went back to the shelter with Elma, and Charlie acted promptly. He didn't see much chance that Rena was mistaken, because on their first trip the girl had sensed strangers long before they could be seen or heard. He spoke quickly to the group, "Rena says we're being watched. Go in the shelters and keep your rifles handy."

Lew stood up, and when Bell hesitated, he grabbed the man's arm and hauled him to his feet. "Do as he says," Lew growled.

As soon as the rest were in the shelters, Charlie stood and waved his arm. "Come on in," he shouted. "Come on in."

He sat and pulled his own gun between his feet. Minutes passed. "Have they gone?" he asked Rena.

"No," she called back softly.

There was a faint rustle, and then three of the filthiest men Charlie had ever seen stepped into the circle of firelight. They were short and squat with wide, flat faces. Thick tangles of hair hung over their foreheads. Their squirrel skin clothing was stained with dirt and grease, scorched by fire. Each carried a short carbine. The leader stepped up close enough for Charlie to see that the muzzle of his gun was big enough to be .44-40 bore. He said, "Howdy."

Charlie returned the greeting.

The threesome stood silently, eyes darting about the camp. Finally, the leader said, "Eat."

Charlie asked Rena to bring the cooked rabbit and make tea. He pointed to the ground beside the fire and said, "Sit."

When they obeyed, the row of socks caught one's eyes. He reached out a hand. "Good," he grunted, touching the sock to feel its thick softness. He started to take it from the string.

Charlie said, "No." The man hesitated, met Charlie's steady gaze, and slowly withdrew his hand.

The leader, who was half a head taller than the others, hitched around the fire until he could touch Charlie's rifle. "Good," he said.

Charlie held it up so they could see it plainly, then ignoring the outstretched hands, put it back between his feet.

Rena divided the rabbit and brought three cups. They wolfed the meat, eyes roving constantly from Charlie and Rena up to the lean-tos that sheltered Elma, Lew and Bell.

When Rena poured his tea, the leader grabbed her wrist. She touched his hand with the hot kettle and he jerked it back with a snarl. Then he grinned and took two small objects from a pocket and handed them to Charlie. They were very heavy for their size and a brown yellow color. Their sides showed tool marks like they had been chopped from a bigger piece. Each, he thought, might weigh 6 ounces, perhaps half a pound. He had never before seen such large pieces of raw gold.

# Chapter 5 – Trading Ends in Trouble

Charlie looked from the two gold nuggets in his hand to the three visitors. The yellow metal was worth $400, even by North Country barter standards, and he wondered why men with so much wealth were wearing such ragged clothing. He wondered, too, why they would carry rifles of such ancient design. It was possible clothing might not matter to them. But he saw the shine in their eyes when he held up his sleek repeater. There was only one conclusion. The men had recently acquired the gold, and had not had a chance to spend any of it.

Meeting the fixed stare of the group's leader, the one who had offered the metal, Charlie tossed the nugget back.

The man's eyes contracted. He gulped his tea, set the cup down, and pointing to Charlie's rifle, said, "I buy." He took one nugget back, and after a short pause, added his own carbine to the remaining piece.

Charlie shook his head. The fellow slowly added the second piece of gold. Then, as Charlie still declined, he reached inside his ragged coat and reluctantly brought out a third. Charlie smiled but shook his head again. The malice in the staring eyes almost made him shiver, but it faded suddenly, and the man grinned.

"We sleep," he announced. Then, to Charlie's amazement, all three men stretched out beside the fire, and resting their heads on their arms, seemed to fall into deep slumber.

Rena cautiously retrieved the three cups and the kettle. Charlie walked over to the lean-to he shared with Lew and Bell.

"They want to buy your rifle?" Lew asked.

"Yes," Charlie replied. "With gold nuggets."

"Where would they get gold?" Bell interrupted.

Charlie started to unlace his boots.

"That," he said slowly, "is a very good question."

He recalled the rumor they had heard at the airstrip about Indians bringing in pieces of gold to trade.

"We mustn't let them get away," Bell said so fiercely Lew glanced at him in surprise. "We must make them tell us where they got it."

Then Elma spoke. "No, we must make them leave. We can't let them stay. We don't know what they might do."

"I'd rather have them by the fire where I can watch them than out in the timber where I can't," Charlie told her. Then he sighed, "One of us will have to stay awake."

He pulled off his boots. The lean-to stood before a string of boulders, and one was big enough to support his back. He leaned against it, pulled his sleeping bag over his shoulders, and said, "I'll take the first two hours."

He looked at the men beside the fire. Despite their thoroughly disreputable appearance, they really were remarkable. They had simplified trail life to a remarkable degree. So far as he could see, their only equipment consisted of the gun and knife each carried plus one short axe. They were traveling without tent, blankets, cooking gear or any store of food. It was possible, he realized, that they were not coastal natives but nomads who wandered continually like the caribou. Either way, it made them an adversary he must not minimize.

It was a long night. Charlie awoke Bell at half past ten. The fire still burned steadily because each time it died, one of the men sleeping near the pile of wood dropped a chunk on the embers.

When his turn came, Bell was hard to arouse. At first he grumbled and protested. Finally, he said, "I want to ask them about the gold. Think they know enough English so we can talk?"

"These fellows may understand better than they let on," Charlie replied. "But better wait until morning."

Two Arctic owls were booming at each other across the width of the valley, and it was some time before he could sleep. Then it seemed more like four minutes than four hours before Lew aroused him for his second turn. Apparently, Lew had let him sleep a little extra because it was after five. Then, as though following an unspoken command, the three men by the fire sat up, stretched and stood. They tugged the skin coats and pants straight and huddled together. There was enough light to show moving hands and jerking heads as they conversed with signs. Then they faced the two shelters.

Charlie cleared his throat deliberately. Without another word, the visitors turned and filed into the timber that surrounded the camp.

It was a sober group that gathered around the fire an hour later. No one had slept well, and tempers were inclined to be edgy. Bell's irritation stemmed from not getting to ask the strangers about the source of their gold. Lew never did like to miss a full meal, and it looked like he would have to do so now. But he agreed when Charlie said they should conserve the food in the packs. They made tea and divided the cooked ptarmigan, planning to break camp promptly and travel until breakfast game of some kind could be shot. Then they would cook a real breakfast. Lew, especially, hoped that wouldn't be too long.

Rena was filling the kettle to make more tea when he said, "We've got visitors."

The three men who had slept beside their fire last night walked in through the trees. The visitors showed no interest in the morning meal. They were smiling widely. The leader came up to Charlie and said, "Caribou. You shoot it." Then he pointed to the rifles leaning against their packs. When Charlie made no move towards the guns, he gestured and said, "Follow. This way."

"OK," Charlie said. "We'll shoot one for you. Come on, Lew."

But the man held up a finger. "Only one should go. Less chance to scare caribou."

That made sense, so Charlie said, "One of you, one of us."

The man nodded and sat down by the fire. One of the others joined him while the third started off, beckoning impatiently. Lew said, "I'll go with him."

He picked up his rifle, checking to be sure he had enough cartridges. Then he held up a hand and said, "See you later."

"You do that," Charlie called after him, and Lew waved to show he fully understood the situation.

Charlie pointed to the kettle of tea. Rena served their remaining visitors another round of the hot drink. She stayed a safe distance away, though, setting their cups on the ground. Neither tried to touch her.

Bell had been moving impatiently about; now he came up with his rifle, laid the .308 lever gun down before the men and asked, "You want to trade for this gun?"

The leader picked up the rifle eagerly and sighted over the barrel. Still clutching the weapon, he brought out one piece of gold. Bell shook his head. The fellow produced a second nugget, and as Bell continued to decline, a third. That, apparently, was the last because the man scowled when Bell still refused the trade.

"Go and get more," Bell said. When the Indian shook his head, Bell suggested, "I'll go with you. I'll help you get more."

Suspicion leaped into the squinting eyes.

A shot echoed back from the hills, and Bell pulled a blue-barreled revolver from under his arm.

"Unload it," Charlie said sharply.

Bell gave him a smug grin. "I already did."

He laid the handgun beside the rifle.

"Can we get enough gold for both?" he asked.

The man was plainly tempted, but still he shook his head.

Bell picked up the revolver. "I'll persuade him," he said confidently and took a cartridge from his pocket.

"What are you going to do?" Charlie demanded.

"Demonstrate," Bell replied. "He'll never resist that. Your partner has his caribou, and now another shot won't scare any game away."

He went over to a large rock and put a smaller one on top. Backing off some 8 yards, he took quick aim and fired. The stone shattered to pieces. Charlie didn't like any of this. But he thought it unwise to let their visitors see divided opinion in the party, so he remained silent.

Bell came back and put the revolver down. "Ready to go and get gold?" he asked, squatting in front of the pair of northern nomads.

Charlie had to admit later that the leader who had done all of the bartering was clever. He picked up his own battered carbine and moved it forward as though to add it to the little heap of gold. Bell grinned and started to say something when the Indian abruptly swung the short weapon up and clubbed him on the head. Bell fell and lay motionless. The second man snarled and swung his gun over so it covered Charlie.

Charlie started to rise, but seeing it was useless, he sank back on his heels and stared at the two men across the fire. The leader grabbed Bell's revolver. He searched the unconscious man's pockets and brought out cartridges for both it and the rifle. He loaded them, picked up the revolver again, put it down and aimed the rifle at Charlie.

In spite of their savage glares and obvious advantage, the two seemed uneasy. Charlie thought they were listening, and what for seemed plain enough, because the first distant shot had unmistakably come from Lew's rifle. What they wanted to hear was a second shot made by their companion's carbine, which would inform them he had taken care of Lew. It was a bad situation. Still, Charlie doubted they would shoot him until they knew exactly what had happened in the other end of the valley. The kettle of water on the fire was boiling. Charlie looked over and said, "More tea?"

He smiled in what he hoped was a conciliatory manner. But the leader only snarled. Charlie picked up a small stick and laid it back on the fire. Then he took a slightly larger one. He had noticed the stake supporting one end of the pole from which the kettle hung had burned partly through. He shoved the piece of wood against the burnt place; it snapped and let the kettle drop. A cloud of steam and ashes surged up before the two men.

Charlie was moving even as the water still cascaded down, staying close to the ground. Both guns exploded almost in his face, but the shots missed him by inches. Before the men could jack fresh cartridges into their weapons, Charlie grabbed a gun in each hand and twisted them free. Then he grasped each man by the throat and cracked their heads together. Then he let them collapse to the ground.

Elma had screamed again at the shots, and Charlie swung around to see if she had been hit. Except for shaking legs and a very white face, she looked all right. He knew Rena hadn't been hurt because she already was rescuing their kettle from the fire.

Charlie went over to Bell and turned the man on his back. A big lump on top of his head oozed a little blood, but he breathed regularly. Charlie hoped he would regain consciousness soon, because he wanted to follow Lew and see if he was having any trouble with the third fellow. It was clear that the three of them had devised the plan to divide their party, and it had worked, or at least the dividing angle had.

Charlie got some water from the creek and splashed it over Bell's face. Bell was as tough as his physique indicated, because he sat up sputtering. He wiped the water from his eyes, touched his head carefully and said thickly, "I'm a fool."

Charlie didn't bother contradicting him.

Bell's glance fell upon the two prostrate men.

"What did you do to them?" he asked.

Charlie ignored the question and said to Bell, "Can you handle them while I'm gone looking for Lew?"

Bell nodded. "I sure can," he said grimly.

Charlie didn't feel sorry for Bell. The man had asked for trouble. Charlie picked up his rifle and ran in the direction Lew and the third interloper had taken. He knew sound could be deceiving, but he doubted that Lew's gunshot had originated from more than 400 yards away.

\*    \*    \*

The stranger took Lew on a northeast course from camp, and in spite of his short legs, he covered ground rapidly. Following, Lew wondered if there really was a caribou. He knew Charlie was skeptical, too, but he hoped they were both wrong because they could use a supply of fresh meat. Lew's mouth watered a little as he thought how easy it would be to cool the liver, tongue and maybe a few thin slices of steak in the ice at the stream's edge then cook them for breakfast.

The ground grew rougher with scattered clumps of branchy birch and aspen. A big white owl lumbered sleepily off on slowly flapping wings. Patches of thin frost masked the tops of the larger rocks. When they were 50 yards from a stand of bigger trees, the Indian raised one hand in caution. He motioned for Lew to precede him, but Lew made the same gesture back. The man grinned and stole ahead.

Lew followed two yards behind.

Most of the ground was covered with gray moss that cushioned their steps. They entered a small grove. A birch had snapped off several feet above the ground and broken down a shorter tree. It made a good blind. They crept up behind it, and looking through the screen of branches, Lew saw a white-necked caribou bull scarcely 100 yards distant. His suspicions returned when he saw that the shot was easily within the range of the other man's antiquated gun. Why hadn't he simply shot the animal himself?

The Indian grabbed Lew's arm and tried to pull him forward. "Shoot," he whispered. "Shoot."

Lew pointed to the carbine, "You shoot," he countered.

The Indian pulled a single cartridge from his pocket, then held up one finger and pointed to his gun.

Lew felt a little ashamed. If the fellow only had one load, it made sense for them to appeal to the party of whites who were so well stocked with high-powered rifles and ammunition.

Lew slipped the safety off his rifle, a .280 sighted in for 200 yards. He waited until the feeding bull stood broadside before firing. The shot knocked the caribou kicking. The Indian ran up, drew his knife and slashed the beast's throat, rather unnecessarily, Lew thought, since the bullet wound was doing a good job of bleeding out.

With his free hand, the man grabbed one of the two raised feet, trying to pull the carcass over so the belly would be up. He moved it only a little, though, and then motioned for Lew to help. Lew put his rifle down and came forward.

When he was four feet distant, the other sprang at him.

Lew knew he didn't have time to recover the rifle. He jumped sideways, barely escaping the keen blade that sliced along his upper arm, shredding the down jacket and wool shirt.

The attacker whirled and stood poised, glaring through slitted eyes. He took a slow step forward, Lew retreated two. Then Lew's foot slipped on a patch of frost and he stumbled. The attacker hurled himself like a human missile, arms thrust forward.

# Chapter 6 – A Bolted Cabin Door

Lew knew he was fighting for his life. But his mind was clear, not panic-stricken. He began rolling sideways before he even hit the ground, and that saved him because his attacker landed sprawling in the exact place Lew had occupied a second before. The knife, sticky with caribou blood, dug into the dirt beside his shoulder.

Lew grabbed for the knife-holding arm, but his opponent jerked it back beyond reach. Lew then shot a short but powerful jab straight into the man's face. There wasn't room for a knockout blow, but it jolted the man enough that he pulled back. Lew rolled again, scrambled to his feet, and started towards the rifle he had discarded in order to help move the caribou carcass. But his adversary made two quick, crouching steps and again stood between Lew and the rifle.

Lew backed off, watching as his enemy stepped to one side and then to the other. The man seemed completely confident. He held the blade low, just right in his fingers.

Lew recalled the advice of a judo instructor about the only effective way for an unarmed man to defend himself in such a situation. It had to be timed right, and there were risks involved.

When the attacker telegraphed another lunge, Lew fell to the ground and lashed out with both feet. One boot struck the short-legged man in the groin, the other landed slightly higher in his belly. The fight drained from the man like gas from a burst balloon. He dropped the knife and sat down. Lew jumped up then dove to the rifle. He was breathing hard, and his legs didn't want to function right. He picked up the bolt repeater, checked the breech for a loaded chamber, and wiped the perspiration from his face. Walking back to the caribou, he took the other man's carbine. Then he kicked the knife towards him.

"Get up," he said, "and get busy."

The man looked sick. His coppery skin had turned livid, and his eyes seemed to have retreated farther into his skull. He sat motionless, staring back with venomous hate.

Lew raised the carbine like a club. "Get to work, or I'll break this over your head," he said.

The fellow slowly limped over to the carcass. Lew moved away several steps and released the safety catch on the rifle. It could be the man was just as skilled in throwing a knife as in hand-to-hand combat, and Lew was determined not to be caught off-guard again.

Considering his features were still pained and that his hands shook a little, the man did a good job field dressing the caribou. Then he reached for the short axe that had fallen from his belt during their struggle. Lew backed off some more, remembering hatchets also are throwing weapons, even more deadly than a knife.

Lew remembered hearing shots earlier, and he wondered what they meant. They had come from the direction of camp, and while he was confident Charlie could handle the other two men, still he was relieved when he heard Charlie call. "Up here," he answered.

The Indian was chopping along the spine to divide the carcass when Charlie reached them. The fellow raised a bitter face, realizing his companions had failed as dismally as himself.

"Have any trouble?" Charlie asked.

Lew nodded. "He came at me with the knife when I put my gun down to help roll the caribou. What happened with you? I heard shots."

Charlie told how the other two visitors had launched their own sneak attack back at camp.

"What are we going to do with them?" Lew asked. "They're going to be a problem, aren't they?"

Charlie nodded. He had devoted some thought to it, but hadn't found a really satisfactory solution.

"If we just turn them loose," Lew observed, "they will follow us and try for revenge."

"I know," Charlie agreed. "But maybe we can pull their teeth so they won't be so dangerous. Suppose we let them see us cache some of the meat with their guns and knives in a tree. Then we use them as packers today. They can carry the quarters of meat we take and also Elma's load. Then tonight, we release them and they can come back to recover everything. That will give us a two-day start, and I doubt if they will try to overtake us then."

Seeing Lew still seemed dubious, he added, "We'll take their ammunition, of course. They can't live very long without it, so they must reach a trading post to buy more. The nearest store is Caribou—by the time they get there, we'll have a three-day start."

When the man finished dressing-out the caribou, they relieved him of the knife and axe. Then he sullenly hoisted the rear quarters to his back. They weighed perhaps 70 pounds, and Lew figured that was load enough to prevent him starting more trouble.

As they walked, Lew said, "That plan of yours has a weak point."

"Several," Charlie admitted. "Which are you thinking of?"

"They'll make a fast trip to Caribou for more cartridges. But after they get some, what happens then? Do they hang around and jump us somewhere on the back trail?"

"I thought of that," Charlie said. "But we have so much to do before we can start back; let's worry about it then."

They saw the blue column of smoke rising from the campfire before Lew spoke again, "I'm wondering where they got that gold."

"I doubt they mined it. So it was probably stolen."

"From the Driscolls?" Lew asked tentatively.

Charlie shook his head and told Lew the chunks offered him were solid pieces carrying tool marks indicating they had been cut from a larger piece. "It isn't placer gold, the kind Dirk and Dorina would get from their uncle's claim."

Walking through the little clump of trees surrounding camp, they saw two very unhappy fellows sitting beside the fire. Bell stood a few yards off, covering them with his rifle. The faces of the pair turned even more glum when their companion staggered in with his load.

The taller man by the fire was rubbing his skull slowly. When Charlie glanced at Bell, the latter nodded. "Sure," he said. "I thought he should know how it feels to get zapped with a rifle stock."

Bell walked slowly around the captives, menacing them with his weapon. "They're thieves and killers," he growled. "We should shoot them right now."

"Let's give them breakfast, first," Lew said. Bell shot an angry glance at him. Then his scowl relaxed. "OK. But I'll see they don't get away while you're breaking camp."

Rena whetted her knife on her hide mukluk then started to slice caribou liver, tongue and steak. She filled the skillet and put the balance on short sticks to cook before the blaze. The three captives darted quick glances at each other. But then they accepted the food eagerly.

When the gear was packed, Charlie told the trio they must carry the meat and Elma's pack. This looked like such an easy penalty for their attack, they brightened visibly. Some of the leader's arrogance returned. He pointed to Bell and said, "He took my gold."

"Of course I took it," Bell retorted. "Why not? They were going to steal all we had. And cut our throats, too."

Charlie motioned him out of earshot. Then he said quietly, "I want you to give it back."

Bell bristled. "I will not. They lost all claim to proper treatment."

"This has nothing to do with ethics," Charlie replied. "It's a matter of survival. Returning their gold will give them less reason to follow us and cause more trouble. You know it's pretty easy to jump a party in this wilderness."

"You're going to turn them loose?" Bell asked incredulously.

"You know we can't shoot them," Charlie said dryly. Then he explained his plan. "If they have something to trade for ammunition, they'll come back for their carbines then travel on to Caribou as fast as they can. Without the gold, they're broke and the guns are useless. Then their only chance of keeping alive this winter is to follow our trail and wait for a chance to murder us for the gold and our rifles."

Bell thought it over. "I guess you're right," he admitted. He took the three chunks of yellow metal from his pocket. "It sure is pretty," he said as he handed it over to Charlie.

Charlie cached the three carbines, the three knives and the short hatchet in a tree with the front quarters of caribou meat. Searching the trio, he found a total of eight cartridges, all, as Charlie had suspected, of .44-40 caliber. He smashed each load between two rocks then held up the gold and said, "Tonight, I'll give you these and you can start back for your guns."

The man to whom Elma's pack had been given refused to shoulder it. "Gun," he growled, "must have gun."

Bell lifted his rifle, but Lew stepped in.

"Let me handle this," he said.

There was a time when Lew practiced magic tricks enough to become quite proficient. He thrust a hand under the rebel's nose. A cartridge appeared in his fingers. It was one for Lew's rifle, but he thought the man would be too surprised to realize it.

"You hid this one?" he demanded.

The man pulled away with a grunt and rubbed his nose.

"Get moving," Lew said.

The man stared warily, looked perplexed, then leaned over and picked up the pack. Elma planted her booted feet firmly before Charlie and said, "I won't let him touch my pack."

Bell solved that problem. "He can carry mine; I'll take yours."

Charlie drew in a deep breath of relief when the party finally moved off for the northern end of the valley. They had lost much time and could never reach the Driscoll cabin in four days as they had planned. He doubted, too, if they would be able to make the cabin where Sam Harmon lived by tomorrow night, although he planned to travel as late each day as Elma could keep her feet. He was anxious to see the old prospector. Sam would be their first reliable source of information on just what had happened to the Driscolls since last fall.

Lew was walking last in line. Elma dropped back beside him. "Where did you learn sleight of hand?" she asked.

"I'm just an amateur," he grinned. "I don't suppose you ever heard of Glass-eye Johnson? I never met him, but he was a legendary fur buyer in the Yukon. He used parlor magic to impress the natives. Of course, they were much more superstitious back then. I doubt if I spooked this fellow much just now. But I did surprise him."

He shoved the parka hood back from his face and walked bareheaded for awhile. "One of Johnson's favorite tricks," he said, "was to pretend to poke out a fellow's eye. Johnson had a pair of glass eyes that were very good imitations—one light, the other dark so he could use the best match. He'd palm one first, and you can imagine how it would scare an ignorant fellow to see what he believed was his own eye in Johnson's hand. Then he would pretend to put it back and buy the fur for about half the going price."

"Sounds like a real stinker," Elma said shortly.

"I believe that was the general impression," Lew concurred.

Charlie drove them hard all day. The weather had taken on an ominous look. The wind grew sharper and carried an occasional spit of thin, hard snow. A heavy snow, though improbable that early, was possible and would make their Spartan camp uncomfortable. It would also delay their progress on the trail.

Charlie decided to keep the three men until morning. That would give their party an extra day's lead.

There had been a gradual change in the fellows. The sullen anger had left their faces, and since it looked like carrying meat and a pack would be the only penalty for their attack, they laughed and talked and occasionally broke out into a kind of chant with a rhythm emphasized by clapping hands and stamping feet.

That night, the party ate an all-meat meal, consuming so much caribou steak it looked like there would scarcely be a half of one of the quarters left after breakfast. Charlie doubted if the Indians would try to slip away or make trouble, but he decided someone had to stay awake.

As before, the trio slept close beside the fire. When Lew got up to relieve Bell a couple of hours past midnight, he found the private investigator dozing with closed eyes. Bell denied he had been asleep, said he had only shut his eyes to keep out the fire light.

Something like an impasse threatened after breakfast when Charlie told the strangers they could go back for their guns. The leader smiled and shook his head. "You are good men. We carry loads all the way, OK?"

This perplexed Charlie at first. But after all, they had been fed well, the work was light according to their standards, and moreover, if they remained, there might still come a time when they could steal a rifle or some other gear. Charlie replied firmly it was not OK and then motioned them off.

When they still hesitated, Bell took up his gun and came towards them. The smiles faded, and they scurried over the rocky ground. When they were about 100 yards away, Bell sent a bullet over their heads. His scowl relaxed at the spurt of speed that produced.

Charlie and Lew added the remaining meat to their own loads. It was another hard day on the trail. But despite gradually rising ground and detours about steep cliffs, they covered mile after mile. Rena lead the group unerringly and without hesitation. There was almost an hour of traveling light left when she pointed ahead and said, "Sam's cabin."

The cabin wall chinking had been freshly packed with clay, and there was a winter pile of tree limbs and trunks with a stack of axe-cut chunks at one end. The main difference was one hide nailed to the leeward wall. Last year, there had been two. Light showed in the window, and they could smell wood smoke.

"I hope Sam's sourdough keg is working," Lew said.

Elma looked at him coldly. "I hope this man can tell us something about my friends," she retorted.

"I believe he can," Charlie said. "If anyone knows the situation, Sam does." He stepped up on the flat stone before the door and knocked. His companions grouped closely behind him.

There was no response. Charlie hammered the split log panel again. The knock sounded dull and muffled because this was bear and wolverine country and any opening in a cabin wall had to be closed solidly and strongly to resist their marauding curiosity.

"Try the door," Lew suggested. "Maybe he's asleep."

"It's bolted," Charlie said.

Almost a minute passed. Lew leaned forward suddenly and put his ear against the wood. "Somebody's moving in there," he said. Then he struck the door two vigorous blows. The sounds within ceased ominously, and the seconds dragged by interminably.

## Chapter 7 – A Gun in His Back

The situation voided all customs of North Country hospitality. They believed Sam Harmon was in his cabin because Lew had heard him moving around. Yet for some reason he did not answer and open the door. Charlie walked to the window and tried to peer through, but a hanging shirt blocked his view. He came back to the door.

"We going to stand here all night?" Lew demanded. "I'm hungry and tired, and if we got to put up our own camp, we better start now."

Before Charlie could reply, they heard a bar moving. Then the door slowly opened a few inches, and silhouetted by the dim light inside, they saw a face. Or part of a face, because only one eye and one bearded cheek were visible.

"Sam?" Charlie asked.

After a pause the man spoke, "Yes. What do you want?"

"Don't you remember me?" Charlie said. "We were here last fall with Dirk and Dorina Driscoll. You knew their uncle Jim. And you showed us the rocks behind your cabin you figured contained twenty million dollars' worth of gold. Remember now?"

"I guess so," was the cautious reply.

"We came back to find Dirk and Dorina. Are they still living in their uncle's old cabin?"

"The Driscolls? In Jim's cabin? No. They went back home last year. Soon after you left." He started to close the door.

"Wait," Charlie said, jamming his toe in the narrowing crack between panel and jamb. "Aren't you going to let us in? There's a lot we need to ask you. And we thought we might stay overnight."

"Sorry," Sam said. "My wife's afraid of strangers, and I don't have any extra room."

Last year, Harmon had been friendly and talkative.

"We have plenty of meat," Charlie suggested. It might be, he thought, that the old fellow was short of food but too proud to admit it. He reached out like he was going to push the door back.

"No!" burst from Sam's lips. Charlie saw the wiry body flinch, saw panic in the shrewd old eyes.

He pulled his hand back. "Sure," he said quickly. "It's all right. Sorry we bothered you. Give your wife our regards. We're going."

He turned and herded his unwilling companions down the path.

"He's lying," Elma declared. "If they had come home I would know. You've got to go back there and make him ..."

Charlie grabbed her arm, swung her around and pushed her forward. That astonished Elma so much her protests froze on her lips.

"Maybe you're going to stand for it," Bell said. "But I'm not. I'm going back and have a showdown with him."

"You're going to keep on the way you're headed now," Charlie told him. "And don't lose any time."

"You figure to make me?" Bell demanded.

Charlie eyed him dispassionately. "It is tempting to let you go back and get your fool head shot off. But I've got to think of Sam."

He did not say another word until they reached the edge of the stream. "Sam isn't alone," he told them. "Somebody's with him."

"Sure," Bell growled. "He mentioned his wife."

"He doesn't have a wife. Someone has a gun jammed in Sam's back. That's why he couldn't talk."

"You're guessing," Bell said.

"Maybe. But I got a good look at Sam's face when I put out my hand like I was going to push inside."

"Who is it?" Elma demanded.

"Someone who doesn't want Sam to talk to us," Charlie said and then walked over to where Rena had dropped her pack and now sat upon it patiently waiting. "Has anybody followed us today?" he asked.

Last year, the native girl had displayed a startling ability to sense strangers on the trail behind or ahead of them. "I don't know," she said reluctantly. "I thought maybe yesterday, but I am not sure."

"Well, if it was yesterday, that rules out our packers because they were with us," Lew said. "What about Woolman? He seems to be carrying on the foul traditions of his family. It wouldn't surprise me if he walked in on us tonight, like his old man did last fall."

Charlie started walking.

"Where are you going?" Elma asked.

"To find a camp," he replied.

"But you must do something. Unless we talk with Harmon, I may never find my friends."

"We'll do something," Charlie assured her. But he had to admit to himself that he didn't yet know what that might be.

About a quarter-mile upstream they found a campsite sheltered by trees and rocks. After he had started a fire, Charlie struck his axe in the butt of a fallen tree. He had been thinking about the problem of Sam Harmon, a serious matter because if an armed man was holding him captive, and he was pretty sure one was, that fellow would have a tremendous advantage in a solidly built cabin. But he thought he had figured out a plan of attack.

"Watch things here," he told Lew. "Remember, Rena said we may have been followed."

He started off, and Bell called, "Wait, I'll go, too."

"No," Charlie replied. "If I need help, I'll come back for you."

As Charlie strode off through the dusk, Bell watched him, scowling. His eyes fell on Charlie's pack. "Is the guy crazy?" he demanded. "He forgot to take his rifle."

"If he needed it," Lew grunted, "he'd have taken it."

"But he said the fellow in the cabin with Harmon had a gun. And there may be two of them," Bell persisted.

"There might be three," Lew said.

Bell just stared at him.

Charlie's plan for rescuing Sam was based on the assumption that someone must leave the cabin to bring in wood and water. He didn't know just when that might be, but odds were good Sam hadn't yet had a chance to make the nightly trip to stream and wood pile. It was too early in the season for Sam to store several days' supply in the cabin, as he would later when the deep snows came. It was possible the man or men wouldn't let Harmon leave but would handle the chore for him. Either way would suit Charlie.

A cabin in the North is always built with its back to the prevailing west wind. That wall is generally built of the best fitting timbers and chinked tightly. It also is made without a window or door.

Charlie planned to take advantage of this. Dusk had deepened almost into night when Charlie reached the windward cabin wall, but there was enough light when he glanced around the corner to reveal the piles of wood only a score of feet away. The chill bit through his clothing as he waited. He swung his arms vigorously to keep warm.

Somebody in the cabin stirred the fire, and sparks drifted from the flue. Voices reached his ears, but the words were muffled. Still, it sounded like grumbling. He wished he had Lew's keen hearing.

Then the door creaked on its wooden pole hinge and he saw a figure approaching. It was too tall for Harmon, and the fellow carried a rifle in one hand. It looked like there was more than one intruder.

When the man reached the wood pile, he put his gun on top of the chunks and began to load one bent arm. It may have been uneasiness or just chance, but not for a second did he turn his back on Charlie.

The fellow finished loading, picked up his gun and started away. Would there be a second trip for wood, or would the next be to the stream with a pail for water? Charlie favored the first possibility, because the man had taken just a few pieces and the night promised to be cold. So he ran to the rank of chopped sticks and crouched behind it.

Again the cabin door creaked. Charlie couldn't risk looking, but he knew he had decided right when he heard boots scraping the ground coming his way. The fellow laid his rifle on the wood again, so part of the stock hung over the side. Charlie reached up, grasped the butt and pulled it slowly forward. Despite his caution, some part of the weapon scraped, and the sound seemed as loud as a gunshot in the still woods. Charlie heard the indrawn breath that would be followed by a cry of alarm, so he dropped the gun, and shooting both arms across the top of the pile, gripped the man's neck with one hand and covered his mouth with the other. That choked off most of the cry, but not all.

A voice called from inside the cabin, "Pete? That you?"

Pete was swinging his arms wildly, but he was too close to land an effective blow. Charlie pulled the man closer and whispered, "Tell him you dropped a chunk on your foot," he ordered. "Don't make me break your neck."

The flailing arms dropped. Charlie carefully released the fellow's mouth. "Better be convincing," he added then swung his captive to face the cabin and stooped behind him. A second man appeared at the corner. Charlie felt Pete stiffen, like he planned further resistance, so he tightened his fingers. Pete hoarsely repeated Charlie's instructions.

The other man hesitated and then said, "Well, hurry it up. I'll wait to bar the door." He went back inside.

Both voices had seemed vaguely familiar, but Charlie didn't spend any time trying to remember why. He picked up the short rifle. "Get a load of wood," he ordered. "A big one. Then walk ahead of me and go in just like I wasn't behind you, and no tricks."

The other man had pulled the door almost shut, which helped because it reduced the amount of light escaping. He shoved it wider when Pete reached the step. Charlie moved closer, and when Pete gained the sill and halted, Charlie shoved him hard. Pete stumbled and the wood in his arms scattered over the floor. Charlie was inside instantly. When the other fellow started to bring up his gun, Charlie shoved the one he carried against the man's belly. "Drop it," he ordered. The weapon landed with a thud. Both men backed off, eyes filling with fear.

Charlie's eyes swept over the single room. He had expected to find Sam tied up, but he was wrong. Sam stood beside the bed with bare feet. The gray eyes were as keen as before. Catching Charlie's glance, he said, "They took my boots so I couldn't run. Am I glad to see you," he added.

Charlie looked at the pair he had disarmed. It was Bert and Pete, the pair who worked for the original storekeeper Woolman, father of the young man who now managed the store in Caribou.

"What happened?" he asked Sam.

"These buzzards knocked on my door and asked if they could come in to warm. Of course I let them in. What else could I do? I couldn't let you in because they was holding a gun on my back."

"I know," Charlie assured him.

"I figured you did. Well, after they got warm, they began to ask me about gold. I told them I washed out a little every year, enough to keep me in grub, but that was all—which is the truth. They also asked about the Driscoll boy and girl. I told them I hadn't seen either of them for a long time. But that wasn't true."

"They didn't go home last fall?" Charlie asked.

"Of course not. I said that because I didn't know if that rat," eyeing Bert, "would really shoot me. But I couldn't take any chances. Besides, I knew you'd come back."

Sam started pulling on his boots.

"They said they had heard about a real rich strike of gold somewhere in the region and thought it might be mine. So they pulled up their guns and made threats. Then they searched my cabin. When they didn't find anything worth stealing, they made me give them my money. I only had about thirty dollars."

"Who's got it?" Charlie asked. Pete put a hand in his pocket and produced the money. He acted like he might toss it on the floor, but when he met Charlie's gaze, he stepped over slowly and laid it in Harmon's outstretched hand.

"Thanks," Sam said, and it was clear he wasn't addressing Pete. "I was worrying about how I might get rid of them," he continued. "Then you knocked on the door and they got real mean. They wouldn't let me open it, but finally I convinced them you wouldn't leave if I didn't get rid of you. One had his rifle poked in my back, the other kept jabbing at me with a knife. I think they recognized your voice, because it made them nervous. When you asked about Dirk and Dorina the knife made me jump. You saw that?"

Charlie nodded. "I was sure you weren't alone."

"I knew what the knife jab meant. So I said the Driscolls had gone. I figured those fellows didn't want anybody to find them. But you did come to hunt them up, didn't you? And you brought strangers this time. Who's the woman and the man?"

"The woman is Dorina's close friend who worried when she didn't hear from them. So she came to see if they were in trouble. The man is an investigator she hired."

Charlie looked at his watch. "Lew and the others are making camp a little ways up the stream. Will you go and bring them? We can sleep in the cabin tonight, can't we?"

After Sam left, Charlie motioned Pete and Bert into a corner and sat down on one of Sam's low split-log stools. "You work for Woolman?" he asked.

"Woolman's dead," Pete replied.

"I mean his son. You work for him?"

"In a way."

Charlie stared at him. Pete scowled and moved his feet nervously. "He offered to pay us for anything we could find out about Harmon and the Driscolls," he finally said. "And about a strike of gold."

Charlie remembered that the two letters Dorina had mailed in the post office at Caribou spoke of people watching them. "You've been spying on the Driscolls for a while, haven't you?"

Both denied this vigorously. "But we did pass their cabin several times," Pete said. "We didn't stop."

"Why not?"

"The brother shot at us. So we stayed away."

"Why didn't you shoot back?"

"We couldn't do that," Bert said.

"No, you couldn't risk it," Charlie said. "There might be inquiries that would bring up how Jim Driscoll had died. I always thought you murdered him."

"I told you we found him dead," Bert said sullenly. But his eyes shifted uneasily. The rest of the party arrived soon after that.

"I didn't work hard at making camp," Lew said. "I had a good idea we'd be sleeping here." Then he grinned at Pete and Bert. "Never know who you'll run into."

They ignored him. But Pete said, "Hello, Rena."

The girl looked at him calmly.

"You steal people's money," she replied.

Harmon chuckled, "They took mine—but I got it back!"

Elma was bristling. "This man won't tell me a thing about my friends. He says you told him not to."

"I wanted to save him telling the story twice," Charlie said. "All he has told me is Dirk and Dorina are still here. They didn't go home last year. Later, we'll start Sam talking." And, he told himself, that shouldn't be hard, either.

"Well, I'm glad to know that much," Elma said haughtily. "Of course, I only pay your wages. Would it be out of line if I asked who these fellows are?" Her eyes swept over Pete and Bert sitting on the floor back of the stove, and Charlie explained some of the background and their tie-in with Woolman.

Sam's sourdough keg was working, and he began to mix out biscuits. Lew sliced caribou meat, and Rena unpacked the cooking kit.

Sam pointed at Pete and Bert and said, "We got to feed them?" Then he added, "Don't answer. I know we have to. But what then?"

Charlie muffled a yawn. The hot room made him sleepy.

"We turn them loose," he said, "without guns or knives."

It had almost become a habit to confiscate weapons from the men they encountered along the trail.

The little room was crowded, but Elma found space to pace back and forth. It was plain to see she was still angry. Once, she began in a belligerent voice, "I want to know ..."

But Charlie pointed significantly at Bert and Pete. Elma was angry, but she wasn't stupid. She stopped abruptly.

After supper, Charlie motioned Pete and Bert outside. They went quickly almost eagerly, a combination that made Charlie wonder if they might have not so far to go to procure supplies and probably another rifle. The light packs they were carrying seemed to indicate this. He wondered, too, if he was loading his own back trail with peril. But again, he didn't see a good option. They couldn't hold the pair prisoner indefinitely, and he didn't trust old Sam with the pair of snakes.

He closed the door. "All right, Sam, tell us about the Driscolls."

To his surprise, Harmon seemed reluctant. Then he began, "I came from their cabin yesterday..."

"How are they?" Elma interrupted.

"I don't exactly know," Sam replied. "You see, they weren't there. The cabin was empty."

# Chapter 8 – Bullets Bar the Door

That brought a sharp reaction from Elma. She jumped up and pointed a finger at Charlie. "You told me they were still there," she accused. "What are we going to do now?"

"Wait," Sam protested. "I didn't say they had left. I said they weren't home. Chances are they were out hunting or prospecting. Their gear was there," he paused nervously, "but it was a mess. Somebody had ransacked the cabin, scattered things over the floor."

"Bear or wolverine?" Charlie asked.

"No, the door was shut and no animal shuts a door when it leaves. Nothing was broken or eaten, either. It was people alright; I saw muddy boot prints on the floor. Could have been the pair that just left. I didn't ask because they'd only lie."

Charlie nodded. "Tell us about last fall and winter," he said.

"Well, I went over and helped them, at first. But the girl and her brother learned quick. Of course, they made mistakes, but they learned from that, too. They panned gold until the stream froze. Then we went hunting and laid in some meat. I helped them cut firewood. Guess I spent five or six weeks with them altogether."

"Did they ever go into Caribou?" Charlie asked.

"Never, and that was kind of funny. They turned me down every time I suggested we make the trip. I got grub for them, had John bring it on his dog sled. It's cheaper and less work to hire him for one or two trips than to feed dogs myself. So they had plenty of grub. They did run short on clothing, but their Uncle Jim had left some things. Last time I saw her, Dorina was wearing his clothes."

"How did their claim pan out?" Lew asked.

"I don't know. They never told me, and I didn't ask. But I know they hit at least one good pocket early on; I helped them clean it out. If there were others, I couldn't say."

"Go on," Elma urged impatiently.

"Not much more to tell," Sam replied. "Soon as the ice thawed in the spring, they panned the creek again. And they did a lot of looking for other prospects, too. This ain't the first time I found them gone. But it was the first time the cabin was tore up."

"Maybe somebody is trying to scare them so they'll leave,"

Charlie suggested.

"Could be," Sam admitted.

"Did Dirk and Dorina store gold in the cabin?" Charlie asked.

Sam shrugged. "I don't know. They never told me what they found, just gave me a little extra to pay for the supplies I got for them. This spring, when I arranged for the last load to come out, Dirk gave me two small chunks of gold to pay for his share. I never saw any like them before, and that was a mistake, because the chunks started the rumors. I didn't tell anyone it wasn't mine, and John never knew the Driscolls got most of the stuff he hauled. I always had him leave it here and then they packed it the rest of the way to them. They worked hard to keep things hidden, and I didn't care one way or the other."

"Last year," Lew said, "you told us how melted gold from a deep vein can flow up to the surface through a crater, or what prospectors call a pipe. The pipe can have a lining of pure gold, and you can cut it out in pieces. Were Dirk's chunks that kind?"

Harmon looked at him quickly.

"Could be," he said slowly. "I never seen a pipe, myself. Or Dirk could have melted some dust down in a bar so it would store easier. Dust can get spilled and lost, you know."

A snore came from Bell's direction. His chin had gradually dropped until it touched his chest. Harmon stood up. "I've talked too long," he said. "It's time to turn in. You can draw cuts for the bunk."

"We have sleeping bags and air pads," Charlie told him. "So you keep it." He hung a tarp from the ceiling to enclose a small space for Elma and Rena. Sam loaded the stove with wood, shut damper and door slide, kicked off his boots and climbed into the bunk. It was made of poles padded with wild hay and set 4 feet high to avoid the floor drafts. Charlie and Lew spread their beds beside the door.

Lew thought it was nearly midnight when Charlie pressed his shoulder. He sat up, was going to speak, but his companion silenced him with a shove. "Follow me in five minutes," Charlie whispered.

Lew lay back in his sleeping bag until he saw Charlie silently close the door behind himself. Then he pulled on his boots and walked cautiously to the door. He had it half open when Bell stirred and said sleepily, "Where you going?"

"Out," Lew said laconically. "I drank four cups of tea."

Charlie stood just outside the door waiting. Lew drew it shut, and they walked away. "What do you think of this business," Charlie finally asked.

"I don't like any of it," Lew admitted. "Too many loose ends. What do you think?"

"I'm worried about the Driscolls. If they aren't in deep trouble now, there's a chance they will be soon."

Lew nodded. "Especially if they've hit the jackpot."

"Sam believes they have. But of course, he won't talk. If he's right, that might explain why they avoid Caribou. But they must go somewhere to ship gold home. It isn't worth much up here."

Charlie thought in silence a few moments. "I figure their cabin is about 20 miles from here. What do you think?"

"Eighteen or twenty," Lew replied. He noticed Charlie had his rifle. "You going tonight?"

"I think I better. Maybe there is no reason. But suppose you planned for something to happen to Dirk and Dorina. Then you learned four of their friends were this close. What would you do?"

"Get there first," Lew declared.

"Exactly. So I'm going tonight. I won't take a pack. Anything you can't carry in the morning leave with Sam. And don't tell anybody until then. I don't want to be missed before daybreak. As I remember the trail, it follows the stream all the way. I can't miss their cabin. Well, see you tomorrow," Charlie said and then struck his companion's shoulder lightly before striding off into the night.

Lew watched until he was out of sight then returned to the cabin. "Shut the door," Bell growled. "You're letting in the cold."

The fire was low when Lew next awoke. Laying split sticks on the coals, he blew up a little flame. When he glanced at the bunk, he saw Sam watching with quiet pleasure.

"Been a long time since somebody built a fire for me," he said.

Rena started breakfast. Bell awoke then, and Elma appeared a little later. Slices of caribou steak were sizzling in the pan before they noticed Charlie's absence.

"Where'd he go?" Bell demanded.

"He was worried about the Driscolls and thought one of us should get there as soon as possible."

"We should have all gone together," Bell exclaimed.

"He can travel twice as fast alone," Lew replied.

Elma's eyes were angry. "I don't believe you," she finally cried. "I think you planned all the time to steal Dirk and Dorina's gold. That's why you were willing to come with me for low pay. Now your partner's gone on ahead so we won't be there to stop him."

She turned to Bell. "Watch him," she said.

Lew glanced at Bell and then said, "The only place I'm going is to the stove to fill my plate. And you," he looked calmly at the angry girl, "better come, too. It will be another hard day on the trail, so eat plenty. Don't you ever use your head before you sound off?"

He slid pieces of meat onto his plate, filled a cup with tea.

"If we wanted to steal the Driscolls' gold, if they really have any, which nobody knows for sure, we could have done it last year. We brought them out here. We found the pocket their uncle had stumbled on and then covered up, and we showed it to them. I doubt if they would have located it themselves. Then we showed them how to use a pan. We left some caribou meat so they wouldn't starve. So let's not have any more talk about us being thieves. It spoils my appetite."

Elma flushed, and her eyes dropped. But she still seemed defiant.

"Why did he leave in the middle of the night without telling me?" she demanded.

"He told me," Lew said. "And he left suddenly because he realized just how much danger might threaten your friends right now. It would have taken this party at least an hour to get started. It took him five minutes. Then he made double time on a 20-mile trail."

"What kind of danger?" she asked anxiously.

"That, I don't know. But the quicker we eat, pack up and go, the sooner we can find out."

"Maybe I ought to go with you," Sam suggested.

"OK," Lew replied. "You can carry Charlie's gear. But should you leave your cabin now? Bert and Pete might come back. I wouldn't be surprised if they set the place on fire."

"I'll stay," Sam agreed. "But what about their guns?" he pointed to the short rifles in a corner.

"Keep them," Lew advised. "They could prove useful."

He cut supper meat from the remaining quarter of caribou and left the balance with Sam. "We made a pretty big hole in your flour," he apologized. "Maybe this will help."

They shouldered their loads and moved towards the door. Bell stepped out first, but he didn't stay long. A gunshot echoed through the frosty air, and a bullet smacked into the log wall about level with his waist. He yelled and jumped back inside.

"Somebody just tried to kill me!" he panted and jammed the door bar in place.

"Everybody get down on the floor," Lew ordered. "He may shoot through the door."

They waited tensely. Minutes passed. Finally, Lew unbarred the door and shoved it open several inches. Then he put his parka hood on the end of a stick and shoved it out. Another shot smashed into the cabin wall, near the ground but a couple of feet away.

"Nobody's that lousy of a shot," Lew muttered. Then he went over to the stove. There was a little tea left, and he poured out a cup.

"You know," he said, "that guy doesn't want to hit anyone. He missed both times by several feet. We hear the gunshot the same time the bullet hits, so he isn't that far away, either. Probably down by the stream where he could have drilled Bell like a sitting rabbit."

He took a drink of tea and added, "I think he just wants to keep us trapped in here so we can't take the trail to the Driscoll cabin."

"That proves they are in danger," Elma cried. "Aren't you going to do something? We can't just sit here all day!"

"We can if he keeps shooting," Lew told her. "I'm not going to take a bullet if we ignore his warnings. There's a risk, too, he might hit one of us by mistake. Nothing will happen to Dirk and Dorina. Charlie's there now, and he'll see to that."

"You have a lot of confidence in him," Elma declared.

"You will, too, after you've been with us longer. My guess is there's only one man outside. The others have gone on, and when they have a good start, he'll leave, too."

Half an hour later he shoved his parka hood out through the door again. There was no shot. He repeated the stunt. When it brought no reaction, he opened the door wide and said, "I think he's gone now."

He looked over at Bell and asked, "Want to try it?"

Bell regarded him warily. "Why me?" he asked.

"You drew the first shot. And it landed wide."

"What is that supposed to mean?"

Before Lew could reply, Elma pushed past them. "I'm not afraid," she said and stepped outside. The others followed.

Sam said, "So long."

Lew thought Sam's voice sounded wistful. When they had almost reached the stream, Lew looked back. The old prospector still stood in the doorway watching.

\*    \*    \*

Charlie's eyes quickly adjusted to the darkness. His watch

showed a few minutes before midnight when he left the cabin, and he thought he could cover the 20 miles in less than 8 hours. He walked fast and even ran where the trail was smooth. Still, this was no time or place to risk a twisted ankle.

Even if there was no emergency, a fast trip would settle one way or another his increasing uneasiness about the Driscolls. Ever since Lew and he had stepped from the plane back in Caribou, incidents had occurred that disturbed him. A kind of mystery surrounded Dirk and Dorina, beginning with the letters that awaited them in the abandoned post office. It was queer, too, that nobody in Caribou knew or would admit they knew anything of the brother and sister.

The trouble with the rough Native trio on the trail seemed unconnected. But now he wasn't sure. They possessed rough chunks of gold, like those Dirk had turned over to Sam Harmon to pay for supplies. The encounter with Pete and Bert was more significant. Past experience showed them willing to commit almost any crime. They had admitted a tie-in with the younger Woolman and by association his partner Breed. Charlie thought this tie-in might be more than casual.

The streamside trail led over a rough outcrop of rock then dipped into a narrow valley filled with dead brown grass. Charlie started running again, and as he ran, his mind reviewed other incidents connected with the Driscolls that bothered him. The efforts brother and sister had made to keep everything secret were getting harder to comprehend.

Either he had overestimated the distance or he had traveled faster than expected, because Charlie's watch showed six o'clock when he sighted the Driscoll cabin. Blue smoke rose easily from the top of the stone chimney.

Charlie paused for a moment to study the cabin. He changed his rifle back to his right hand and walked forward. "This time," he told himself, "I'm going to get the answers to a lot of questions."

# Chapter 9 – Breed Gets Out of Line

Charlie decided not to give the loud shout that customarily heralds a visitor to a cabin in the North. Pete and Bert had said Dirk shot at them when they approached. So, keeping out of line with both door and window, he moved forward from an angle. He hoped breakfast was started, or that at least there would be hot water for tea.

Standing to one side of the door, Charlie heard someone inside and rapped smartly. The sounds stopped. "It's me, Charlie," he said.

He heard the wooden bar slide back, and a voice said, "Come in."

When he opened the door, Dorina was pointing the muzzle of a rifle barrel at him. She was dressed in a man's jacket and overalls, and her blonde hair was cropped close. But despite the dark streaks beneath her eyes, the bad haircut and ill-fitting garments, he thought she looked fit and even more attractive than he remembered.

"I got your letter," he said.

"Sorry about the gun," she replied. "But I had to be sure."

Charlie closed the door. "Better slip the safety on," he said.

"It isn't loaded. We ran out of cartridges a month ago. Sam ordered more for us, but they haven't come in yet. Where's Lew?"

"He'll be along this afternoon."

The room looked the same: slab table and benches, packing-box cabinets, and a wood-burning stove that stood on the fireplace hearth with its pipe shoved up the flue. But there were two bunk beds now, and beneath the peeling mirror, someone had contrived a sort of dressing table. Several bottles and a tube lay on its top.

"Where's Dirk?" Charlie asked.

"He left before daybreak. Someone is watching us. So we go early so they can't follow as easily." She pushed a hand over her forehead. "I stayed here to rest, but I fell asleep and had the most terrible dream. It frightened me so much …"

Then she melted like new snow before a chinook blast, stepped forward and fell against Charlie, hands clutching his coat. "I'm so glad you came," she cried, her shoulders shaking with suppressed sobs.

"It's all right," he reassured her. "When do you expect Dirk?"

She stepped back, looking a little embarrassed.

"I better sit down. I'm still shaking. Dirk said he would return before dark. He will be early tonight because this is the last trip. We…"

She pressed her lips together and stopped speaking.

Charlie said, "You have a friend named Elma."

"Elma Nash? How do you know about her?"

He smiled. "She'll be along shortly with Lew and also an investigator she hired to help find you."

"Elma, here?" he asked looking a little dazed.

He nodded and then explained the entire situation. Dorina finally smiled and then said, "Elma can be a bit overbearing. But it was good of her to go to so much trouble. And you, too."

She walked over to the dresser. "I must look like a ghost," she said picking up a tube that once contained lipstick. Then she set it down again. "How did you get here so early and so far ahead of the others?"

"I was worried about you and Dirk. When we saw Sam yesterday, he said you were gone when he last checked and that your cabin had been searched. Since one man can travel faster, I came alone."

"You walked all night?"

"Just since midnight."

"You must be starved," she declared. "I'll cook breakfast right away. Do you like rabbit? It's the only meat we have now."

"Love it," Charlie assured her. "Let me help."

"Sam showed me how to snare them," Dorina said. "Hard to believe, isn't it? I mean the change since we met."

She shuddered and then went on. "I'll never forget last winter. I read a book a long time ago that told about what the author described as a 'white hell.' He must have lived here before he wrote it."

"We thought you would leave before winter," Charlie said.

"So did we," she replied. Then some of the distrust and suspicion crept back into her face, and her lips clamped shut.

"Don't talk about it if you don't want to," Charlie said. "But I think you will have to confide in someone, and soon."

"I know, but I want Dirk to be here."

"Want to tell me where he is?"

She hesitated, made a fast decision. "He is at our gold mine. Not the one Uncle Jim discovered, but a new one we found. We named it 'Caribou Claim' because Dirk stumbled on it when trailing one."

"How did your Uncle Jim's claim pan out?"

"Not so good. There were a few pockets, and we finished them quickly. Then, when we were planning to leave, Dirk found our mine."

"Is that where you got the chunks you sent to Caribou?"

"We shouldn't have done that," she admitted. "We had panned gold. I think Dirk was just trying to impress Sam."

She took something from her pocket and laid it in his hand. It was a tool-marked piece of gold. He gave it back. "I keep it where I can touch it when I get afraid," she explained simply.

After breakfast, Charlie went outside and chopped wood. Carrying it inside, he said, "Your pile is getting low. When Lew comes, we'll chop down a few dead trees and drag them here."

"I hope we won't need them," she replied. "If possible, we want to leave before winter. Now that you are here, I think we can."

He pushed a bench over against the wall. Leaning back, he said, "I may doze off. If I do and you hear anybody outside, wake me before you open the door."

The combination of fatigue, a warm room and a full stomach dropped Charlie into deep sleep. Although it seemed like just a few minutes, it was four hours later when Dorina roused him.

"They're coming," she said. "But I count four."

"I forgot to mention Rena. You remember Rena, don't you?"

He went to the window in the south cabin wall and rubbed his sleepy eyes. The approaching party was so close he saw instantly this was not Lew and his party.

"It isn't Lew," he told Dorina. "You know the older Woolman who gave us so much trouble last fall? He died and his son took over."

She nodded. "Yes, we knew that."

"It may be the son and his partner, a man named Breed."

"What do they want with us?" she asked doubtfully.

Something clicked in his mind. "I think you know," he said slowly. "Is that why you stayed away from Caribou and tried so hard to prevent people knowing you were here?"

She didn't have to answer; her face said it was true.

"There has to be a showdown sometime," Charlie continued.

"I'm glad you're here," she said, and Charlie had the same thought. Standing back from the window he watched Woolman, Breed, Pete and Bert approach.

"When they knock at the door," Charlie said, "agree to let two enter, but that's all. Tell them Dirk is away."

"Will there be trouble?"

"I don't know, but don't unbar the door until they agree."

When the knock came, Dorina said, "Who is it?"

"Woolman from the store at Caribou. You knew my father, I believe. I have a business matter to discuss."

"My brother isn't here. Can you come back later?"

Charlie knew Woolman would likely welcome an opportunity to browbeat a girl he believed to be alone.

"Sorry. I must see you now."

"You can't all come in," Dorina replied. "Just two. No more."

"That's OK," Woolman said smoothly. "Pete and Bert will go back to the stream." Then he added, "You boys can build a fire."

Dorina slid back the bar and pushed the door wide. Woolman stepped in with Breed close behind. "Thanks," he said. "This matter won't take long. I know you'll be sensible ..."

His voice broke off abruptly, the sight of Charlie wiping a smug smile from his face. "What are you doing here?" he demanded.

"Just visiting an old friend," Charlie replied cheerfully.

Breed stepped forward, pale eyes angry, his voice a sneer. "My, my," his thin mustache curved in a smirk. "Nothing like rekindling an old flame. Not that I'd blame you," he added, glancing at the girl.

It was the smirk that did it. The flush tinting Dorina's face helped, too. Charlie had already decided there was only one way to handle a man like Breed. He stepped forward and clipped the chin below the sneering mouth. Charlie could move fast, and although he had to take two steps before the swing, Breed only had time enough to get his hands halfway up before the blow landed.

The crisp blow hurled him backwards into the cabin wall, still on his feet but head wagging. One hand dropped towards his belt.

Charlie picked up his rifle. "Don't do it," he warned and shot a glance at Woolman. The storekeeper was too astonished to prove a menace. "If you have any real business to discuss, and can do it decently, go ahead. If not, get out."

"We don't want trouble," Woolman said quickly. "Breed didn't mean anything. It was just a joke. Isn't that right?"

"Sure," he muttered. "Just a joke. I'm sorry, Miss Driscoll."

Then he looked at Charlie with cold, calculating eyes.

"I have a business matter to discuss," Woolman continued. "When it is finished, we will go. May I sit down?" When she nodded, he pushed a bench up to the table. Then he took a small, thick book from his pocket. It looked like a ledger. Charlie moved back to the bunk and lowered the butt of his rifle to the floor.

"When I inherited my father's business," Woolman said, "I found some accounts that had not been paid. Among them was one for James

Driscoll. He was your uncle, I believe?"

Dorina nodded and said, "He is dead."

"That's right," the storekeeper replied. "But debts are not canceled out when a man dies."

"Or is murdered," she retorted.

"All the evidence points to a natural death," Woolman said smoothly. "Pete and Bert found him dead in his bunk, a fact they are ready to swear to in court."

"How much is the bill? And how do I know it is genuine?"

"Only $160, and quite authentic. Every item was entered in my father's handwriting. That, too, can be verified. At first, I decided to write the debt off. Then I discovered you and your brother were living here, and thought that as his heirs, you might want to settle the account. The law specifies all debts of a deceased person must be satisfied before property can be inherited."

Charlie had to admit he was right. He also had an idea the store account was just window dressing, and the real kicker was coming.

Dorina sat in silence a few moments. She looked at Charlie. He nodded, and she said, "Of course, I must consult with my brother. But I don't mind saying now I approve of paying our uncle's debt. But we can't give you the money today."

"That is all right," Woolman said. "Any time that's convenient. Now I can reinstate the account as collectible and balance my books. Perhaps you would like to add to it or start one of your own?"

His eyes roamed about the sparsely furnished room. "I have a large stock at the store, and everything is priced reasonably."

"Thank you," Dorina replied.

Woolman made pencil notes in the ledger, turned back some pages. "There's one more matter," he said. "The grubstake agreement your uncle signed with my father—I found that, too, in his papers. I'm sure you are familiar with contracts in which the prospector pledges a share of any ore he mines in exchange for financial backing and supplies?"

Dorina nodded. "He mentioned it."

"I would like an accounting on that, also. I am surprised you have let it go so long and did not come into Caribou to report. I was entitled to that consideration." He studied her keenly. "You have discovered an unusual type of gold, according to the nuggets sent in for supplies."

Charlie glanced at Breed. The man had settled down on the floor. His eyes, too, were fastened on Dorina's face. Until now, they had stayed directed towards Charlie in an unpleasant way.

"What share does this agreement give you?" Dorina asked.

"The usual 50 percent that is customary in all mining country."

Her cheeks flushed with anger. "I don't believe my uncle signed such a contract. He always got any money he needed from Dad."

Woolman spread his hands. "I have only a copy here, but the original is at Caribou. You can check it when you come in. You know your uncle's signature."

The anger in her face was replaced with a look of hopelessness. Charlie saw he had guessed right, and this was why she and Dirk had made every effort to keep their activities secret. He didn't know if the grubstake agreement was genuine. Judging from his experience with the Woolmans, he thought it could easily be a forgery. Regardless, it was time to throw a monkey wrench into Woolman's artfully contrived mesh. So he said, "There's a matter you may have forgotten. Assuming this grubstake contract is genuine, it only covers gold they may have taken from the uncle's original claim. Any discovery they may have made themselves after they arrived is their exclusive property."

The cunning in the storekeeper's face told Charlie the man had already considered this and still planned to take advantage of Dirk and Dorina and claim half of all the gold they had mined. "It will be hard to prove which claim produced what, won't it?" he asked.

"And that will be your problem, not theirs," Charlie replied.

Woolman got up slowly, his eyes still fastened upon Dorina.

"I am serving notice now that a proper accounting must be made of all gold in your possession before you leave Caribou. Don't try to take any away. If you do, I'll stop you."

"By law?" Charlie asked quietly.

Woolman walked to the door. Opening it, he pointed at the rifles he and Breed had stacked against the wall before entering the cabin.

"There's the law up here," he said.

Breed turned in the doorway and told Charlie, "Be seeing you."

Charlie had no doubt he would.

# Chapter 10 – A Man is Missing

Woolman's declaration that he would use force if necessary to prevent the Driscolls taking any of their gold out of Caribou at first surprised Charlie, but even if he had a legitimate claim upon the gold they had taken from the uncle's claim, he must know he had none on anything the brother and sister had discovered themselves. Still, Woolman seemed confident he could collect half of the yield from both mines. That confidence not only puzzled Charlie, it worried him, as well.

He stood in the doorway watching Woolman and Breed walk to the bank of the stream and join Pete and Bert. He said to Dorina, "How much gold did you pan from your uncle's claim?"

"A little less than six pounds. We weighed it on a balance with a pound package of soda as the counterweight."

"About $3,000," Charlie calculated. "How does that rate with the gold you found on your own?" Then, as she hesitated, he added bluntly, "You know you need me and Lew to help you take it out. You also know we won't rob you, but we must know the score. Woolman's too confident, and that makes me think he knows something I don't."

He went over to the stove and shoved in more wood.

"You haven't answered my question," he prompted.

"With the gold Dirk brings today," she finally said, "we will have at least a hundred pounds. That was our goal, and we want to leave."

"That's at least fifty thousand dollars," he said. "A very nice stake. You and Dirk must have done a tremendous job."

She flushed at the compliment.

"The problem now is to get it back home. With Woolman and his men watching the trail, it won't be easy. Had you made any plans?"

She shook her head. "Nothing definite. We thought Sam might help. And Dirk said if anybody tried to stop us, he would shoot."

Charlie thought that sounded exactly like Dirk.

"The trouble with that plan," he said, "is they'll shoot back."

"You will help us?" Dorina implored.

"Yes. But we should clear up this grubstake business first. If we do, Woolman will have no legal grounds to interfere. That probably won't stop him, but it puts us in the clear. Do you have your uncle's signature, something we can check against Woolman's contract?"

"I have a letter, but it doesn't have his full legal name. He signed it 'Uncle Jim.'"

"That's not as good. But maybe we can run a bluff. Tell me, are you willing to split the first three thousand with Woolman?"

"I guess so," she said hesitantly.

Charlie went back to the door and stepped outside. The four men stood in a huddle around the fire Bert and Pete had started. Charlie shouted, "Woolman! Come back tonight when Dirk is here, and you can figure out a settlement."

But Woolman shook his head emphatically. "No. This time, you come to me. I'll be camped about a mile north near the stream. I'll give you until ten in the morning. Then we take action." He turned and started off in a northerly direction. His companions fell in behind.

"What are they up to?" Dorina asked.

Charlie shrugged. "They may want to check the claim your uncle staked out to see how much digging has been done. That might help them estimate how much gold you have recovered; at least it will provide material for argument. How far away is the other mine where you get solid chunks of gold?"

"About two miles. I hope Woolman doesn't go there."

"Can anybody find it?"

"I don't think so. There is no trail, and we gather the pieces of stone we chip away and drop them in a deep canyon."

She sat down on a bench. "I don't know why I shouldn't tell you. The gold comes from what Sam calls a pipe. I think he mentioned that last fall when you were here with us. He says molten gold is forced up through a fault in the rock. When the pressure ceases, the gold in the fault hardens and forms a lining. That is what we found."

She looked down at her hands. "See these calluses? The pipe is just a narrow crack. We chisel a full day to uncover half a pound of gold. We have earned every cent, and I won't let Woolman steal half."

"The gold isn't cached in the cabin, is it?"

"We know better than that. Sam told you he found our things scattered around. Well, it wasn't the first time somebody got in to search. No, the gold is in a safe place. Near the …"

He raised a hand. "Don't tell me," he said quickly. "I don't want to know. And I wish you didn't, either." He leaned down to close the stove draft. "What I would like to know is why Woolman is so confident. Making you come to him tomorrow is just more proof."

"Do I have to go?" she asked.

"You or Dirk, and Lew or I will tag along, if you like."

She turned grateful eyes toward him. "I'm glad of that."

It was late afternoon when Lew and their party arrived. Charlie met them out in front of the cabin.

"Sorry we're late," Lew said. "We lost an hour getting started."

"How are Dirk and Dorina?" Elma demanded.

"I haven't seen Dirk, but I know Dorina is OK. Why don't you give me your pack and go on ahead to see for yourself?"

Then he said to Lew, "What about that late start?"

"Somebody kept shooting at the cabin so we couldn't leave. Anybody else been here today?"

"Yes, Woolman, Breed, Bert and Pete."

"Surprised to see you?" Lew asked with a sly smile.

"Quite," Charlie grinned. "They came about that old grubstake contract the senior Woolman claimed to have with the uncle. The contract is what the son plans to push."

"Didn't we agree Woolman lied about it?" Lew asked.

"Yes. But even so, it may be better to compromise on it if we can prevent bigger trouble. Woolman acts very confident, like he holds all the cards. We better go in now. I'm glad you brought meat, but someone will have to go hunting tomorrow, or everybody eats leftover rabbit." Lew groaned at that one.

Inside the cabin, Dorina and Elma were both talking at the same time. As usual, Rena had taken over the kitchen to prepare supper. Bell had pulled off his boots and sat by the stove, eyes half closed.

When Charlie went out for a pail of water, Lew followed.

Charlie told him about Woolman's demand for half of everything Dorina and Dirk had discovered, including the gold from a mine found after the uncle's death. "And I'm not sure he will settle for that. His confidence worries me."

"What about the other mine?" Lew asked.

"They have about a hundred pounds of chunk gold. It's legally their own, and they're determined to keep it." He glanced at his companion. "I told Dorina we'd help them get it out."

"Sure," Lew nodded. "We've got to help them. And if they only found three thousand in the original claim, then the ones we filed probably aren't worth working."

"That's my idea, too," Charlie replied. "We might find a pocket or two, but there won't be a pipe like Dorina and Dirk found. You have to look for those in higher, rougher ground."

Dorina met them at the door. "I'm worried about Dirk," she whispered. "He should have come home an hour ago."

Charlie motioned her outside. "What did you tell Elma?"

"I said he was hunting. But she keeps asking about him."

"Suppose we wait another half-hour. Then, if he hasn't returned, I'll try to find him. But you will have to come and show me the trail."

When the 30 minutes had passed without any sign of Dirk, Charlie said, "I'm going out to meet him. He may have too much of a load to make it back by mealtime without help. Dorina is coming, too. She knows the route he took."

Bell said, "I'll go with you."

Charlie shook his head. "We need you here. Don't forget, there are four hostile men outside, and they may start trouble."

"He's right," Elma declared, and Bell sat down reluctantly.

At the door, Charlie said, "Don't wait supper for us. We'll eat with Dirk when we return."

"I'm frightened," Dorina confessed when they reached the stream and turned to follow it north.

Charlie looked at her with understanding. It wasn't the first time loneliness, doubt and uncertainty had caused her agonizing fear. But she had managed to come through with courage left to endure. There was no question she and Dirk had earned every cent of the gold they found, and he was even more resolved to help them keep it.

They followed the stream half a mile then turned. "We come this way from the mine," Dorina said, "so we can hide the gold. In the morning, we use a shorter route straight from the cabin."

The ground rose sharply and grew more rough. "We should have met him before this," Dorina was saying in a taut voice when a disturbance among the rocks ahead startled her to a quick halt. There were rattling noises, like something fleeing through the stones and loose gravel. Dorina screamed, "Dirk!"

"It wasn't a man," Charlie told her. "I'd guess caribou. Regardless, it would take four hooved feet to make that much noise."

Dorina led him unhesitatingly through a series of ridges and low cliffs. A mile farther on, she stopped below one of the cliffs and pointed. "Halfway up is the opening to our mine."

She called cautiously, "Dirk!"

When there was no answer, Charlie climbed up to a narrow pit that slanted down into the cliff. The pit was about 4 feet across and deep enough to hide a tall man. But there was no one inside.

Dropping in a lighted match, he caught a brief glimpse of the vein. It was just a crack perhaps 2 inches wide. The realization of how much work brother and sister had expended here hit him like a blow. They had chipped away tons of stone by hand to expose the gold lining and retrieve it.

As they climbed down, Dorina said, "Dirk must be in trouble."

Charlie was thinking the same, but all he said was, "We'll return over the short route. If he's had an accident, he'll be waiting there for help." Then he added, "I suppose we passed close to the place you hide the gold, and there was no chance of missing him there."

"We walked within 20 feet of it," she said wearily. "It's a hollow tree with a small hole in the top through which we drop the chunks we chisel loose. The space must be deep or we would have filled it before now. No one would think of looking for gold in a hollow tree."

Charlie agreed with that, provided they had not left a visible trail with the daily visits. If they had, no woodsman would miss the inference. But he kept that thought to himself.

"Since you will leave soon, you better bring the gold to the cabin. Say tomorrow morning? There are enough of us to protect it now."

Some of Dorina's dejection disappeared at that prospect, and when they saw the cabin, light streaming a welcome from the single window, conveying as it invariably does to wilderness travelers a promise of warmth and comfort, her voice was almost cheerful.

"He may be here right now. And I have worried about nothing."

"I want you to go on alone from here," Charlie said. "When you reach the cabin, stand for a moment in the doorway so I can see you. If he's there, signal me by raising your hand. Then I'll come on in. But if he isn't, do nothing. Then I'll check Woolman's camp up the stream."

Her voice had regained the tone of fear when she spoke. "You think he's with them? Why don't you go inside with me now?"

"I'm staying here because I want to do this job alone, and I don't want to argue with Lew or Bell about it. You can tell Lew later. But just tell everyone, now, that I'll come along later."

"You haven't had anything to eat," she protested.

Charlie touched his coat pocket. "I have a chunk of pemmican; it'll do until I get back. And who knows," he grinned, "Woolman and Breed may invite me for dinner."

Watching her walk away, Charlie felt deep pity for the disappointment that lay ahead for her. He was sure Dirk had not returned while they were gone. He unwrapped the pemmican, bit off a small piece and stuck it in his cheek. The cabin door swung open. Dorina paused, silhouetted by the light. Even at that distance, he saw her shoulders sag. Then she went inside and closed the door.

Charlie strode swiftly towards the stream. He had noticed that everyone traveling along the little river followed the eastern bank. Because he wanted to arrive undetected, he decided to take the western side. As he remembered it, the water was almost a foot deep at the riffle. He pulled off his boots and socks and waded across.

The gravel was sharp and the water quite cold. On the other side, he sat on a big rock and rubbed his feet briskly with his hands. Then he replaced the foot gear. As he reached for his rifle, a bullet zipped past his head and then a gunshot reverberated through the valley. He rolled off the rock and crouched behind it. The shot had been murderously close. If he hadn't stooped for the rifle, the bullet would have hit him.

He shoved the barrel of his rifle forward and settled in alongside the protecting cover.

# Chapter 11 – A Fight by the Fire

Because he was stooping for the rifle, Charlie had not seen the lancing flame at the muzzle that must have accompanied it. Consequently, he had no clue about the location of the man who had pulled the trigger. He believed, however, the fellow was some distance away, probably upstream from the direction of Woolman's camp.

It was certain he had not been waiting in ambush, because in that case he would have seen Charlie ford the stream and fired then. Such a shot would have been much easier. He waited a few minutes to see if there would be more shots and then looked for a route of escape. There were other rocks strewn along the stream bank, and one some 6 feet behind his present shelter looked like it would do.

Charlie checked the articles in his pockets, rearranging them so they couldn't spill out. The rifle would prove awkward, but he made it safe by unloading the chamber and locking the bolt. Then, grasping the weapon with muzzle shoved inside his coat so it couldn't collect dirt, he started rolling. It took fewer revolutions of his body than he had expected, and he reached the new boulder without drawing more fire. He was so near the moosewood bushes and stunted aspen trees bordering the stream he didn't bother to roll again but just scampered into the dark cover. Then he stopped, reloaded his rifle and headed north.

It was about half an hour before he saw their fire. As expected, the camp was on the other side of the water. The shot he had escaped prompted strong caution, so he walked past the camp a quarter-mile, planning to cross over the stream and approach from an unexpected direction. While passing the campfire he tried to see just how many were seated around it, but because of the trees he could distinguish only two heads. He hoped one belonged to Dirk. The young fellow probably was there, but if he wasn't, Charlie had no idea where to look. There was a slight chance Dirk had accompanied Woolman and Breed willingly. More probably, he had been forced.

Charlie located another shallow riffle and again removed his foot gear to wade across. He spent a little more time rubbing the circulation back into his feet this time. There was timber for cover, but trees mean dead limbs and fallen leaves that might snap or rustle, so Charlie moved slowly, testing each step.

Coming closer, he saw the party was camping without any tent or canvas shelter. Instead, they had erected a low wall of cut brush to break the wind. The fire was large, and it looked like the men also lacked blankets and were depending upon it for warmth. Moving in, Charlie saw the backs of two men sitting on the near side of the blaze. Another he thought was Pete came up with an armful of sticks and dumped them on the blaze. When a piece of loose bark flared, Charlie saw one of the men opposite was indeed Dirk. The young man seemed as lean as before, but his shoulders looked broader. Charlie saw a dark spot on his face that could be a bruise or merely dirt. A pot sat on three rocks over some coals raked out from the main fire. Pete went to it and poured himself a cup. Charlie thought it was tea, and as the fellow drank, his own stomach knotted up from emptiness.

Pete splashed some more steaming liquid in the cup and planted himself before Dirk. "Smells good?" he asked. "Too bad."

Woolman spoke next. "You're going to tell us sometime. Why make it hard on yourself?"

Dirk looked up belligerently. "No" was all he said.

Charlie couldn't see if Woolman gave a signal, but Pete drew the steaming cup back and flipped its contents at the prisoner's face. Dirk ducked just in time to receive the hot liquid on his forehead and cap. He struggled to stand but fell back onto the ground. Charlie saw then that although his hands were not tied, his feet were. He rolled away from the fire, furiously rubbing his scalded forehead.

Charlie knew he had to do something, and do it fast. A cup of hot tea might not sound dangerous, but boiling liquid could blind a man for life, and Dirk might not be so fortunate again. Charlie realized he could put a bullet into at least three of the four kidnappers before they could respond. But he never was one to shoot first from an ambush.

Pete turned to the steaming pot, evidently to prepare another devilish torment. Charlie aimed at the base of the fire and pulled the trigger. A cloud of sparks, ashes and smoldering embers shot into the air. Pete caught a face full, dropped the cup and screamed loudly. Bert, who had been sitting beside Dirk, seemed just as effectively blinded. Woolman whirled about rubbing his eyes as he staggered away into the shadows. Only Breed escaped serious consequences. He sprang up and ran towards a cluster of rifles laid around the base of a small tree.

Charlie was running for them, too, and he reached them first. That didn't stop Breed from trying. He made a desperate lunge, and Charlie planted a foot on the rifle the man was trying to pick up. Then he brought the side of his hand down hard on the base of Breed's neck. The man slumped over and lay motionless.

Charlie saw Woolman backing warily away, swung up his rifle and said sharply, "Hands over your head."

Then he heard muffled cries coming from beside the fire and saw that in spite of his tied feet, Dirk had managed to pull Pete down and was hammering the blinded fellow with his fists.

Charlie went back to the rifles. There were three: a couple of short models that looked like .30-30 or .32 Special belonging, he thought, to Woolman and Breed, and Dirk's 9mm Mauser. Evidently, Bert and Pete had not been able to replace the weapons left in Harmon's cabin. Charlie gathered them up. They made an awkward load, but he carried it around the fire and stopped the two struggling men.

"That's enough," he told Dirk. "I need your help."

"I don't know who you are, but I …" Then his eyes went wide. "You're Charlie! You got Dorina's letter, didn't you? She was sure you'd come back. I thought we'd never see you again."

Charlie dropped his knife on the ground. "Cut your feet loose. Then go over and get Woolman's pistol. Don't get between us, either."

The thongs about Dirk's ankles had been tight, and it was several seconds before he could take a step. But when he was able to stand, he managed a swagger on his way over to the storekeeper.

"It was a good stunt to shoot into the fire," he said. "Of course, I could have handled them if you had given me a little more time. But I'm glad you saved me the trouble."

Relieving Woolman of his pistol, Dirk added, "I've a notion to sock him. He certainly has it coming." His hand touched the dark spot on his cheek, and Charlie saw then that it was a deep bruise.

"Unload their guns," Charlie ordered. "And then pick up your own and watch them. When did they get you?"

"I was on my way home. They stepped out of the brush already covering me with their rifles. How did you know I was here?"

"Your sister and I looked for you on your regular trail. When we didn't find you, I figured Woolman had brought you here. You know he wants half of all the gold, not only what came from your uncle's claim but any from the claim you found yourselves?"

"I'll see him in blazes first!" Dirk declared.

"He'll probably end up there," Charlie agreed.

"I ought to work him over," Dirk cried. "I ought to work all of them over. They need to be taught a lesson."

Charlie shook his head. "Not now. Dorina will worry until we get back. Let's start now."

"What will we do with these rats?"

"Well …" Hard, strong fingers suddenly clamped about his neck and strangled the words. Charlie remembered too late he had not checked Breed to see if he had recovered. Obviously, he had.

The fingers were strong, and Charlie could hear the man's eager breath behind his shoulder as he drew them tighter. Charlie's senses swam and the bright firelight began to dim. Then he cleared his head with an effort, saw Dirk coming in with raised gun, and managed to choke out, "This is my fight."

Throwing his head and shoulders forward, Charlie catapulted his attacker over his head and upon the ground before him. This broke Breed's grip, but he twisted cat-quick trying for another.

He jolted Breed with an uppercut, and then crashed alternate rights and lefts into the man's twisted features. Breed staggered, but he was a tough and seasoned fighter. He dropped his head behind his shoulders and warded off most of Charlie's blows with his arms. Then he advanced swinging. His blows were wildly aimed, but two landed, and both rocked Charlie.

Realizing this would be no easy victory, Charlie shifted to the defensive, blocking the swings and giving ground. The maneuver worked as he hoped. Breed felt a false advantage, pressing forward, swinging wilder and faster. Charlie's footwork prevented any real injury. No man, not even one with Breed's iron muscles, could maintain such a pace for long. When Breed finally drew away, Charlie thought this might be it. But he was mistaken. Breed charged forward as savagely as before. Yet he was breathing hard and fast, panting, and Charlie stopped giving ground.

Planting his feet firmly, he met the slugging attack in kind. Breed retreated; Charlie pressed him harder. One of the man's eyes was closed, and Charlie aimed for the other. It was brutal work, but since force was the only thing such a man respected, it was necessary.

The end came rather quickly. Breed tried to regain the initiative, but his arms had lost their strength. He made another wild swing that left his chin wide open. Charlie stepped closer and unloaded on it. Breed landed on his back, and Charlie knew the fight was over.

Dirk said admiringly, "I never saw a better fight in the ring. I've boxed a lot, myself, and I sure don't want to take you on!"

"This wasn't boxing," Charlie said shortly. "It was fighting." He picked up the guns belonging to Woolman and Breed and smashed them over a rock. "You have Woolman's pistol?"

Dirk nodded.

Charlie got his own rifle and walked over to the storekeeper, who still stared back defiantly.

"Listen carefully," Charlie said, "because I will only tell you once. You don't get a cent's worth of any gold the Driscolls found themselves. They will give you half of what came from their uncle's claim—provided you have a grubstake contract and it's real. They'll check your copy with letters to verify the signature. And they will pay the debt on your store books, too. We're leaving tomorrow. If you're smart, you won't try to stop us. The next time anybody shoots at us, we will shoot back."

He moved around the fire and confronted Pete and Bert. They raised frightened faces. Pete had been pretty well hammered by Dirk. Charlie looked down at them grimly. "I'm getting tired of you," he said. "The next time we meet, I don't care where, I'll give both of you a worse beating than Breed just got."

Charlie turned to Dirk and said, "Let's go."

Dirk fell in step beside him and said, "I see Dorina has told you about the gold. They were trying to make me tell them where we had it hidden. They admitted they had searched the cabin twice."

A minute later, he added, "You were pretty free with our gold, weren't you? Promising we'd give it to those rats."

"If the store account and grubstake contract are real, Woolman is legally entitled to it," Charlie said shortly. He had begun to remember what a pain Dirk could be.

"I think you were out of line," Dirk continued. "Next time ..."

"You talk too much," Charlie said. "I told Dorina we'd help get you and your gold out. And we will. But Lew and I are running this show. We'll do whatever we believe is right. So keep that in mind."

They walked in silence after that.

"How is Lew?" Dirk finally asked.

"He's fine," Charlie replied. Then he added, "There's an old friend of yours at the cabin. A Miss Elma Nash."

"My gosh! What does she want? I thought I had gotten rid of her when we came north. I wish she would stop chasing me."

"I wish she would, too," Charlie said, "For her sake. She was worried enough to hire an investigator to hunt you up. Then she came herself to be sure he hadn't overlooked anything. She's paying his wages, Lew's and mine to see you get home safely."

Following another silence, Dirk said, "You are right. I talk too much, Elma is a good scout. And I'll tell her when we get back."

When they walked through the cabin door, Dirk hugged all of the women, including Rena. Charlie didn't know if the girl was more surprised than the sister, or vice versa. Dirk could be likable when he chose, and he made the choice now. He thanked Elma sincerely, and then he made light of his recent misadventure, which suited Charlie very well. Rena had a kettle of caribou meat and dehydrated vegetables simmering on the stove. She made tea and they ate ravenously.

"We also had a little excitement," Lew said. "Bell thought he heard someone behind the cabin. So he went out to check."

Charlie looked up. "Didn't I tell you to stay inside?"

"Slow up," Bell protested. "I don't take orders from you. I take them from her," he jerked his head toward Elma.

Elma nodded. "I thought it was all right for him to see if anyone was spying on us. Go on, tell what happened."

"Somebody was hanging around," Bell continued. "I chased him up the river. Then he must have waded across, because when I saw him again, he was on the other side. I sent a bullet over his head as a warning. I don't think he'll be back."

"Was Dorina here when you came back?" he asked slowly.

"Yeah, she had been here about a quarter-hour."

Charlie's first thought was to tell Bell who it was he had shot at across the stream. And to emphasize in equally emphatic words that instead of the bullet passing over his head as a warning, it had actually missed by a narrow space. Then he sank back on the bench.

Could Bell really be that careless? Charlie decided this was a matter meriting more serious thought. So when he spoke, Charlie merely said, "We've got a job to do early in the morning. We'll get the hundred pounds of gold Dirk and Dorina cached on the trail to their mine. Then we head for Caribou."

He stood up. Most of his muscles ached, and some were very sore. He walked over to unroll his sleeping bag. "It will be a busy day," he added, "so get some sleep."

# Chapter 12 – The Enemy Tries Again

Disturbing thoughts and aching muscles kept Charlie awake for some time after he crawled into his sleeping bag. He wondered if Bell had actually mistaken him for a snooper. He doubted his blunt warning to the storekeeper and his partner would prevent further trouble there. They would be packing more than a hundred pounds of raw gold on their return to Caribou, and he believed their enemies were unscrupulous enough to take extreme steps to steal it. He forced the troubling thoughts out of his mind and finally fell asleep.

In the morning, one look at his face in the polished steel kit mirror decided Charlie against shaving. His cheeks were puffy with several cuts, and his lips were swollen. Rena had awakened first and already made a fire. He heated water and washed. His hands were in good shape despite the heavy hammering they had given Breed.

There was much excitement in the little cabin over the coming trip to the gold cache. Eating breakfast first was almost a burden, except for Lew, who ate with his usual display of enjoyment and capacity. The tension mounted even higher when they assembled outdoors. More than $50,000 worth of gold is no ordinary matter, and none had ever seen so much in a pile. This included Dirk and Dorina, because they had dropped each day's gleanings in the hollow tree without seeing the growing pile.

When Rena said she would stay at the cabin to scour their cooking gear and clean it for the trip out, Charlie decided he should remain, too. There were enough people going without him to carry the metal, with Lew and Bell to guard it in case they were attacked. Charlie didn't think it wise, either, to leave their packs or the cabin unguarded. And a rest would do him good. So he poured a cup of tea, and sitting by the window, watched the others walk briskly away.

Dirk had given Dorina his rifle so he could carry the axe. In daylight, the hollow tree they had chosen as a cache looked more like an old snag, the trunk mostly devoid of bark and gray with age. Yet it had not decayed much, because when Dirk swung his first blow, the axe bounded back with a ring. He planned to cut through the seasoned wood near the ground. Then chunks of gold would spill out.

Dirk slanted his next stroke more, and the blade dug in. Dorina,

Elma and Bell crowded so close Lew feared one might be hit when the axe swung back. He wanted to crowd in, too, but decided someone should be alert to possible trouble, so he moved back several yards and shot quick glances around the thinly timbered area.

Dirk had developed into a good axe man. He sank a blow that went through and reached the hollow. When he pried the chip away, three little sausage-shaped skin bags tumbled out.

"That's the dust we panned from Uncle Jim's claim," Dorina explained. "The chunks will come next."

Dirk struck the body of the snag twice. "It's cracked open," he said. Stopping, he thrust his arm into the opening.

Coming closer, Lew saw he had begun to tremble. Dirk grabbed a dead limb and shoved it up and in.

"It's gone," Dirk said dully. "The tree is empty."

"Someone stole it," Dorina cried.

"Then why didn't they take the bags?" Elma asked.

It was a good question. Lew walked around the stub. Except for a few black streaks he suspected were caused by a previous fire, the wood was unmarked. There was only one conclusion.

"It was a second-story job," Lew announced. "The gold was taken out through the top opening."

Their eyes fastened upon it, hardly 4 inches wide, almost round with smooth, polished edges. "Impossible," Dorina said.

"It's not impossible," Elma concluded. "They could drop a piece of wood covered with glue and tied to a string in the hole. Gold would stick to it when they pulled the wood back out."

Lew shook his head at that. He had expected better from her.

The ground about the tree was ridged with rock ledges, some barely higher than the surface, others rose as much as several feet. Lew began to walk among them, kicking at the little piles of leaves and trash that had blown between.

"What are you doing?" Bell asked.

"Looking for gold," Lew replied.

"He's nuts," Dirk said. "So were we to hide it here."

Lew glanced up. "No person took it. Why would a man fool around with glued wood on a string when he could chop it out. If I'm right, animals took it and we'll find the stuff close by."

"What kind of animal?" Dorina asked.

"Tree squirrel, maybe a pack rat. A dozen kinds of rodents live around here. It could even be a squeaker."

"Why would an animal take the gold?" Elma asked. It was easy to see she hadn't bought his theory.

"Didn't like to have its tree nest spoiled," Lew suggested. "Maybe the stuff was cold to sleep on. I don't have all the answers."

Then he added, "You might help."

They moved reluctantly away from the tree.

"Look for a crevice," he told them. Then, "No, don't bother. I think I've found it."

That brought them running. Lew had discovered another cache of cured grass laid by for the winter season, and when he reached behind it, his fingers closed on what felt like sharp-edged pebbles. He drew a handful out and dropped it on the ground. The pieces were dull yellow, unmistakably raw gold.

Everybody crowded closer. Dirk had stopped trembling, but now Dorina was shaking. They leaned down eagerly to grab the chisel-marked chunks. This included Elma and Bell, so Lew warded them off with his arms. "Take it easy," he said. "The stuff won't run away. Since it belongs to Dirk and Dorina, I think they should gather it up. You brought the bags?"

Dorina produced four, made of hide with thong-laced seams. She put Dirk's rifle down, and kneeling beside her brother, held the bags while he filled them. Elma, Bell and Lew gave them room.

"Don't you wish it was yours?" Bell whispered.

Lew just grinned, but Elma looked indignant. "I certainly don't," she declared. "Dirk and Dorina need it so much."

The brother and sister had filled three sacks and were starting on the fourth when Bell picked up Dirk's rifle and said, "Quite a cannon."

Dorina was tying the last sack. It wasn't as full as the others, but when she lifted it over in the row, it seemed plenty heavy. Lew thought once more this was going to be an awkward load on the trail. Then he sensed motion behind him, and a sharp voice said, "Drop your gun."

Lew froze but kept a firm grip on the rifle. He turned only his eyes sideways, glimpsing Bell standing six feet away. One of the man's hands held his own and Dirk's rifle. The other was leveling a short, blued handgun.

"Is this a joke?" Lew asked, although he knew it wasn't.

"No," Bell said. "And I won't tell you again to drop that rifle." The hammer of his revolver clicked into full cock.

"I don't think you're going to kill all four of us," Lew retorted. "Those sacks of gold aren't that valuable."

"Who said anything about killing?" Bell replied. "I'll just put a bullet in your knee. And don't think I won't. If your partner hears the shot, he won't pay any attention because he said last night we must hunt for meat."

Lew realized the man had it all planned out, so he let his rifle slide through his fingers to the ground. He looked at the Driscolls. Their faces appeared stunned. But Elma was more mad than afraid.

"Put that gun away," she ordered. "Have you gone mad?"

She came forward with determined steps. Bell fired a bullet into the ground before her, showering her feet with dirt and gravel.

"Next time, I shoot your legs out from under you."

"When did you sell out to Woolman?" Lew asked. "Clear back when you bought the corncob pipe?"

Bell's teeth showed in a smug grin. "Woolman and I made a deal on my first trip in, when I reported to Elma that there was no sign of the Driscolls. Now, back away from those sacks, and the rifle. Move!"

"I'm going to kill you for this," Dirk grated, rage choking off his voice. "Let's rush him," he said to Lew. "He can only shoot one of us before the other gets him."

"The gold isn't worth your life or mine," Lew replied.

"That's good advice," Bell approved. "Those sacks may look like a small deal, but I know a market where they'll bring eighty thousand. Keep that in mind. For that kind of dough, I will use my gun."

"I suppose you're waiting for Woolman?" Lew suggested.

Bell flashed his teeth again. "And it won't be long. I marked the trail plainly for him to follow."

Lew remembered the man had walked last in line. He looked anxiously at his own rifle, but it was more than 10 feet away, and seeing that glance, Bell motioned him farther away with his revolver. Lew was worried, but he was curious, too. He wondered just how they planned to finish this deal. Woolman was an established merchant and Bell a licensed investigator, both with standing and recognition that made them unlikely candidates for wanton murder.

Unfortunately, Lew's curiosity was soon satisfied. Four men ran in through the timber from the direction of the river. They were the storekeeper, his partner Breed, Pete and Bert. Lew knew about the fight last night, but he was surprised to see how badly Charlie's fists had marked Breed. And Pete's face was in no better shape.

Bell assumed the role of leader. "Take these rifles and watch them," he said. He walked over and picked up Lew's repeater. "I've wanted to handle one of these a long time." He leveled it, sighted over the barrel. Then he worked the bolt, caught the ejected cartridge in his hand, and shoved it back in the chamber.

Woolman was frowning. "You should have waited until we had them all together. What about the other man?"

Bell waved the rifle confidently. "Leave him to me. I'll do the job because you boys haven't done so good so far."

He pointed. "There's the gold. Put it in your packs. Give me a half-hour start and then come to the cabin."

He tossed Lew's rifle in the air, caught it and strode away.

Breed held Bell's rifle, Woolman had picked up Dirk's and given it to Pete. Ignoring Dirk, the storekeeper spoke directly to Dorina.

"I'm sorry you didn't settle this matter yesterday, Miss Driscoll. If you had, we could have avoided this trouble. I'm taking possession of the gold under the terms of my grubstake contract. I'll give you a receipt, and when you come to Caribou, we will have our accounting."

Lew regarded the storekeeper almost with admiration. The guy was slick. A receipt for four bags of gold chunks was indefinite, and he suspected there would be a big shrinkage before anything reached Caribou. And there was nothing the Driscolls could do about it. The burden of proof would be upon them, and since the bags had not been weighed and there was no court or other legal machinery in that small settlement, it was anybody's guess how much farther they would have to journey to seek justice. By that time, the gold would be on the other side of the world.

Lew shrugged. It was up to Charlie, now. Suddenly, a shiver of cold fear played up his back. The investigator had indicated Charlie as the only one to worry about, and it would be easy to explain a shooting on the trail as an accident. He looked around desperately. There was no chance he could break away and warn Charlie.

\*  \*  \*

Charlie finished the cup of tea and leaned back against the cabin wall. He was getting drowsy. The last two days and been hard. And he was not as young as he used to be.

Rena came back from the stream with sand to scour the cooking pots and skillet. Glancing out the window, she said, "Bell is coming."

"Bell?" repeated Charlie. "Wonder what he wants?"

Rena spoke again, "He has Lew's rifle."

The lethargy left Charlie. He returned to the window, saw that the girl was right. Bell had a good gun of his own, and Lew had never been one to loan his. When Bell's footsteps sounded outside the door, Charlie stepped over to the hinged side, so when it opened it would conceal him. Bell paused in the doorway. "Where's Charlie?" he demanded.

"I'm here," Charlie said quickly, reaching past the man and grasping the rifle stock. For a moment, Bell acted like he would resist, then his arms relaxed.

Charlie said simply, "Lew always leaves his rifle outside so it won't condense moisture."

Then he gave the repeater to Rena. "Put it outdoors against the cabin wall, will you?" Then he looked at Bell. "Anything wrong?"

"No," Bell replied evenly. "I came back first because I wanted to talk with you alone."

Charlie nodded. "Sit down. Might as well be comfortable." He pushed a bench beside the table. Then he moved the other seat to the opposite side so they faced each other across the table top.

"Go ahead," he said. "Talk."

Bell grinned disarmingly. "OK. It's really simple. This has been a hard trip, and we've taken a lot of risks. I just thought we should get a little more than wages. Say a nominal share of the gold?"

"I thought Miss Nash offered you a bonus?" Charlie said.

"Sure. But I don't know how much it will be." He dropped a hand down and scratched his hip. "It might not pay for the danger."

"Well, it's a thought," Charlie said slowly, looking in the man's face but also watching the dropping hand in his peripheral vision. When he saw it move lower, he knew it was time to act. The idea of carrying a short handgun in the top of a boot was by no means novel.

He shoved the table into Bell. The man brought up the groping hand instinctively to catch the table and protect himself. Charlie grabbed him by the hair and smashed his face down on the table.

Bell was persistent. His hand went for the boot again. Charlie lifted him by the hair with one hand and swung with the other. Recalling his bout with Breed, and wanting no repeat performance, he put everything he had into the swing.

Bell lifted off the stool and slammed to the floor.

Charlie had a moment of doubt, wondering if he might have guessed wrong. But it passed when he leaned over the unconscious man and jerked a short blue revolver from the top of his right boot. He backed away and glanced at Rena. She had watched with impassive features, apparently without any fear.

"I don't like him," she said calmly.

He picked up the water pail and splashed some in Bell's face. Bell sat up gasping. Charlie grabbed his wrists, bent them around to his back and lashed them together with a boot lace.

"You know," Charlie told him, "I was suspicious of you from the first day. But the clincher came when you walked back carrying Lew's rifle. Lew would never allow that."

He jerked the man erect. "Now," Charlie added, "we'll go get the others. And I hope for your sake nothing has happened to them."

He pushed the man out the door, grasped his own rifle and followed. "We'll be back soon, Rena. You might have water boiling for tea and dinner."

They had gone a mile when Charlie heard voices. He jerked Bell behind a stand of spruce trees and warned, "Keep very still."

Elma, Dirk and Lew approached. Behind and herding them along with rifles came Breed and Pete. Woolman and Bert were last in line. Charlie put his rifle down and drew Bell's revolver. Pushing the man before him as a shield, he stepped out just as Lew was opposite. "Drop the guns," he said sharply. "My rifle's behind me, Lew. Get it."

Pete raised his rifle but couldn't shoot with Bell shielding Charlie. "Drop it," Charlie said. "Remember what I told you last night?"

He dropped the gun. Lew had Charlie's rifle now, and he was moving around to flank the gang. The whipping Charlie had given Breed the night before had taken all of the starch out of the man.

Dirk came up to Bell. "Untie his hands," he ordered. "I won't strike a man with his hands tied behind his back."

Charlie pushed Dirk back. "There has been enough of that," he said. "These fellows won't bother us anymore."

Charlie cut the thongs from Bell's wrists and gave him a shove. "Go with your friends," Charlie commanded, "and if I see your face again, you're going to be sorry."

"I'll see he loses his license," Elma declared.

"OK," Charlie agreed. "Do that. But first we have to get to Fairbanks. It may be weeks before another plane puts down."

"Isn't this the 12th?" she asked. "I ordered my pilot to return on the seventeenth. We can reach Caribou in five days, can't we?"

"Like a breeze," Lew grinned.

*The End*